ONLY
THE
CHILDREN

BOOKS BY S.A. DUNPHY

ONLY THE CHILDREN

S.A. DUNPHY

bookouture

Published by Bookouture in 2024

An imprint of Storyfire Ltd.
Carmelite House
50 Victoria Embankment
London EC4Y 0DZ

www.bookouture.com

ISBN: 978-1-80314-723-9
eBook ISBN: 978-1-80314-722-2

PROLOGUE

THE TEMPEST

*'This thing of darkness I
Acknowledge mine.'*

— WILLIAM SHAKESPEARE

THE CHILDREN

It felt as if the world was trying to throw them off its surface.

They didn't know what to do, so they held on to each other and fought the fear and nausea and tried to find comfort in being together.

'Are we going to die?' the little girl asked through her tears.

'Hold on to me and keep your eyes closed,' her older brother said. 'Try to think about something else. Think about that day we went to the zoo.'

She tried, but the sounds and the motion and the dizzy sickness wouldn't allow her to focus on anything else.

One moment they were plunged downwards with such force they could feel their stomachs lurch and heave, the next they were thrown skywards with a violence that was terrifying, as it seemed they would surely fly from their seats and hit the roof of the low room they'd been told not to leave.

Crates of food were stacked around them, forming a cubicle in which they huddled, and their worst fear was that amid the rolling and quaking these would topple over, crushing them. So they made their way into the corner and wrapped their arms around each other once more, and the oldest boy told them again and again that it would be alright, and the little girl cried and whimpered in terror, and the middle child remained stoically silent, although they could feel him trembling. And when at one stage the whole room tilted over to the side so severely it seemed it would never right itself, he gripped his siblings' arms with such ferocity, his older brother was sure his fingers would leave bruises behind.

But in spite of it all they held on to one another, the three children.

Even in the midst of such terror, they had each other.

The storm hit at 3.46 p.m., fifteen hours after they'd left Oslo, the weather front coming across the murky waves of the North Sea with a roar the likes of which Mike Bernie, the *Dolphin*'s pilot, hadn't heard in twelve years of seafaring.

He reached above his head and pulled down the handset for the ship's intercom. Pressing the button so he could address the entire ship's complement across the *Dolphin*'s loudspeakers, he said: 'Storm's here, and it's going to be a bumpy one. Make sure everything is secure and hold on to your arses. This is going to last a few hours.'

The eight-person crew had known hard weather was coming, and the *Dolphin* was designed to withstand even severe storms and remain on schedule, so when the storm came screaming from the north-east, Mike wasn't particularly concerned. He'd brought ships through treacherous seas before and didn't see any reason why this one would be any different, even if the sound of that gale was sharper than he was used to – a demonic howl that made him shudder in spite of himself.

Peering through the windows of the observation deck, Mike surveyed the expanse of ocean all around them. The *Dolphin*'s bridge was the control centre of the huge vessel, the highest point on the boat, and gave him a clear, unobstructed view of the surrounding water. It might have been mid-afternoon, but the sky was already dark, roiling clouds blotting out any trace of the sun. Rain lashed across the seascape at an almost horizontal angle, and suddenly Mike felt the ship rise and then lurch as it dropped into a trough that felt like it was sending them to the ocean floor.

Through the rain-battered glass, the pilot could see nothing but charcoal-coloured water, and the *Dolphin* seemed to hang suspended for a long moment before the mass of ocean beneath her gathered, and the ship surged skywards again, like a cork popped from a bottle.

Mike hadn't been seasick since his days as an apprentice seaman, but his stomach turned over just for a second. As he fought the unexpected nausea, the ship was hit portside by a wave so large the *Dolphin* was fully underwater for a second. The impact caused the vessel to list to starboard. This wouldn't have been a problem had a second wave, coming from the same direction, not hit before the *Dolphin* had a chance to right herself. Mike, holding on to the edge of the primary navigation desk for all he was worth, had a brief instant of panic.

We're going to get turned over, he thought. *I never believed I'd see it, but I think we are.*

But just as he was certain the vessel was going to roll, the ship, its hull creaking against the strain, fought its way upright and crashed forward through a wall of brine. For a moment, Mike could see the cloudy sky and felt a rush of gratitude, whispering a prayer of thanks to the generations of nautical engineers whose wisdom had gone into the construction of this indomitable ship.

Grabbing the intercom again, he called out: 'All hands report in. That was a hard one.'

It was sailing protocol to check the welfare of the crew intermittently during severe weather.

'Fine in engineering.'

'Me and Kieran are on cargo deck three and we're good.'

Each station signed in. All except for the galley.

'Derek, sing out please.'

Still nothing.

The wind screeched like a tortured soul. Rain slapped on the windows of the observation deck like a thousand fists desperate to get inside.

'Derek, you're worrying me, man.'

A door to Mike's left opened and Oliver, the *Dolphin*'s captain, came up from below decks. He was ten years older than Mike's thirty, his short blonde hair speckled with grey, his thin face sporting a bushy beard that Mike privately thought made him look scruffy. Adding to his looking less than tidy, today the captain's face was battered and bruised, looking as if he'd just had an altercation with an angry docker and come out the worse for it.

'What happened to you?' Mike asked, grimacing at the painful-looking cuts and scrapes.

'I opened the cupboard in my cabin and the storm had shaken loose a lot of what was inside. It fell out on top of me. I can't believe I was so stupid.'

Mike wasn't sure he did either, but he had more pressing things to worry about.

'Derek missed the call,' the pilot said, turning back to the desk.

'He's probably pissed. Or asleep. Or both.'

'Will we leave it an hour and try again?'

Oliver considered. 'No. It's early to be pissed, even for him. He doesn't usually take anything until after he's prepared the evening meal.'

'Want me to go?' Mike offered.

'Sure. I've got it here. Once you've confirmed he's okay, take a break. You're overdue one.'

'Thanks, Captain.'

'Let me know our cook is alive. We're due to arrive in Rosslare in ten hours. Grab some sleep and be back here to help me dock.'

'Will do. See you soon.'

And putting on his jacket, Mike Bernie went out into the tempest.

2

It took the pilot no more than fifteen seconds to get from the bridge to the doorway leading down to the galley, but within those few moments he was soaked to the skin by rain that fell in sheets. The yellow weatherproof jacket kept his upper body mostly dry, but despite having the hood up, water was blasted into his face by the ferocious force of the gale, and rivulets ran down his neck and soaked into the back of his shirt.

Shivering, he descended the narrow metal stairs three at a time until he reached the door to the ship's kitchen and pushed it open.

'Derek, do you think you're above standard safety protocols?' he called out as he entered. 'Is a simple "yes, all is well" too much for you?'

The galley was long and low ceilinged: one side of the space consisted of a hob and a counter; the other was covered in store cupboards and a tall fridge. The swarthy chef, however, was nowhere to be seen.

Mike strode over to the cooking station, scouting about to see if the ship's cook had, as their captain suspected, been imbibing alcohol before his usual drinking time. There was no sign of early boozing however. In fact, the bottle of cheap vodka Derek kept in the cupboard at his knees was stowed in its compartment, held in place by a plastic ring to prevent it from getting broken as the vessel dipped and rolled in the waves.

Mike paused for a moment, considering where the cook might be.

As the ship took another lurching dive, he reasoned that Derek might have fallen foul to seasickness. This in mind, he ducked out of the galley and, using the walls to keep from falling, made his way to the toilet at the other end of the hallway.

He banged on the door with his fist. 'Derek, are you in there?'

There was no reply. The wind shrieked and bellowed outside, echoing and booming against the hull, making Mike feel very small and vulnerable, even within the sturdy vessel. He reached for the handle, turned it and pushed the door open, expecting to find the wrinkled and untidy form of the cook bent over the toilet, purging his stomach and moaning.

The bathroom was, however, empty.

Mike wondered if Derek might have gone to one of the other bathrooms, deep within the bowels of the ship, but couldn't see any reason why he would. It made no sense, particularly if the man was sick.

He was standing gazing into the open door, trying to work out where to look next, when, from the corner of his eye, he detected movement.

It was so slight, he wondered if he might have imagined it – just the vaguest flicker of shadow at the end of the corridor. Mike thought it might just have been a flurry of rain that had blown in through the door, which he thought he'd closed but was, in fact, swinging open.

The pilot walked quickly to the end of the hall and reached to fasten the hatch when, through the lashing rain outside, he spied a slender figure as it disappeared behind a bulkhead on the deck.

His first thought was that it must be Derek, but the cook was a large, bulky man, and this individual was small by comparison, moving with a speed and grace he'd never witnessed in the galley master.

In fact, there was no one among the crew who matched the physicality of the person Mike had just seen.

What the hell is going on? he wondered.

The deck was off limits for any member of the ship's complement during such hard weather, and there wasn't a soul aboard who didn't know that. Mike realised he was now faced with not one but two problems: Derek was missing, and someone else (identity as yet unknown) was at large on the deck during a freak storm.

There was nothing to be done but to go out there and attempt to bring whoever it was back inside. Mike pulled up his hood and plunged into the elements.

Using rails bolted to the side of the hull and to each bulkhead, he made his way painstakingly along the deck. Visibility was limited – he could discern objects only about a metre in front of him – and every now and again the *Dolphin* rolled so violently he was literally taken off his feet, only his grip on the safety rail preventing him from landing on the deck and sliding towards a watery doom.

Mike felt a jolt of real terror, a white-knuckle panic that threatened to overwhelm him for a moment, and, like a reflex, wrapped his arms about the rail and pulled his knees up to his chest, temporarily unable to move. Being on deck in a storm of this magnitude was genuinely life-threatening, and with the rails slick with rain, the threat was even more acute.

But like all sailors who spend their working lives traversing a medium that seems intent on killing them, Mike knew there was nothing to be gained from focusing on the what ifs. Given a choice, he wouldn't be in this position, but that, in truth, was the point: the moment one of the passengers on the boat he was piloting found themselves in peril, it was his sworn duty to get them to safety.

Even if he didn't have a clue who they were.

Coming back to himself, he loosened his grip very slightly and inched forward, finally reaching the end of the deck. He could still see no sign of the mysterious passenger.

Standing in the midst of the elemental fury, he shielded his eyes with his hand and peered through the downpour, desperately searching for any sign of the figure.

He was about to give up and head back inside when, to his horror, something grasped him by the ankle, making him cry out in shock and jump.

Looking down, he saw that the individual he'd witnessed leaving the safety of the corridor was now crouched at his feet. He only saw the person for a moment, but he had time to note piercing eyes set into a pale face and that they were lashed to the rail with a strand of shipping rope.

'We have to get back inside!' he shouted, his words barely audible over the roaring gale.

The stowaway (he was now sure they weren't a member of his crew) gazed at him with those piercing eyes, and then the ship tumbled again, and the stranger made a sharp movement so fast Mike barely registered it. It caused him to lose his balance and tilt backwards, his arms pinwheeling, his whole body becoming weightless, just for a second, before gravity took hold. And then he was gone, dropping like a stone from the deck of the ship he'd steered and loved for more than a decade before crashing into waves that reached up and swallowed him down into the relentless dark of the sea.

PART ONE

WASHED UP

'I, poor miserable Robinson Crusoe, being shipwrecked during a dreadful storm in the offing, came on shore on this dismal, unfortunate island, which I called "The Island of Despair."'

— DANIEL DEFOE

3

Detective Inspector Tessa Burns stood on a sand dune overlooking Ballymoney Beach in North Wexford, her hands shoved deeply into the pockets of her green parka, the hood up, obscuring her shoulder-length dark hair, which she usually wore tied up in a ponytail. Tessa was five foot six and had a strong build: broad shoulders that tapered to a slim waist and legs that, while not long, were powerfully muscled, though the blue jeans she habitually wore tended to cover that fact. Her face was strongly featured, laughter lines around her mouth showing that, despite the nature of her work, this was a woman who laughed a lot, and despite her thirty-eight years, her forehead was smooth. Her green eyes had flecks of brown through them. She didn't think of herself as attractive, but most who knew her did, although Tessa Burns wasn't the kind of person who entertained such comment.

She was all about her job.

There was a wind coming in from the Irish Sea, and while it was only September and a mild evening when Tessa had left Dublin a little over an hour ago, it was now just after 7.30 p.m., and there was a distinct chill in the air.

Ballymoney was as pretty a beach as one could hope to see. The section Tessa looked down upon was on a curve in the shoreline, and directly below her was a shelf of rock which stepped down to a bed of what appeared to be perfectly round stones that ran right to the water. The stone and shale only served as a short break in a perfect spread of yellow sand that skirted the shoreline until it vanished round the next curve, perhaps a kilometre to Tessa's left. The ocean was grey in the autumn evening light, the waves that washed onto the shore capped with white foam.

The idyll wasn't as peaceful as it might have been however.

A mix of vehicles were parked on the beach below her: she could discern the white and blue of the Irish police force's Garda patrol cars, the orange-and-yellow check of coastguard jeeps, and dotted among them the fluorescent yellow-and-green of ambulances. People milled here and there, coming and going from the huge object that lay, tilted at an angle, just on the tide-line, so long most of it remained in the crashing surf: the grey looming hulk of a cargo ship, run aground on Ireland's treacherous south-east coast.

Tessa peered at the crowd of responders and picked out the figure she was looking for, one that was far taller than the others and considerably broader at the shoulders – her colleague, Detective Danny Murphy. The huge man was making his way up the beach, and she hauled her right hand out of her pocket and vigorously waved at him.

Obviously consumed by what he'd just been doing, the big detective didn't notice her at first, and Tessa increased the sweep of her arm until he looked up and returned the gesture before breaking into a jog and coming to meet her.

'So what's the story?' Tessa asked when he was standing at her side.

'You're looking at the *Dolphin*, an Irish ship bound for Rosslare that left Oslo three days ago. It went out of radio contact in a storm on the first day of sailing and never reported back in again.'

'They've been missing for two and a half days?' Tessa asked, looking up at Danny, eyebrows raised.

He was six feet four and weighed in at 240 pounds, putting him just over sixteen stone, almost all of which was muscle. This afternoon he was dressed in a thigh-length jacket over black jeans. A grey flat cap was on his head, and beneath it, his dark hair was cut close. His sharp-featured face was clean-shaven, and Tessa knew his blue eyes, which continued to dart here and there about the beach, saw everything.

If she were to ask him in two hours' time how many police cars there had been on the strand while they'd been there, he would be able to tell her exactly and would probably know the registration plates of most of them.

'We're only a bit up the coast from Rosslare,' Tessa observed. 'They almost hit their target – just overshot it a bit.'

'It wasn't by design,' Danny replied. 'There's only one crewmember on board, and he wasn't in any position to navigate.'

Tessa cocked an eyebrow at her partner. 'Could you be a bit more specific?'

'Someone cut his throat. I'm not a pathologist, but it looks like he's been dead for hours. The ship drifted here.'

'Do we have a suspect?'

'Not yet. The state pathologist is half an hour away, so hopefully she can give us something to go on with the deceased. Forensics are on their way but won't arrive for a few hours yet – they're coming directly from a crime scene in Roscommon. We've got the recordings from the security cameras, and we're downloading the ship's logs. So I'd say we've got enough to get working on.'

'Okay. Dawn said there are other people on board though.'

'There are, yes, though we're not considering them as being directly involved in the murder.'

'And what do they have to say?'

'Nothing, as yet.'

'You've been talking to them?'

'I've talked *to* them, yes. They're just not answering.'

Tessa sighed and gazed down at the grounded ship. She'd had little experience of the sea, and the freighter seemed like an alien vessel, an object from another world that had lived a life completely unknown to her.

'Are they still on board?'

'Yes. I wanted to move them, but the local sergeant is refusing to budge until someone with authority gets here.'

Tessa laughed cynically. 'Who does he think is coming?'

'I told him my team leader was on her way and that she had the direct authority of the commissioner.'

'Oh you did, did you?'

'I did, yes.'

Tessa sighed and hunched her shoulders against the wind. 'Alright,' she said. 'Let's go and take a look.'

And together they trudged down the sand dune to the beach and its ghost ship.

4

A ladder had been set against the *Dolphin*'s hull that allowed them to climb aboard. Tessa thought the deck seemed surprisingly empty when they reached it, just a long flat space with a couple of what looked like steel boxes rising from it to break the metal plateau here and there. There were a couple of winches, one on each side of the boat, and near the end was a structure that seemed to be constructed from glass, which she figured was where the steering wheel was – or whatever mechanism was used to control a vessel like this.

Tessa wondered if the ship's emptiness was somehow seeping out, and making the whole thing seem even lonelier and more desolate than it normally would have been. The grey, rolling waves stretched out into the distance behind the *Dolphin*, frigid and uncaring.

She shuddered.

'Where are the survivors?'

'Below,' Danny replied and led her back out onto the deck to one of the metal boxes, which had a door set into it.

The entrance opened onto a dark and narrow stairwell, and Tessa followed her guide as he descended. The steps led to a long corridor with doors on each side, just wide enough to accommodate Danny's build (in both height and girth). It seemed to go on forever, and at the end was another stairwell, which they also went down, only to find yet another long walkway.

The whole place smelled of seawater and disinfectant, and she didn't like it one bit.

'Nearly.'

They reached the fifth door on the right, and Danny paused for a moment.

'They're in here. There's a social worker with them at the minute, but she's got nothing out of them either. Maybe you'll have better luck.'

'I'm banking on Maggie and Pav working their magic, but I'll give it a go,' Tessa said, referring to their colleague and her ever-present terrier-mix dog.

'Okay then,' Danny said. 'Let's get you introduced to the new arrivals.'

He ducked through the doorway, and Tessa, who didn't need to duck but found herself doing so anyway, followed.

The room was small and cramped, full of bulky packages of tinned goods, all wrapped in clear plastic, cardboard trays containing bottles of drinking water and various other food-stuffs. Tessa could see that a stack of bottled water had been pushed aside to reveal a narrow space in which someone had placed three camp beds. Seated on one of these were three children: two boys and a girl; Tessa put them at perhaps six, eight and ten. The eldest – he was certainly the tallest of the three, even sitting – had almost white-blonde hair, while the middle child, also a boy, had a shock of red. The youngest, the little girl, was dark-haired with fine features.

For all these differences, there was a clear familial similarity. Tessa reckoned it was a safe bet to assume they were siblings.

The kids were all dressed in warm clothes: jumpers, jeans and stout shoes, and they seemed clean and well fed. Tessa could see no marks of violence, and while there was a stillness about them that spoke of shock or trauma, they didn't appear terrified. They sat huddled together, but their expressions were neutral, and they watched her and Danny as they came in with interest.

It was as if they'd suddenly materialised on this marooned boat out of nowhere, beamed aboard from some other place. As if by magic.

A woman with a thick plait of hair down her back was sitting on an overturned crate just opposite the three waifs, and she stood when the detectives came in. Her jumper was so bright the colours showed through the jumpsuit she was wearing.

'Gloria, this is my team leader, Tessa Burns.'

'Gloria,' Tessa said, shaking the proffered hand, then she turned to the three children and smiled.

'Hi, guys,' she said. 'I'm Tessa, and Danny and I are police officers who work especially with kids who are in trouble. We're here to try and help you, find out where your family is if we can. Or if your mam and dad aren't around anymore, or are in hospital or in prison, we can arrange for you to see them if you want to, and find out where your carers are – or get you new ones.'

The children showed no sign of understanding her but continued to eye her with huge, liquid eyes.

'What we also do is try to work out why kids like you find themselves all alone and in trouble in the first place. But it would be a real help to us if you could start by telling us your names and where you're from.'

No response. Just more silent stares.

'Are you from Norway?' Tessa asked. '*Norge?*'

The use of the Norwegian word for what might or might

not have been their home country elicited no more of a reaction than anything else the detective had said.

'I already tried something like that using Google Translate on my phone,' Gloria told her. 'If they speak Norwegian, it'll make your job harder, but so far, there's no indication what their first language is.'

'The job wouldn't be worth doing if it wasn't hard,' Danny said in a voice that suggested he wasn't altogether happy about this fact.

'Okay,' Tessa said. 'Our friend, Maggie, should be here shortly, and she's the expert on working with traumatised kids. I don't think this dank little room is the place for her to do her thing though. And it's a priority to get them medically checked out.'

'Agreed,' Gloria said. 'One of the paramedics has given them a once-over, but with your permission, I'd like to take them to Wexford General for a full examination. Your colleague could see them there?'

'I'll tell the sergeant to release them,' Tessa said. 'And I'll call Maggie and tell her to follow you. Do they have any stuff? Toys? Other clothes? Wash gear?'

'Local boys have been combing the ship,' Danny said. 'And they've found nothing.'

Tessa blinked. 'But their clothes look fresh on today.'

'And they all smell of soap,' Danny agreed. 'It's weird.'

Tessa thought about that but could make no sense of it. Deciding it would have to wait, she said: 'Kids, would you like to come with us? We need to get you checked out at the hospital, but after that, maybe you could have some ice cream?'

Once again, no move or reaction.

In desperation, Tessa held out her hand.

And slowly, painstakingly, the dark little girl tentatively reached out and took it. Tessa felt an explosion of compassion in her chest. There was something so gentle about the action, as if the child was saying: *Okay. I'll trust you. But please don't betray that trust.*

The detective met the child's eyes and tried to communicate in her gaze that she wouldn't. That she would, in fact, do everything in her power to honour the faith this lost urchin was placing in her.

The children took each other's hands, forming a daisy chain with Tessa, who then led them – followed by Danny and Gloria – through the dark chilly corridors, up the metal steps and out onto the deck.

There the strange cargo stood, blinking uncertainly in the early-evening light, before looking back at her and then around them at the curving, stony beach.

'Welcome to Ireland,' Tessa said. 'Or should it be welcome home?'

The children made no comment.

5

Tessa and Danny waved goodbye to the children, safe in the knowledge that Maggie would take care of them at the hospital, then turned back to the ship.

'You're certain no one else is hiding out on the ship? Has it been thoroughly searched?' Tessa asked as they trudged back across the sand.

'The coastguard has been all over it. They're certain no one else was on board.'

'Is it possible someone jumped overboard before it ran aground?'

'I interviewed the woman who called it in,' Danny said. 'A Mrs Maureen Gaffney. She watched the *Dolphin* from when it was several miles out and came down to the beach before it was driven up onto the sand by the tide. She insists no one could have jumped off without her seeing.'

'You think she's reliable?'

Danny shrugged. 'She's elderly but has all her wits about her. Told me her father had a boat, so she seems to know what she's talking about. And she spends her days watching the shoreline – she's into wildlife and such. I think we can take her testimony as good.'

They headed back up the ladder and stopped at the top. A young, uniformed guard, his face pockmarked from acne, watched impassively as Danny and Tessa donned white over-alls, complete with hoods to cover their hair and prevent any follicles from contaminating the crime scene, and pulled plastic coverings over their shoes.

When both detectives were suited up, Tessa asked the guard: 'Where's the vic?'

'On the bridge.'

Tessa looked about her but couldn't see anything that looked remotely like a bridge. 'Am I missing something?'

'It's what they call the control room,' Danny said. 'Where they steer the ship. It's the glass building over there.'

She'd been right about that part at least.

'You're going to have to explain the nautical lingo to me for a while,' Tessa said as they walked across the desk. 'I was in the army, not the navy, so I'm not in my comfort zone.'

When they entered the ship's control centre, they found another person dressed in similar protective gear leaning over a body – it was slumped in a chair in front of a panel covered in buttons, dials and screens, all of which were dark and inactive.

'Hello, the house,' Tessa said.

The figure straightened up, revealing he was almost as tall as Danny, but with a slim and rangy build. Tessa was immedi-ately struck by a set of very pale blue eyes that showed a keen intelligence, but the face mask didn't reveal much more.

'DI Tessa Burns and DS Danny Murphy,' she said in intro-duction.

'Coastguard Chief Officer in Charge Jim Sheils,' the man said. 'You're not from any of the Wexford stations.'

'We've been sent from Harcourt Street,' Tessa replied.

'We're a special working group reporting directly back to the commissioner.'

'She feel we aren't capable of running the case ourselves?' Jim Sheils asked, turning back to the dead man.

'You'd have to ask her that,' Tessa said dryly. 'What have we got, Chief Officer Sheils?'

'We have the ship's captain, one Oliver Patrick Burgess. It looks as if he was at his post when someone came up behind him and cut his throat.'

Tessa moved forward to get a closer look.

The man in the pilot's seat was small and thin to the point of possibly being underweight. He had a dense beard that did nothing to hide the bony angles of his face, and, as Chief Officer Sheils had reported, a wound had been opened in his throat that ran from one side to the other, revealing the glistening white structure of his larynx. Blood had soaked into the heavy woollen jumper he wore, drying to give it a brittle, almost plastic look.

More of the late Captain Burgess's bodily fluids had pooled on the console in front of him, and the floor about him was blackened with it.

Tessa cast about but could see no drips or drag marks to indicate that Sheils' hypothesis wasn't correct.

'Murder weapon?' she asked.

'Haven't found one yet,' the chief officer replied. 'I'm not an expert, but I'd put money on us discovering one of the kitchen knives missing though. Looks like that cut was made by a big blade.'

'And you'd be able to recognise that?' Tessa asked, probably more tersely than she'd intended.

Sheils looked over at her, and she saw annoyance flash in those impossibly pale eyes.

'I know you're in the sticks now, DI Burns, but we know how to do our job here too. In fact, I don't know why you're here at all. This murder occurred while the *Dolphin* was at sea, making this case the coastguard's jurisdiction. If you don't mind my saying so, neither you nor Andre the Giant there are coast-guards or even nautical experts.'

'We're here because of the passengers downstairs,' Danny said.

'Why don't you go and see them then and let me do my job?'

'The state pathologist will be here shortly,' Tessa said. 'I'll be back then to talk to her.'

'I'll be wanting a word with her myself,' Sheils said, but he'd returned his attention to the crime scene and, it seemed, had lost interest in his war of words with the detectives.

6

Maggie Doolan steered her electric wheelchair into the family room in the paediatric wing of Wexford General Hospital.

The chair was an impressive-looking piece of kit, one Maggie had personally modified over the years, amping up the motor, adding a small laptop computer on a platform close to her right hand should she need to do some online investigating while out and about. Beside the laptop was a cradle containing Maggie's mobile phone. A scabbard that held an extendable baton was built into the panel at her right leg, and a similar one on the left-hand side held a can of pepper spray. Just beside that was a red button which, if pressed, activated an alarm loud enough to shock most assailants into momentary inaction – but just long enough to give her the upper hand, while hopefully also bringing assistance.

Maggie was thirty-two, with a strong, angular face that contained deep laughter lines. Today her long auburn hair was worn loose about her shoulders, and she was sporting a black leather jacket over a plain white T-shirt and black jeans, her feet shod in Doc Marten boots. On Maggie's knees sat a small, black-and-white terrier-mix dog – Pavlov, her closest friend and work colleague.

As a family liaison officer, Maggie's job involved making traumatised families feel safe and secure, guiding them through the process of a police investigation, which could be deeply distressing. Pavlov helped with that no end. He was gentle, warm-hearted and was particularly patient and affectionate with children, enduring tight hugs and tolerating having his ears and tail pulled with remarkable stoicism, seeming to understand the manhandling would stop once the children understood he wasn't going to run away.

Once that dawned, the healing could begin, and Pavlov was always instrumental in that process. Lots of kids wouldn't talk about their experiences unless the little dog was curled up beside them. And many parents were no different, seeming to need his comforting presence before they felt safe enough to open up.

Maggie soon came to understand that she and Pavlov were a team, and when Tessa had approached her to join the new task force, it had gone without saying that she and her canine friend came as a package.

The family room the pair now entered had a worn floral carpet and a couch that was upholstered in some kind of green felt-like material. A flat-screen TV hung from the wall, showing the animated children's show *Booba*. On the floor, each sitting cross-legged and watching the TV intently, were the three children Maggie and Pavlov had come to see.

A woman dressed in a colourful patchwork jumper, a long plait slung over her left shoulder, was sitting on the floor beside them, looking far less comfortable than the kids.

'Hello, everyone,' Maggie said cheerfully as she gently powered the chair inside, making sure not to scuff the door frame – despite the Irish laws around accessibility, Maggie had learned long ago that some doors were simply too narrow to accommodate an electric chair.

'You must be Maggie,' the woman said, standing up stiffly and extending her hand.

'And you must be Gloria. This is Pavlov, and we're very pleased to meet you.'

They shook, and the social worker gingerly patted Pav, who raised his head in acknowledgement.

'And who do we have here?'

'Um... I still don't have any names,' Gloria said.

'That's okay,' Maggie replied, rolling up to where the children were sitting. 'Hey, guys, can we mute the TV for a bit? You can get back to your cartoon soon. I'd just like to talk to you for a little while.'

Three pairs of eyes turned to look at her for a moment before returning to the screen. Maggie waited to see if there might be a delayed reaction then cleared her throat loudly.

'Guys, do you understand me? I'd like to have a quick chat with you, and I think that would go better if the sound was turned off. As much for your benefit as for mine. So how about it?'

This time not so much as a single gaze was thrown her way. Maggie watched the trio closely. They were all pale complexioned, and while each child had startlingly different-coloured hair, their locks all had the same thick texture and had been cut in slightly old-fashioned styles, making Maggie think of kids in movies from the early 1980s – *ET* or *The Goonies* perhaps. Their clothes were all clean and looked new but were similarly slightly out of fashion. The outfits all consisted of jumpers and jeans, but the cuts and designs seemed to be of another era.

What an odd group they were.

'Pav, will you help me out here?' Maggie asked her friend quietly.

The dog stood up in her lap and barked sharply three times.

The sound was piercing and wholly unexpected, and the three kids (not to mention the social worker) all jumped. Now all three of the unusual children were staring at Maggie, and this time they didn't look away.

'I don't know if you spotted Pavlov when I came in,' Maggie said, piloting the chair over to the coffee table, where she spied the TV remote nestled among the boxes of games and puzzles.

She picked it up and muted the cartoon.

'I know he startled you just now, but he's actually really friendly. Would you like to pet him?'

None of the kids moved. Maggie rolled a bit closer, so she was within reach, and made an exaggerated motion of stroking Pav's white furry back.

'See? He really likes it. Just as long as you're gentle.'

For what felt like forever, none of the children moved. Maggie wondered if this might be the first time Pavlov had failed to elicit a response, but then, slowly, the smallest child, a dark-haired girl, came up onto her knees and reached out a pale hand.

'That's it, sweetie,' Maggie said. 'This is my friend Pavlov, and he's very pleased to meet you.'

The child touched the dog cautiously, and when the animal didn't move, she became more confident, running her hand from his head down to his tail in gentle strokes.

'There you go,' Maggie said, smiling. 'See? He's very gentle. I think he likes you.'

The little girl turned to her siblings, a grin of happiness on her face, and following a scurrying motion, the red-haired boy was also pressed up against Maggie's chair, gently petting Pavlov.

'There's room for one more.' Maggie grinned, looking over at the eldest of the three.

He scowled at her and turned back to the now muted TV.

'That's okay,' Maggie said, tossing the remote towards him –

it landed on the floor at his feet. 'You can have the volume back on as long as it's not too loud.'

The boy eyed her suspiciously but picked up the device and hit the volume. Instead of keeping it low however, he turned it up as loud as it could go, the sound of the jaunty, comical music deafening in the small room, the speakers on the TV buzzing and rattling with each bass note. His two siblings covered their ears, and Pavlov whined in discomfort.

'Hey! Turn it down please!' Maggie shouted over the din.

In a fit of temper, the lad hauled back his arm and flung the remote directly at the family liaison officer as hard as he could. It was a good throw, well balanced and deftly performed. The controller spun once, straightened and would have hit Maggie right in the forehead had she not, in a calm movement that looked almost languid, reached up and plucked it out of the air just before it reached its target.

She hit mute again and rolled over to the boy, who pretended to ignore her.

'You don't know me,' she said, 'so I'm going to give you a pass on that one. But listen carefully, because this is important. I've only got two rules. Rule number one: we're working together because bad things have happened, and we're all a bit stressed and a bit angry, and that's okay. But no matter what we're doing, whether that's drawing or playing a game or even just chatting, we all do our best. It doesn't matter if you make a mistake or if things don't always go right once you've tried your best – you can still feel good about what you did because you worked hard at it. Rule number two: no one hurts anyone, even themselves.'

The boy slowly turned to look at her. Maggie thought she saw some remorse in his blue eyes, but she couldn't be certain.

'Okay then,' she said and turned the volume back on – but at a normal level.

The other two children continued to play with Pavlov, and Maggie turned to Gloria.

'Well done,' the social worker said, sounding tired but relieved. 'That's more than I've managed in four hours with them.'

'None of them threw anything at you?'

Gloria laughed. 'You know what I mean!'

'You didn't have my secret weapon,' Maggie said, winking at her. 'Wasn't a level playing field.'

'You're kind,' Gloria said. 'I don't believe you, but tonight I'll take it. The coffee they've left for the families is cheap instant shit. I'm going to go to the canteen to get a decent cup – will I bring you one?'

'Please,' Maggie said. 'And how about some juice or 7Up or something for the kids?'

Gloria smiled, nodded and left.

Maggie watched the kids playing with Pavlov – all three of them now – and knew this small victory meant little in terms of the struggle to come. She sensed these children were carrying secrets that would bring a darkness with them once they were unearthed.

But darkness was something Maggie and her team were accustomed to dealing with.

7

Leaving the ship behind, Tessa and Danny drove the five kilometres into Gorey, where they parked outside the police station, at the southern end of the busy town's main street.

Gorey had all the hallmarks of a small town that had expanded rapidly during Ireland's recent economic boom. Built on a hill, the main thoroughfare snaked downwards, with various side streets branching off it on either side. Only an hour from Dublin, it had, over the past decade, become part of the commuter belt to Ireland's capital city, with housing estates sprouting up on its outskirts and a large shopping centre and industrial estate adding to the sense that this was only the beginning of that expansion.

Yet Gorey retained its small-town charm, with lots of little cafés, old-world bars and antique shops scattered amongst high-end clothes boutiques and gastropubs.

Sergeant James Tibbett, a grey-haired man with a large paunch and kind grey eyes, met them at the door and welcomed them in.

'The guys from the coastguard are going through the logs

and manifests and will give us an update as soon as they have anything useful, but in the meantime, we've been looking over the security tapes,' he told them as they settled into his office.

The sergeant had more tea and biscuits waiting for them on a tray, and Tessa helped herself to a mug.

'Anything showing up yet?' she asked.

'Well there's days of tape to go through, so I've put three men on it, but there are a couple of things they've come across already that are... well they seem very damn odd,' Tibbett replied.

'We're all ears,' Tessa said, taking a sip of her tea and noting, with some disappointment, that it wasn't Barry's, her favourite brand. Danny and Maggie often pointed out (not quite jokingly) that Barry's tea was her only real addiction.

'Take a look at this,' the sergeant said, turning the screen of his desktop around so they could all see it. 'This is lower deck one, and we're looking at the first day out of Oslo, at about the two-hour mark.'

The image on the screen was grimy, the light poor, but they could still clearly see two men fighting. One was large, swarthy, wearing an apron over what looked to be a grey tracksuit. The other was a smaller man with full beard, his hair closely cropped. The bigger man was pushing the smaller, shoving him, and seemed to be yelling as he did so. Then he grabbed the smaller man by the scruff of his neck and began bludgeoning him about the head with his other fist.

'The freight company has sent us the files on the whole crew, complete with photographs, so we can identify anyone who shows up on the footage,' Tibbett said. 'The big one is Derek Sherlock, the ship's cook. The smaller is Oliver Burgess, the ship's captain.'

'Are we watching a mutiny taking place?' Danny asked.

'If we are, I don't think it was successful,' Tibbett replied.

As they watched, the captain, who'd just been thrown backwards by the cook, reached behind him and pulled a safety axe from where it was hanging on the wall.

'That's given him something of an advantage,' Tessa said as he flung himself at the cook.

The rest of the altercation was quick and bloody.

'Is there any indication of what started the row between them?' Tessa asked.

'No. But have a look at this.'

Tibbett fiddled with the laptop and pulled up video of another hallway in the boat, identical to the one Tessa and Danny had traversed to get to the children. The light was dim here too, but the passageway could be seen well enough. Figures came and went, and the sergeant identified each one in turn.

'So we're at three hours, see?' he said, indicating a clock in the top-right corner of the screen. 'It happens at the three hours-and-seventeen-minutes mark.'

They waited as the minutes shot past in the sped-up footage.

'Here it is.'

A figure appeared at the end of the corridor, seeming to pause at the bottom of the stairs for a long moment before shooting very quickly up the hallway, moving past the camera and out of sight. Tessa watched carefully. This individual seemed smaller than any of the others they'd seen so far – not exactly childlike, but they didn't seem an awful lot bigger. They were dressed in a jacket that hung almost to their knees, the hood of which was pulled up, obscuring their face.

The footage, dim though it was, captured what could only have been a strand of long dark hair that had escaped from the folds of that hood.

'Is it a woman?' Tessa asked.

'It could be a small man with long hair,' Danny ventured.

'Yeah,' Tibbett agreed.

'Seeing as you haven't introduced this particular person, I'm guessing we're not looking at a member of the crew?' Tessa said.

'No. I've sent a screenshot of this to the freight company who own the *Dolphin*. They don't know who she is. There were no female crewmembers, and none of the male sailors have long hair or this person's physical attributes.'

'Does she show up again?' Tessa asked.

'My guys have only been able to view a little over six more hours. We have her in two more locations. Or him. Or them. You don't know what's right to say these days.'

Tessa waved that off. 'Have the children shown up on any security cameras yet?'

'No. Not a sign of them.'

'Could they be the children of one of the crewmembers?'

'That was our first thought. Only two of the men aboard had families, and they've all been accounted for.'

Tessa sighed and sat back, picking up a bourbon cream from the plate and taking half of it in a bite.

'Are all the goods aboard? Has anything been stolen?'

'Nothing as far as we can tell. A man from the Dublin office of the shipping company is on his way. He'll have to give the last word on that. But to be honest, Tessa, this doesn't look like a robbery to me.'

'What does it look like then?'

'I'm damned if I know,' Sergeant Tibbett admitted.

Tessa poured more tea for herself – it wasn't Barry's, but it was better than no tea.

'So,' she said, 'we know Captain Burgess killed the cook, Sherlock. But we don't know why, and we have no idea what happened to the rest of the crew – we have to assume they're dead, but we don't know how they died or who killed them. We don't know who that strange woman is wandering about the ship, and we don't know who the children are, how they got on the ship or why they were there.'

'That about sums it up,' Tibbett said.

'Heartening, isn't it?' Tessa replied, reaching for another bourbon cream.

8

Tessa and Danny stood in the car park beside Tessa's red 1984 Ford Capri. Cars cruised by on the road, people on their way to dinner or the movies, living lives that didn't involve lost children or missing sailors.

'What do you make of it?' Tessa asked her colleague.

'I'm not sure yet. It's a strange one.'

'I'd like to know why the captain killed the cook. From how I viewed the fight, it looked as if the cook started it.'

'Well the captain finished it,' Danny said. 'Being at sea, cooped up on board a ship for hours, maybe days at a time, tensions must run high sometimes.'

'Yes, but these men are surely all used to that,' Tessa said. 'Do we think the captain killed the rest of the crew?'

'It doesn't seem likely. A boat of that size, wouldn't he need at least some crew to dock it safely. And if he killed the rest of them, who killed him?'

'That is a very good question,' Tessa replied.

'Could the strange woman on the security footage be another one of the kids, one we haven't found yet?'

'I wondered that too. Size-wise looks like she could be. Or

we might have been looking at a small adult. So it could just as easily be their mother.'

'Why isn't she still with them then?' Danny wanted to know.

'Maybe the plan was to get the kids to Ireland. They're here, so her work is done.'

'Why bring them here though?'

'Maybe their father is here,' Tessa suggested. 'Or their grandparents. Or a well-off aunt or uncle.'

'Shouldn't we have a note to that effect then? Or something to tell us that was the intention?'

'It's possible we just haven't found it yet.'

Danny shrugged. 'Can we be certain the rest of the crew are dead?'

'We know no one jumped overboard as the ship was approaching the strand,' Tessa said. 'Could another ship have picked them up at sea?'

'That would mean someone with resources was in on it. Could the shipping company have something to do with it?'

'The transport of three small kids? Why would they?'

'I've no idea. It doesn't make sense. None of it.'

'That's what we're here for,' Tessa said sagely. 'To find sense where before there was none.'

'You never told me that when you asked me to join your team.'

'I didn't want to put you off.'

'So what now?' Danny asked.

'Come on – let's drop our bags at the hotel. I want to get back to the ship to talk to the prof – I have a few questions for her about the captain's death. How he died might give us a clue as to who killed him and why. It would be good to get a look at the ship's logs too. They might just hold some information we could use. You go to Rosslare and try to catch the harbourmaster before he leaves for the day – see what you can learn about the crew of the *Dolphin*. I'd be interested in knowing if any of them have criminal records, or if the *Dolphin*, or any of the other ships from this freight company, has a reputation for smuggling or any other illicit activities.'

'I can dig into that.'

'I know you can. With a bit of luck, Maggie'll be able to get a bit more out of the kids than we did.'

Danny nodded and walked to his black Volkswagen Golf GTI, following her out of the car park and through the town, before turning right off the main street towards the Ashdown Park Hotel, where the commissioner had rooms booked for them.

The sun was low in the sky now, but their day was far from over.

CHILD #3 (THE LITTLE GIRL)

She and her brothers' lives were suddenly a blur of new, strange faces and funny accents. Before arriving in Ireland, they'd been told to speak to no one, and they stuck to what they'd been told. It wasn't difficult – everyone thought they couldn't understand English – and it was easy to stay silent.

Gloria, the lady in the brightly coloured jumper with the old-woman braid, was nice enough, but she seemed cross with them.

Maggie, the woman who came in the wheelchair with her wonderful little dog, was different though. She'd got kind of cross about the TV, but she'd got happy again really fast, and the child could see right off that this woman was kind.

And Pavlov!

What had surprised the girl about the little dog was that he'd seemed to understand everything anyone said to him right away – and not just words. As none of the children had been talking, when they'd played with him, they'd used looks and signs to tell him what they wanted, and he'd understood and done everything right away.

The best thing about Pavlov though had been that he'd made her feel good – kind of warm and snuggly and safe. The girl had known right away that he cared about her and wanted her and her brothers to be okay. When he'd snuggled into them on the couch in the dark little room where they'd watched TV, it had been the first time she'd believed she could actually be happy now everything had changed.

With Maggie and Pavlov here, maybe things would be okay. All she had to do now was make her older brother believe it.

9

'They mostly kept themselves to themselves,' Tom Doran said to Danny.

They were in his office in the headquarters of Rosslare Port Authority, which was based in a single-storey building in Rosslare Harbour, a busy, milling port that catered for passengers as well as freight of all kinds. Through the window, the detective could see a line of cars boarding a huge ferry, which he knew was bound for Fishguard in Wales. Beyond the ship, the sea looked dark and choppy, and the sky had taken on a darker hue than it had worn in Ballymoney. Danny was glad he wouldn't be making the crossing – he expected there would be a lot of seasick people on the Irish Sea that night.

The room itself was a mess of file boxes and folders which seemed to have been dumped here, there and everywhere. Danny had to move two fluorescent jackets from a chair to sit down, and he noted four coffee mugs on the desk in front of him, two of which had healthy crops of mould flourishing in them.

Doran was a barrel-shaped man, his cheeks pitted with old

acne scars, his steel-grey hair cut close to his head. The shirt and tie he wore didn't even come close to disguising the fact that, despite being in charge of human resources, as well as running administration for the port, Doran was and always would be a docker at heart. At some point he'd been promoted up the ladder and now spent most of his time in an office doing paperwork, but it was clear to Danny he didn't belong there; was in fact almost ashamed that this was what he'd been reduced to.

'You knew them? I mean, to speak to, what they were like?'

'I knew Oliver, the captain, pretty well. He'd been sailing all his life. I used to run into him back in the early 2000s when he started coming through Rosslare. He was a quiet guy. Thoughtful. He'd open up when he'd a few drinks in him, and then he might talk a bit.'

'What did he talk about?'

'Sailing. The sea. Places he'd been. Ships he'd sailed in. People he'd sailed with. He was a real old salt was Ollie.' Doran paused, looking Danny dead in the eye. 'We're talking about him and the crew in the *past* tense. You know that, don't you?'

'I do. Oliver was murdered, Mr Doran. As to the others, there's no record of the *Dolphin* making landfall anywhere other than Wexford, and none of the lifeboats had been launched. That leaves us with no other conclusion than that the other seven crew members went overboard. If they haven't been found alive by now, they won't be.'

'That's grim.'

'If you can propose a version of events that might offer hope for their survival, I'd like to hear it.'

Doran smiled sadly and shook his head. 'Your reasoning is sound. I can't argue with it.'

'Can you think of any reason why someone would wipe out an entire ship's crew?'

'Do you know any sailors, Detective?'

'No. I'm afraid I don't.'

'Most men who spend their lives at sea are an odd bunch. People are drawn to the life for different reasons. Some commit to it because seafaring is in their family, and they want to continue the tradition. Those are probably a tiny minority these days. Others do it because they enjoy the lifestyle – you're literally on the job for two months, off for a month. The money is good. You don't have to spend too much time around your family, and that offers a kind of freedom. It suits a certain mentality. Others like the sense of community they find on board a ship. A lot of sailors are orphans or have been in care, or the armed forces. They crave that feeling of belonging to something.'

'I can understand that,' Danny said. He'd lost his parents in a car accident when he was four and had grown up in a series of foster homes. For him, the Gardai had fulfilled that desire to belong to something bigger than himself, to have a huge family who would always accept him.

'Then there's the last group, and while I haven't seen any research on the subject, I suspect they're a much bigger subset than most of us in the industry would like to think.'

He stopped for a moment, and Danny had the impression he might change his mind and clam up entirely. But after some brief contemplation, he continued.

'There are lots of people who take to the seas because they're running away from something or somebody. If you sign on as a member of a ship's crew, you could quite easily disappear for eleven out of the twelve months of the year if you really wanted to, and that twelfth month you could spend any place you wished – all you'd need to do is disembark anywhere the vessel puts in to port and rejoin her when she next passes that way. Most shipping companies don't ask for a lot of references or paperwork, and a hell of a lot pay their crews cash in hand.

You want to use an alias? No one's going to do much checking. Once you can pull your weight and you don't spend your shifts with your head in the toilet from seasickness, no one gives a damn what you did in your previous life.'

'Was there anyone like that on the crew of the *Dolphin*?' Danny wanted to know.

'I didn't know them well enough to tell you for sure, but... if I had to guess, I'd say their galley cook, Derek Sherlock, had a past. He certainly was a man who knew how to cause trouble – and how to put an end to it too. I saw him take down five men in a bar fight once. A row he started, by the way, because one of them had taken his seat when he went for a piss.'

'So you're saying what happened on the *Dolphin* might be connected with Derek?'

'No. I don't think I'm saying that. You asked me if any of them had enemies. I'm damn sure he had. That's all.'

Danny made a mental note to recommend a deep search into Derek's character and history.

'Does this kind of thing happen often, in shipping?' he asked.

'What? Ships arriving at their destination without their crew?' Doran asked incredulously. 'No. It does not happen often. Which is why stories like, for instance, the *Marie Celeste*, are remembered and pass into legend.'

Danny nodded and stood up. 'Thank you for your time.'

'You're welcome. I don't think I've helped you much, but if you need anything else, you know where to find me.'

'I'll be sure to do that.'

The detective was almost at the door when he paused. 'Is anyone you know particularly pally with Derek?'

'Yes. There's a chap who works in one of the storage yards, name of Quigley, who I've seen drinking with him on more than a few occasions. Those places run around the clock, so you might still catch him.'

'Which storage yard?'

Doran told him, and Danny thanked his host and left him to his work, returning to the Volkswagen with more questions than answers.

10

Professor Julia Banks was a short, heavyset woman who sported a neatly cut grey bob, which was now obscured by the hood of her protective suit. When Tessa got back to the *Dolphin*, she'd found her standing by the control panel of the bridge writing notes on a clipboard. The body of the captain was still in its chair, and Chief Officer Jim Sheils was speaking quietly into a mobile phone, his back to her as he looked out the large windows at the waves.

It was beginning to get dark, and a light rain was peppering the waves and giving the seascape an amorphous, hazy quality.

'I've been waiting for you,' Julia said as Tessa closed the door behind her. 'The commissioner told me the Burns Unit was on the case, so I figured you'd put in an appearance sooner or later. Good it's sooner though, as the techs want to bag our deceased friend here.'

'I was needed in Gorey,' Tessa explained. 'What have you got for me?'

'Well everything I say here is with the proviso I haven't had him on my table yet, but from what I can gauge at this stage, he's been dead for approximately twenty-four hours, and while it's never possible to say with one-hundred-per-cent accuracy, the only wound I've been able to detect so far that would be liable to prove fatal is the one that opened his throat, severed his windpipe and almost bisected the carotid artery.'

'Are you saying he has other wounds?'

'Oh yes. He was in some kind of physical altercation. If you look closely, you'll see bruising about his right cheekbone, his lower lip has been split and there's distinct soft-tissue damage about his abdomen.'

'So he put up a fight?' Tessa asked.

'An amateur might think so,' the pathologist said. 'But no – these were received some time before his throat was cut. Hours before, in fact.'

'How can you tell?'

'They'd started to heal. That doesn't happen when you're dead. Look, let me show you.'

She walked over to the dead man and, using her pen as a pointer, indicated the area on the right side of his face.

'See here? I know there's a lot of blood, but I cleaned away a small area and you can see the discolouration – kind of a grey/yellow. The area is also slightly swollen – rigor will have lessened it, but when he was alive, this whole side of his face would have been puffed up and painful. Someone struck him a fair blow to the face.'

'I can see the split lip now too,' Tessa said.

'Yes. Same thing – his lower lip is slightly enlarged on that side, and you can see the split has scabbed over. If you look at his stomach, you can see clear patterns of bruising and discolouration. He took quite a pounding. To be honest, when we open him up, I wouldn't be surprised if we find some internal damage. The bruises have a large circumference, which means somebody with a big fist delivered the blows. Big fists are usually backed up by large bodies.'

'Oliver was obviously one tough cookie,' Tessa observed.

'He was, which makes it interesting that he doesn't seem to have put up any kind of fight when he met his demise.'

'There's no sign of a struggle?'

'None. The blood always tells a story, and the tale here is that the blood just flowed. So no thrashing about, no desperation. In fact, I wouldn't be surprised if this gentleman was asleep at his post when someone snuck in and cut him. He was dead before he even regained consciousness.'

Tessa nodded. 'And the murder weapon?'

'A large blade with a single cutting edge.'

'Like a cook's knife,' Chief Officer Sheils said, walking towards them, his phone call clearly over.

'Precisely,' Julia said.

'See, DI Burns,' Sheils said, and even though he was wearing a face mask, Tessa could tell he was grinning. 'We're not quite the hicks you might have thought here in the south-east.'

'I never thought you were,' Tessa said, exasperated. 'Look, I think we got off on the wrong foot. Can we start again?'

'Can you two take your professional rivalry somewhere else?' Julia asked pointedly. 'I have a body to bag and a report to finish.'

'Yes of course,' Tessa replied, embarrassed.

'The rep from the shipping company is just a few miles out,' Sheils said. 'Consider the hatchet buried for the moment, DI Burns.'

And he stalked past her and out the door.

11

Seamus Quigley, *Dolphin* cook Derek's drinking companion, was a large, jowly man who looked to be about fifty, his receding hair, which was still dark, gelled back on his head. He had a florid face, a potato-like nose with a maze of burst blood vessels, and tiny close-set eyes.

When Danny found him at 7.30 that evening in a huge warehouse a quarter of a mile from the terminal, he was piloting a forklift with remarkable speed and ability. So focused was he on the task at hand, it took the detective four full minutes to gain his attention. Once Quigley saw he was being hailed, he paused, staring at Danny, after which he waved in acknowledgement and then finished placing the pallet his vehicle was transporting on top of a stack – one of thousands in that room alone.

This done, the swarthy man steered the forklift over to a bay by the wall of the storage unit, dismounted and approached the policeman.

'You're the Garda Mr Doran told me was asking after Derek,' he said, extending a sweaty hand for Danny to shake.

Quigley was wearing a set of oil-stained blue overalls which were unbuttoned to midway down his flabby chest. Danny noted with some distaste that the man didn't appear to be wearing anything beneath them, at least not on his upper half.

'Yes. I'm Detective Sergeant Danny Murphy. I believe you were a friend of Derek Sherlock's?'

'Was?'

'You haven't heard about the *Dolphin* then?'

'The ship? What about her?'

'She ran aground in Gorey yesterday evening. The crew were missing, all except the captain, who was dead. It's certain the others were all lost at sea.'

'*What*? How? I mean, Derek had been a sailor most of his life. He'd survived storms, hijacks, mutinies and one bastard of a captain who confiscated his private stash of booze for more than half a three-week sailing.'

'Can we go somewhere and talk, Mr Quigley?'

Quigley thought about that for a moment then nodded. 'Let's go for a smoke.'

'I don't smoke actually,' Danny said.

'You can watch me then.'

The greasy-looking man led Danny through a maze of stacked pallets, most of which seemed to contain myriad sacks of animal feed, and out a metal door that opened onto an almost-empty car park. He took a Silk Cut Purple box from the breast pocket of the foul overalls and a cheap, orange plastic lighter from the hip pocket, and fired one up, blowing a plume of smoke into the darkening night.

'What do you want to know?' he asked Danny after he'd taken a couple of deep inhales.

'How long is it since you've seen Derek?'

'I dunno. Three months maybe.'

'Did he call you when he was in Wexford?'

'What? Call me? No, we'd run into one another in Chas-by's, a pub in the harbour. I go there most evenin's after work, and Derek, he'd go there sometimes when he was home for a few days. Look, I'm a hard drinker. I know that. Prob'ly an alcoholic, though I don't like the word. Just a fuckin' label if y'ask me. I can go on a ten-day bender and be totally fucked up, then I might not touch the stuff for a month. Then I'll go hard on it again for a while, then ease off. Does that sound like an alcoholic to you?'

Danny thought that that sounded exactly like an alcoholic, but he just shrugged non-committally.

'Derek, he was the same. I can get kind of loud when I gets enough into me, 'specially vodka, and he is – sorry, was – like that too. People di'n't always want to be around us, so we got to drinkin' t'gether when we ran into one another.'

'What kind of a man was he?'

'D'in't I just tell you?'

'You told me he was a heavy drinker who was loud when he was drunk,' Danny said. 'I imagine there was more to him than that.'

'Oh,' Quigley said, stubbing out his cigarette against the wall and taking out another. 'Well yeah... yeah, course there was.'

Danny looked at him expectantly.

'He could be funny, like.'

'How? Did he tell jokes?'

'Sometimes, but they was *never* funny. Usually they was kind of nasty. Cruel, like.'

'Could you tell me what you mean by "cruel"?'

'Like he told me one about Jews in concentration camps. I don't remember the bit that was s'posed to be funny, only that it wasn't. I'm not a educated man, but I knows right from wrong. I told him I di'n't like it.'

'But you say he could be funny in other ways?'

'Yeah. He tole me stories about some of the places he'd been and the scrapes he got into. They was always funny.'

'What kind of scrapes?'

'He told me one about bein' thrown out of a brothel in Hamburg cause he tried to take the money back off the girl he'd been with when she wouldn't do this particular thing he wanted cause he wouldn't take a shower. Now *that* was a funny story.'

Danny thought it was, actually, pretty unpleasant, though he couldn't decide if it was in as poor taste as a joke about the Holocaust. He decided to just push on.

'Did he have a family?'

'If he did, he never said anythin' about them.'

'You say he'd been sailing all his life?'

'Well, for a long time.'

'Do you know what he did before that?'

'Um... well... I...'

'You do know that lying to a member of the Gardai is a crime, Mr Quigley?'

'He told me he'd been in prison once. I think he went to sea after he got out.'

'Do you know where he was in prison?'

Quigley just shook his head.

'Was he from Wexford?'

'He said he grew up in Dublin.'

Danny nodded. 'What did he serve time for?'

'He said he was in a gang when he was younger, and they was into some bad stuff.'

'Bad stuff?'

Quigley nodded.

'Can you be more specific?'

'That's all he said. It ain't really the done thing to ask a guy about that kind of stuff unless he decides to tell you himself.'

Danny let that one go. It seemed to him that Derek bringing it up in the first place was an invitation to ask about it, but he sensed that Quigley wasn't the most astute of individuals. Such social nuances were liable to escape him.

'Anything else you can tell me about him?'

'He seemed to be sad. I mean, he seemed *very* unhappy. Not just that he was an alcoholic but as if he was carrying something. As if he had a' – Quigley searched for the right word – 'a *burden*, y'know?'

'Did you ever ask him about it?'

'Naw. I asked him if he was okay once. That was about as far as it went.'

'What did he say?'

'Um... he said: "No, I'm not okay. I owe a debt and I'm forced to repay it every day, and it weighs heavy upon me." Or something like that.'

'He told you he owed someone a debt?'

'Yeah. He definitely used the word debt.'

Danny pondered that. 'Is there anything else you can think of?'

'He had tattoos. Lots of them. On his chest, his arms, one that came up almost to his neck. I thought it was just a sailor thing.'

Danny knew those types of tattoos were, in fact, often a sign of gang membership, but he kept that information to himself. He wasn't sure it would mean anything to Quigley anyway.

'Can you remember any of them?'

'One was the Madonna and Child; it was on his chest – I saw it once when he called for me here last summer and he had his shirt off. He had a ship too, on his shoulder. And I remember he had a crown on the back of his neck.'

Danny mentally noted all of these. He was certain each tattoo had a specific meaning, and he was pretty sure Maggie would be able to figure it all out in about five seconds flat.

'Can you think of anyone who would want to hurt Derek?'

'No,' Quigley said. 'But I di'n't know many who liked him neither.'

12

The agent from the *Dolphin*'s company, Farnogue Freight, arrived at five past nine that evening. He was a diminutive, grey-haired man who could have been fifty-five or sixty-six, wearing a grey suit over a yellow shirt and dark-blue tie.

Once he'd parked his black Volvo on the beach, he made a direct line for the *Dolphin*, completely ignoring the police and coastguard who still dotted the beach. The sky was completely dark, clouds obscuring most of the moon and only a smattering of stars visible here and there above the strand.

The wind had grown even colder and more insistent.

Tessa intercepted the grey-clad man just as he reached the ladder leading to the beached vessel's deck.

'Can I ask you to state your business, sir?' she asked, holding out her ID.

The man eyed the detective with thinly veiled disdain and held out an ID card of his own, his photo, name (Eric Stafford) and the company's logo clearly visible. Tessa noted the man had a clipboard under his left arm, and there were several pens in the breast pocket of his jacket.

'I'm here to inspect the cargo and to see if the ship can be saved as an ongoing concern.'

A very slight Kerry accent was audible in the shipping agent's voice, but you'd have to be really listening to catch it. He had an educated delivery, and the detective noted that he could have had a career as a radio presenter or podcaster: his tones were rich and mellow.

'I've been waiting for you,' she said. 'There's one or two questions I'd like to ask.'

'You can talk to me as I work,' Stafford said, seemingly undeterred by the detective's status. 'I have to file a report with my superiors by 6 a.m. As you can imagine, the loss of a ship along with its cargo and all hands has caused a degree of concern at Farnogue Freight. That the vessel has reappeared is something of a relief. I'd like to establish what can be recompensed as regard the losses we believed we had accrued.'

Tessa bristled. 'I'm sure you would,' she said, keeping her breathing level and her tone moderate, 'but you'll pardon me if I suggest the disappearance of six men and the violent death of two others, not to mention the unexpected appearance of three unaccompanied children, trumps your financial concerns.'

Stafford eyed her again, seemingly considering the point.

'If you walk with me as I carry out my inspection, perhaps we can address both sets of concerns simultaneously.'

'Let's see if we can,' Tessa agreed.

They donned the white protective outfits and foot guards and found Sheils on the bridge, bent over an open drawer and riffling through the contents.

'You couldn't have arrived at a better time,' the chief officer said, straightening up, a leather-bound book held in one latex-gloved hand. 'Could you take a look at this for me please? I've read it, and there's one bit I don't understand.'

'I'm here to inspect the cargo and the vessel itself,' Stafford said testily. 'I have no intention of playing detective or helping you to do jobs the tax payer rewards you well for. Would you be so good as to step aside so I may ascertain the integrity of the *Dolphin*'s engines?'

Tessa smiled. 'You can look at whatever you like, but until forensics arrive, you're touching *nothing*. The controls aren't working, anyway.'

'Be that as it may, I was given to understand that I would have access to the vessel in full.'

'As a favour between the government and your employers, you're being given access to every room in an active crime scene,' Tessa said. 'But that doesn't include you laying down countless sets of fingerprints our techies would then have to rule out. So you can wait a while before you start handling the goods.'

'This is most unsatisfactory.'

'Life can be like that,' Tessa said in conciliatory tones that were less than sincere. 'Now, am I to understand you're refusing to assist the police in their inquiries?'

'I beg your pardon?'

'The book,' Tessa said as Sheils brandished it at him. 'My colleague wants you to take a look at it.'

'I'm very pressed for time, Detective Burns.'

'Use whatever minutes you were going to spend fiddling around with the controls. That way you'll still be on schedule. Here.' She produced some gloves. 'Put these on and have a gander.'

The shipping company representative took the proffered hand coverings and put them on stiffly before taking the notebook from Sheils.

'It's a journal, signed by Oliver, the ship's captain,' Sheils said. 'And like I said, there's a bit I don't understand.'

Stafford scanned the small but precise handwriting. Tessa

read over his shoulder and immediately understood what Sheils wanted to know.

'What's to understand? These are the ramblings of a deranged mind,' Stafford said.

Tessa indicated the first paragraph, which read:

I'm writing this because I no longer trust the technology on the Dolphin. This morning, the radar failed, and our GPS hasn't been working since yesterday. After we lost Mike, I've been navigating by the stars. I don't know what's caused this run of bad luck, other than to say we're somehow cursed. Simon believes something evil came on board during the storm, and that it won't rest until we're all dead. There are four of us left. Roy says he saw someone on the deck last night, someone he didn't know – he became hysterical and insisted it was a merrow.

'What does that mean?' Tessa asked, jabbing at the final line. 'What's a merrow?'

'A mermaid,' Stafford said through clenched teeth. 'It seems this crewman believed a mermaid had come aboard, was killing the crew and had started to sabotage the ship.'

CHILD #1 (THE ELDEST BOY)

He pretended to sleep, but he couldn't, because his brain wouldn't stop, and every time he thought he might drop off, another scary idea popped into his head, and he was wide awake again.

Maggie, who'd been sitting quietly in her cool-looking chair reading a book, was on the phone to her boss. The boy liked her, though he wasn't sure he trusted her. Every single adult he'd ever trusted had let him down, and he couldn't see how this woman was going to be any different.

But she did seem kind and gentle, though she was no pushover, and he couldn't wrap his head around that. The boy had met lots of important people, and he'd seen them acting tough plenty of times – had, in fact, been on the receiving end of it more times than he wanted to remember – but someone using kindness to show there might be another way to do things was new to him.

And he loved her relationship with Pavlov, the little dog who was clearly much more than a pet to her. He had, when he was still very young, decided that animals were much better than people. They were honest and didn't lash out unless they absolutely had to. In the city where he went to school, he'd see people going about with dogs of all shapes and sizes, usually being led on leashes, and he sometimes thought these animals didn't look very happy and would probably make a run for it if they could.

Yet little Pavlov wasn't on a leash at all. He could come and go as he wanted, yet he stayed at Maggie's side and seemed to understand everything she said, and he'd tried really hard to let the children know he wanted to be their friend too. The boy thought about the dog's brown eyes, and how they seemed to tell him everything the dog was thinking, and how when he looked into them, he'd seen love and had known how smart the dog was.

Maybe he was getting carried away. And he couldn't afford that.

He and his siblings were in a tough spot. These people were all strangers, and he didn't know what they wanted. Until he knew more, he would keep his thoughts to himself – he and his siblings wouldn't utter a word.

There was stuff going on he didn't understand. For instance, Maggie might be a nice, kind person, but what about her boss? Who was Maggie working for, and what did they want? Were they involved in putting him and his siblings on that boat?

He half-opened an eye and glanced at the woman who, it seemed, would be watching over them for the next while.

Maggie was still on the phone, scratching Pavlov behind one of his ears – the dog was sleeping in her lap. Her back was to the window, and outside he could see nothing but black.

He was about to close his eye again and see if he couldn't catch some sleep when something made him wake right back up again. It was a movement at the window.

Which made no sense, as they were on the second floor of the hospital.

The boy looked again, and sure enough, there it was a second time. It was small, and you would have to be looking to notice it, but as he stared, wide-eyed now, at the darkness, he caught a glimpse of a small figure crouched on the windowsill; of a pale cheek and a wisp of dark hair.

And then he saw her eyes.

It was the woman who'd been on the ship, the woman he'd prayed he would never see again.

But there she was, gazing in the hospital window, her eyes locked on his.

He covered his mouth and tried not to scream.

13

It took Stafford four hours to go through each piece of cargo and satisfy himself nothing was missing. When this was done, he retrieved a set of waders from the boot of his Volvo, donned them and started examining as much of the hull as he could see.

Danny had arrived at 10 p.m. after writing up the notes on his interviews, but it was now going on two in the morning, and he and Tessa watched Stafford from Danny's Golf, sipping tea from a flask one of the uniformed officers had been kind enough to provide.

'What do you make of our man Eric?' Tessa asked.

'He's not like any pencil pusher I've ever seen,' Danny retorted.

'Me either. I don't get the impression he's here just to protect his employers' investment either. When he was going through the ship, I had the sense he was looking for something. And not missing laptops. It was like he kept expecting to find something, and when he didn't, he was relieved it wasn't there.'

'You're suggesting the *Dolphin* was smuggling?'

'It'd give us something to go on if they were,' Tessa said.

'Would it? The children don't fit any picture I've been able to put together. Smuggling doesn't make it any easier a scenario to work with.'

'Doesn't that depend on what they were smuggling?' Tessa asked, giving Danny a hard look.

'You mean people.'

'I do. It would join up a lot of the dots for us. The deaths could be a result of one of their illicit cargo getting loose and... I dunno, going on the rampage.'

'You think that woman on the security footage was being trafficked here against her will?'

'Why not?' she asked.

'If she was able to kill the entire crew single-handed, and disable their navigation systems, don't you think she'd have been too much of a challenge to get on board in the first place?'

'Anyone can be subdued, Danny. But I accept your reservations. I'm just spitballing. I've got no sense of this case yet.'

'Tessa, can I say something to you? It's been on my mind.'

'Danny, you and me are beyond the stage where we have to ask permission to speak our minds to one another. Whatever it is, out with it.'

'Tessa, the woman on the ship... her face wasn't visible on any of the tapes, was it?'

'No. Not that I could see.'

'Do you think she's one of those Faceless people? Like the one that killed your parents?'

Tessa considered the idea. Danny was right – her face hadn't been visible on any of the security tapes. Of course, that didn't mean she'd had it adjusted surgically or that she was a member of this guild, but it was a possibility worth considering.

And if she was, could that simply be a coincidence? Or was Tessa being led towards this lethal group on purpose, by a person or persons still unknown?

'It's definitely worth looking into,' she replied. 'Right now, I just don't know.'

'Me either,' the big detective concurred. 'But I'll bet *he* knows stuff that would help.' He nodded towards the waterline.

The beach was, by now, in darkness, the ship only visible due to the illumination from floodlights the coastguard had set up. In the light thrown by these, Tessa and Danny watched Stafford coming up out of the foam. Waders or not, he must have been chilled to the bone, but if so, he showed no sign of it.

'Let's go and offer him a cup of tea,' Tessa said, and they got out of the car.

The shipping consultant strode up the beach, pulling the braces of his wet gear off his shoulders as he went. He still had his shirt and tie on beneath, neither of which seemed particularly crumpled despite their recent usage.

'Have a hot drink, Mr Stafford,' Tessa called, holding up the flask. 'You'll catch a chill if you don't.'

'I'm quite alright, thank you, Detective. I'll purchase some coffee once I'm on the road. I am, as you know, in something of a rush.'

'How's the ship looking?'

'I see no damage to speak of.'

He'd peeled off the waders now and was folding them precisely.

'Mr Stafford,' Tessa said, 'exactly what is your position within your company?'

The grey man paused for a moment, meeting her gaze. 'I solve problems.'

Tessa nodded slowly. 'You're a fixer.'

'If that's what you'd like to call it.'

'I don't think there's anything else *to* call it.'

Stafford shrugged. 'As you wish.'

'What went down here?' Tessa pressed. 'What happened to your men? Who are the three children my friend is currently watching over in Wexford General Hospital? And what was your *inspection* really all about? Because I'm damned sure your people aren't as deeply concerned about one or two missing bundles of jeans as you'd like to make out.'

Stafford placed his waders into a waterproof bag, sealed it and put it into the boot of his car, which he closed gently. He then opened the rear door and took out the jacket of his grey suit, which had been placed on a hanger suspended from a handle above the rear passenger window, and put it on. This complete, he looked back at the two detectives.

'Have I committed a crime, Detective Burns?'

'None that I can think of at present,' Tessa replied.

'Then why do you address me so accusingly? I assisted you with Oliver's journal, and I've responded to all questions that were within my power to answer. As yet, I don't know what happened to the *Dolphin* and her crew. As far as I can tell given that I wasn't permitted to touch anything' – at this he shot her a pointed look – 'no cargo is missing and there's no structural damage that I can see. Until your forensics team have done their work, I'm unable to ascertain why the navigation systems failed. I have a suspicion investigations will also show the communications were disabled, but why, and how, as yet I can't be sure.'

'What kind of person would have been able to do that?' Danny asked.

'Someone with an in-depth knowledge of the workings of a large ocean-going vessel,' the grey man said.

'Do you suspect one of the crew?' Tessa asked.

'I'm reserving judgement,' Stafford said. 'From the contents of the journal, it looks as if the ship's complement began to suffer from some form of hysteria. So it is possible the issues they encountered came from within. It has been known to happen on deep-sea vessels. Rarely, I'll grant, but it's not unheard of. Certain toxins in tinned foods can bring it about.'

'We'll have our people check the foodstuffs on board.'

'Our ships' cooks use mostly fresh ingredients in their

meals. The trips aren't long enough to necessitate a lot of processed produce.'

'Doesn't that negate what you just said then?'

'I have to allow the possibility someone brought on some tins, or that the chef had a store-cupboard supply my employers don't know about. It is... one hypothesis.'

'I'd like to hear any others you're considering,' Tessa said.

'Well, there's always the chance someone from outside the crew was responsible. You told me of a figure seen on the security cameras. If, as you say, she wasn't a crewmember, then she may be the guilty party. And if the crew were having delusions, she might also be the mermaid the captain's journal referred to.'

'You think she might be a stowaway?' Tessa pushed him.

'Yes, but it's also possible one of the men might have had a girlfriend or mistress or even a sex worker they regularly attended whom they brought on board for the sailing. It's strictly against regulations, but once again, such things do occur from time to time.'

'And the children?' Tessa asked.

'I'm as in the dark regarding that mystery as you are. I don't believe I've ever heard of a similar occurrence. My employers have checked with the families of the crew, and they don't belong to them.'

'Could they have been transporting them for a friend? Free passage as a favour?'

'Unaccompanied?'

'Maybe their escort was killed with the rest of the crew.'

'The only theory I've concocted that might explain their presence is that these children *do* belong to one of the crew but are the children of a... well, a second, hidden relationship. One hears of such things, particularly with sailors who spend long periods away from home. Perhaps one of the crew had a second family his spouse knew nothing of, and his mistress had to go away and had no one to care for her young ones, so our

unfaithful friend had no option but to take them on board with
him for the voyage.'

Tessa had to agree that it was a good working theory. And
one she hadn't considered.

'Is there any way of checking that?' she asked.

'My employers are pursuing it as a line of inquiry,' Stafford
said.

'Will they let us know what they find?'

'They'll report to me, and I give you my word I'll relay any...
relevant information.'

'Who decides if it's relevant or not?' Tessa shot back.

'That would be me,' Stafford said, giving the detective a wry
smile.

'Any final thoughts?' Danny asked, yawning audibly.

'The only one I haven't seriously considered is that Roy, the
ship's mate, was correct,' the grey man said. 'That a mermaid
was washed on board during the storm and killed them all
before setting the ship adrift. But I don't think my employers
would take kindly to my submitting that in my report.'

And with that, Eric Stafford nodded at both detectives, got
into his car and drove away.

'I can't work that guy out,' Tessa said to Danny as they
walked back to their own vehicles.

'I think that's kind of his thing,' Danny said. 'Being
inscrutable. I just hope that, when it comes down to it, he's on
our side.'

'I have a feeling the only side he's on is his employers','
Tessa said. 'I'm just not sure who exactly they are.'

14

Around the time Tessa and Danny were watching Eric Stafford drive away, Maggie woke from a deep slumber.

The three children were all fast asleep in the three hospital beds the staff had managed to fit into the private room that had been provided for them, which was in semi-darkness, the only light from a small bulb above the red-haired middle child's bedside locker.

Maggie had been given a not particularly comfortable folding camp bed, and she lifted her legs out of it and spread them out in front of her, stretching her toes to get the blood circulating.

Pavlov, who was snoozing on the floor, lifted his head and looked questioningly at her.

'I need to pee, Pav,' Maggie whispered. 'Go back to sleep.'

The dog didn't need to be told twice and simply placed his head back on his paws.

Maggie continued to stretch and flex until she felt the muscles in her legs relax, then reached for her chair, parked right beside the camp bed, and pulled herself up and into it. This accomplished, she steered towards the en-suite bathroom.

She was just finishing her ablutions when she thought she heard a sound from the adjoining room – it was only for a moment, but it struck her as material rustling. Assuming it must be one of the children tossing in their bed, possibly disturbed by her moving about, quiet though she'd been, Maggie continued washing her hands. She was drying them when she heard another noise and realised it was the door that accessed the children's room clicking closed.

Someone had come in and gone out again.

In the normal run of things, Maggie would have taken this as simply one of the nursing staff looking in on the kids, but checking her watch, she saw that it was 2.20 a.m. As none of the children were sick (the doctors had given them a clean bill of health) and weren't connected to any machines, drips or monitors, it had been agreed that checks would be done three times throughout the night, and the next one wasn't until 3 a.m.

After placing the towel back on its rail, she opened the bathroom door and peeped out. The three kids were still there, except now the oldest boy, the one with white-blonde hair, was awake and staring at her.

'Hey,' she whispered. 'Was that you up? I just had to use the facilities. Were you looking for me?'

The boy didn't answer but turned his gaze towards the door.

There was something unsettling about the way he looked at it. Maggie didn't see fear exactly but something close to resignation.

She moved fully into the room from the bathroom, turned the handle on the door, opened it and peered out. The corridor outside was all but empty. Ten yards to their left, she could see the lights of a nursing station, and to her right, the corridor stretched off into darkness.

'Was someone here?' she asked the boy.

Slowly, almost ponderously, he nodded.

'A nurse?'

This time, a slow headshake: no.

'A doctor?'

Again a shake. No.

'Who was here then?'

The boy watched her, unblinking.

Maggie rolled out into the hallway and looked up and down, trying to see if anyone was in the corridor. The nurse on duty spied her and waved.

'All okay?' the woman called out, softly but loud enough to hear.

'Has anyone come past this way?'

'No. No one I've seen anyway.'

'Thanks. Just checking.'

Maggie turned to her right and narrowed her eyes to gaze along the walkway in the other direction. The building was long, and at night only service lighting was on, but the family liaison officer could see a good distance relatively clearly.

At first glance it seemed as if the space was empty, but then, as Maggie continued to look, she thought she spied the slightest movement in the shadows of a doorway, perhaps a hundred yards away. Maggie held her breath and kept looking, straining her eyes, trying to make out a shape in the darkness.

'Can you keep an eye on the kids for a few moments?' she called back to the nurse.

'I can do my check now if you like.'

'That'd be fine. I just want to check something myself.'

'Right you be.'

The nurse grabbed an iPad and bustled past Maggie and into the room.

When the door was closed, the family liaison officer steered out into the middle of the hallway. Taking a deep breath, she hit her modified chair's throttle with her right hand and sent it shooting up the corridor, moving through the automatic gears quickly until she was travelling at full tilt. As she raced through the darkness, she pulled the can of pepper spray from its holster and rested it on the arm of the chair, ready for use if necessary.

All the while she kept her eyes on that patch of darkness. It hadn't moved again, and she was beginning to wonder if she'd been mistaken, but she hadn't gone more than ten yards when a figure stepped out of the doorway – though thinking back later, Maggie wondered if 'stepped' was the right word; it just suddenly seemed to be there.

As she barrelled towards it, Maggie thought it appeared to be made completely of shadow. It was small and slight, the head and face hidden by a hood.

'Police – stay right where you are,' Maggie called.

She was only a few yards from the person now, and prepared to ease her acceleration.

Before she could, the shadow person performed a kind of ducking, dodging motion, as if they were on springs. Thinking they were attempting to weave around her, Maggie tried to swerve to match them and felt the chair's left-side wheels tilt dangerously. The flaw in Maggie's modifications was that while the chair could safely go at high speed while travelling in a straight line, it wasn't stable if forced to turn sharply.

The family liaison officer threw her weight onto the left side of the chair, causing it to turn hard, and while her concentration was on ensuring she didn't tip over, the figure leaped to the right and took off down the corridor at a speed she reckoned Usain Bolt would be quite proud of.

Maggie swerved again, this time hard right, and that proved to be her undoing. The chair tipped fully into the direction of the turn and this time toppled over, spilling Maggie onto the tiled floor. Curling herself into a ball as best she could, the family liaison officer rolled for three metres before coming to a halt on her side.

She turned her head to watch the shadowy figure sprint past her and back towards the kids' room and the nurses' station, but there was nothing she could do.

Maggie lay there feeling like a complete idiot and hoping her chariot wasn't damaged, then shook herself and slowly got up. Maggie could stand, and even walk, though these were things she did with difficulty and no small amount of pain. From the children's room, she could hear Pavlov snarling and barking.

'I'm okay, Pav,' she called and began to make her way stiffly towards him.

By the time she made it back to the children's room, the nurse had completed her checks and left the room. Pav was standing on the room's windowsill, staring fixedly at the window, which was now open.

And the red-haired middle child, the little boy, whose bed had been closest to that window, was gone, the sheets on his bed crumpled and bunched but the boy himself nowhere to be seen. Maggie checked the bathroom, then turned on the oldest boy, who was still awake and gazing at her, a look of grim horror on his face.

'Where's your brother?' she asked, trying to keep panic from her voice.

The youngster simply pointed at the now open window, his lip trembling.

Maggie looked at Pav. He barked at her and skittered about as if he wanted to climb out and give chase.

Maggie went back out to the nurses' station to raise the alarm. Then she called Tessa.

* * *

'Uniforms have searched the place and they're gone,' Danny said two hours later.

They were sitting outside the children's room so as not to disturb the remaining two. Maggie's head was lowered, and Tessa knew her friend was beating herself up terribly over what had happened. Pavlov was curled up at her feet, but she'd barely spoken other than to recount what had happened and was now listening quietly as her partners explained what they'd learned.

'We've cordoned off the doorway you saw the woman hiding in,' Danny continued, 'and forensics can sweep it when they arrive later. Maybe it'll give us some clues.'

'CCTV?' Maggie asked, still not looking up.

'Was disabled,' Tessa said. 'The last ten minutes before they shut down was set to play in a loop so no one would notice unless they were looking very closely. Which security obviously weren't. The nurse who'd been in with the kids had popped up the hallway to the kitchen to grab a cup of tea, so she didn't see anything either.'

'The local guys have set up roadblocks on every road leading out of town, and the grounds of the hospital are being swept by men and dogs as we speak,' Danny told Maggie. 'We'll find the little fella. That woman can't have got far with him.'

'How did she get into our room? It's on the second floor!' Maggie said, tears clear in her voice, as well as no small amount of anger.

'A piece of old rope, which she'd probably found in a dustbin or a skip, had been looped around a spot where a drain-pipe was connected to the wall,' Danny said. 'One of the tech guys told me the knot used would have enabled someone to jimmy up and more or less abseil back down. Whoever the woman is, she has some experience with mountaineering.'

'Was this the person you saw?' Tessa asked, holding out her phone, on which was an image taken from the security footage on the *Dolphin*.

'Yes,' Maggie said. 'That's them.'

'What the hell is going on here?' Danny asked. 'The Irish government want to place these children in care, and now the person who maybe murdered everyone on the ship they came here on is popping into their room to say hello and snatching one of the kids back. *Who are these children?*'

'I don't know,' Tessa replied. 'But there is one thing we've learned from tonight.'

'What's that?' Danny asked.

'There are *four* survivors from the *Dolphin*. What interests me is why survivor number four came here and abducted survivor number two.'

'To finish the job?' Danny suggested.

'Why the hell didn't she then?'

'Because Maggie gave chase?' Danny said, continuing his train of thought. 'Number four was being pursued and grabbed the closest kid. Maybe she plans on coming back to get the others?'

'I don't buy it,' Tessa said. 'Three bullets or three stab wounds is all it would've taken. Whoever this person is, they're a professional. They had time.'

'You're saying she didn't want to kill them then,' Maggie said. 'Or me.'

'If she wanted to kill those children, she had the whole voyage to do it,' Tessa said. 'Why wait until they're in a crowded hospital with a member of the Gardai watching over them? It doesn't make sense.'

'So why come here and snatch one?'

'There's only one reason I can think of,' Tessa said. 'I think she's trying to protect them.'

'From what?' Danny asked, looking very confused.

'Us,' Tessa said. 'The state. Whoever took them in the first place. She wants the children safe.'

'You're not just saying that to make me feel better?' Maggie asked. 'Because nothing short of finding that little boy will.'

'I'm not,' Tessa said. 'I think this case just got much more complicated.'

PART TWO

STRANGERS ON THE SHORE

'We build where monsters used to hide themselves.'

— HENRY WADSWORTH LONGFELLOW

15

By 9 a.m. they were all in the playroom in Wexford General's paediatric wing, a bright airy space with big windows, the walls painted with murals of Winnie the Pooh, Paddington and Kung Fu Panda.

Maggie and the two remaining kids had finished their breakfasts first and gone on ahead of the others. When Tessa and Danny came in, she was out of her chair and on the floor, the two kids sitting nearby. The smallest, dark-haired child was perched in front of a doll's house, a deeply serious expression on her face as she arranged the furniture in one of the rooms, arranging then rearranging it in various different layouts. Pavlov, his tail wagging, was standing beside the eldest boy, who had an encyclopaedia open in his lap and appeared to be utterly engrossed.

'You're all looking very busy,' Tessa said, closing the door behind her, trying to sound jovial even though her mind was racing, turning over everything she could think of that might help locate their brother.

'Someone has to get some work done around here,' Maggie shot back, her voice also light even though Tessa could see the pain and tiredness in her eyes. 'I thought the pair of you had decided to have an extended breakfast and leave me and the kids to our own devices for the day.'

'Well, the idea did cross our minds, didn't it, Danny?'

'Not for a minute,' the big detective, whose sense of humour sometimes took a moment to catch up, said earnestly. 'But we just wanted to say goodbye before heading back out.'

Maggie looked at him with genuine fondness. 'Well I'm glad one of you still has a vestige of professionalism.'

The family liaison officer reached over and placed a hand on the child nearest her, the dark-haired girl, before reaching out to her brother.

'I'm just going to have a word with Danny and Tessa here,' she said, addressing the two as a unit and gesturing towards her colleagues.

The children looked at her: the girl's expression was neutral, though the oldest boy's eyes betrayed just a hint of nervousness.

'I'll be back with you in just a moment.'

The children nodded and continued what they'd been doing.

Maggie, using her hands as if they were feet, lifted her bum off the ground and moved to her chair, hoisting herself into it without any apparent effort, using the leg rests and then the arms as if they were a ladder. Tessa had seen her do this countless times before but still noted that it must take a good deal of upper body strength.

When she was securely seated, Maggie piloted the chair over to the corner, beckoning her friends to follow.

'How are things going?' Tessa asked when they were out of earshot. 'Did you talk to them about last night's visit?'

'I did, but they're still not communicating verbally yet,' Maggie said. 'They've relaxed a bit in my presence. They love

Pav, though that goes without saying. But they're still remaining silent.'

'So they still haven't said anything?' Danny wanted to know. 'With the little fella missing, it would help a *lot* if they could tell us something about this woman.'

'Not a word. Not only that, they've not uttered a single *sound*. Not so much as a whimper. The speech therapist is coming by a little later to establish whether or not there's something physiological preventing them from speaking, but I'm still of the opinion that we're dealing with three children who've experienced a severe trauma and are choosing not to talk.'

'Do you think they understand us?' Tessa asked. 'I mean, do they speak English?'

'I believe they do – at least a bit. I've had no trouble getting them to understand me.'

'Are you any closer to knowing who they are?'

'Yes and no,' Maggie said.

'Stop being coy,' Tessa replied, with no humour. 'We both know you're bloody good at what you do. Now spill.'

Maggie reversed the chair, executed a U-turn and rolled back to where the kids were now drawing. Without disturbing their work, she reached down and plucked a page from among the ones scattered on the floor, then returned to her colleagues. She handed the item to Tessa.

'I think this might be true. The girl drew it about twenty minutes before you got here.'

On the page was a drawing of stick figures. Three of them were obviously the children: one was small with long dark hair, another a bit larger with a mop of red, the third larger again with blonde locks. Names had been written above each figure: the girl was Sofie, the redhead Isaac and the blonde Noa.

'This is amazing, Maggie,' Tessa said, beaming. 'You're a fucking magician.'

Then she paused. In the corner of the page, right down at

the bottom on the left, was another figure. It had been drawn completely in black, swathed in what looked to be a long coat with a hood, strands of hair escaping from it.

A word had been etched above it in dark-blue crayon.

Merrow.

Tessa looked at Danny and Maggie in turn. 'Merrow?'

Maggie shook her head helplessly. 'I'm assuming it's our elusive friend's name.'

'The captain had this word in his journal,' Tessa replied. 'It's another word for a mermaid.'

'I didn't see a tail,' Maggie said dryly.

Tessa nodded. 'Come on, Danny,' she said. 'Let's go fishing.'

'I think I'm going to do some fishing myself,' Maggie said. 'Isaac was lost on my watch.'

'No one blames you for that,' Tessa said.

'I do,' Maggie retorted, and Tessa knew arguing with her friend would be pointless.

16

They decided that Maggie would stay with the kids and continue to try and get them to talk. Tessa would return to the *Dolphin* to see if the desk was operational yet so she could access the log, and Danny would investigate the missing crewmembers, in the hope that some shred of information might offer a clue as to why they'd vanished. He'd pleaded to be appointed to the hunt for Isaac, but Tessa pointed out that there were already a large number of uniformed officers on that, and his interview skills would probably bring up more useful information anyway, a fact with which he begrudgingly agreed.

Tessa arrived at Ballymoney at 10.30 a.m., just as a team from Forensic Science Ireland pulled onto the strand. At her instruction, they devoted their attentions to the ship's bridge and observation deck first.

By midday, the coastguard's people were able to examine the *Dolphin*'s computer systems to see what exactly had happened to cause them to fail.

'I'm going to be honest,' Jim Sheils said to Tessa, 'I'm stumped. The entire system is offline. I've been over it from the desk here right down to the generators in the engine room, and I can't see what's causing the fault. Both the main generator and the backup are working perfectly, but the desk is dead.'

Sheils, when not wearing the protective suit, was a tall, dark-haired man in his early forties, with the rugged features of someone who spent a good deal of their time outdoors. Tessa had already noticed his pale-blue eyes, but she could now see the laughter lines about his wide, expressive mouth and the well-groomed beard he sported, which was shot through with grey, although she thought this only added to his character.

Today he was wearing a black sports coat over blue jeans and a black-and-red checked shirt. Tessa noted that he completed the outfit with black Doc Marten boots, which she also happened to favour.

'Can you get it working?'

He looked up at her and grinned. 'You reckon I might be a bit handy with boats?'

Tessa smiled back. 'Look, I know we've had our little scuffle for superiority, but the fact is, I don't and never did underestimate your abilities. I wouldn't be surprised if you could take this vessel apart and put it back together again. And your instincts about the murder were spot on. So let's agree to work this thing together as much as we can and put the competitiveness aside.'

'Agreed.'

'So can you get the desk working, Chief Officer Sheils?'

'Putting it bluntly, DI Burns, I don't know.'

'I'm assuming if you do, there'll be a record of course alterations and... um... other things of that nature?'

'Oh there will, of course. But I'll need to open the whole desk up and go through it one wire at a time until I find the fault.'

'Could it just be down to some kind of electrical malfunction?' Tessa asked. 'I mean, is it possible we're *not* talking about sabotage?'

Sheils sat back in the pilot's chair and ran his hands through his jet-black hair. There was a smattering of grey in it too and some white – it looked as if he'd been painting a ceiling and not been careful about drips. Tessa noted in an idle kind of way that he was as attractive a man as she'd seen in a while. The thought surprised her, as she usually paid little heed to such things, and she pondered it for a second before pushing it aside. Sheils being handsome wasn't going to help her solve the case.

No, a voice in the back of her mind piped up. *But it won't make the process less pleasant.*

Tessa tried to ignore this piece of wisdom and continued listening to the coastguard.

'No, that's not possible,' Sheils was saying. 'Ships all have circuit breakers and safeguards in place to prevent this sort of thing. Someone must have systematically rerouted all of them, and that's not an easy thing to do.'

'So we're talking about a professional here.'

'Not just that,' Sheils said. 'What amazes me is *how* they did it. The bridge has to be manned at all times. To have finished the job, they'd have needed to get in here to do it. And I'm damn sure whichever crewman was on watch would have stopped them.'

'Maybe they tried to,' Tessa said. 'Doesn't mean they succeeded.'

Sheils looked at her grimly. 'Yeah,' he said. 'I suppose it doesn't.'

They lapsed into a silence that was broken when Tessa's mobile rang shrilly – her ringtone was the opening riff to AC/DC's 'Whole Lotta Rosie'.

Sheils raised an eyebrow for a moment then grinned. 'That's a blast from the past.'

Tessa grinned back, suddenly realising she'd flushed a bright pink, and answered. 'DI Burns here.'

'Hello, this is Sergeant Tibbett calling from the Gorey station.'

'Yes, Sarge. What can I do for you?'

'A guy from the tech squad is here – they've managed to get hold of the *Dolphin*'s logs, and we've finished viewing the security footage. I thought you might like to come and have a chat about what we've learned.'

'That's great. I'll be there directly.'

'I'll put the kettle on.'

'Much appreciated. See you in a few.'

She hung up, relieved in spite of herself at the interruption and the excuse to get away.

'You're needed elsewhere?' Sheils asked.

'Yes, I've to head into Gorey.'

'I won't keep you then. I've a colleague who's an electrician. I think I'll give him a call, see if he can't help me solve this puzzle.'

'That's probably not a bad idea.'

'I'll call him now.'

'Fantastic. Right – I'll hit the road.'

Sheils extended his hand, and, oddly uncomfortable, Tessa gave it a quick shake and turned on her heel.

It occurred to her though, as she made the short drive to the police station, that Officer in Charge Jim Sheils wasn't wearing a wedding ring. And she had to admit, that made her happy.

17

While the children were with the speech therapist, Maggie searched for the names Sofie had written on her drawing using every search engine she had access to. Isaac had been missing for a little over nine hours, and she needed to do something to make her feel as if she was helping to bring him back. Finding out who these children were seemed as good a starting point as any.

She tried putting them in with the phrase 'missing', then with 'lost children', then with 'abducted siblings' but drew a blank each time. The children had been photographed by the Gardai who'd arrived on the scene first, and she did an image search using these photos, which similarly resulted in nothing at all – no similar images existed online, Google informed her.

Next, she entered the names into the Garda PULSE computer system in the hope the children had been reported missing somewhere in Europe.

But to Maggie's frustration, the names didn't bring up any useful hits.

She sat back in her chair and scratched Pavlov behind the ears.

Maybe Sofie was trying to fool her, giving her incorrect names. But why? What did she gain from such a ruse? Wouldn't it make more sense for the kids to just not furnish her with any names at all? Okay, so she'd wasted half an hour on a wild goose chase, but it had hardly caused the case to grind to a halt.

The other possibility was that the children weren't, technically, missing at all. She'd read of women forced to have children in captivity, their progeny subsequently taken from them to be sold, often into foreign adoptions with wealthy families. Could that be the case here? It didn't seem likely, as these were clearly siblings, and Noa, the eldest boy, looked to be ten at least – who would keep such a group for so long and look after them to such a degree if their plan was to auction them off? Kids born into what amounted to slavery wouldn't have been kept together and certainly wouldn't be so healthy and well cared for.

Maggie had to admit she was at a loss.

She had more luck with *merrow*, though she wasn't sure it helped enlighten the case any further. Merrow, Google told her, was an archaic Irish term for a type of mermaid.

The men on the *Dolphin* believed a mermaid had somehow come aboard. The kids called the woman Merrow. And there was precedent in the mythology for children being spared by these creatures.

'But none of that's possible,' Maggie said to Pavlov, who sighed sympathetically and wagged his tail a couple of times. Which didn't help much either but made her feel a bit better.

Whoever the Merrow was, she had Isaac. And Maggie was determined she was going to get him back.

18

When Tessa got to the police station, she was told Sergeant Tibbett was waiting for her in his office with the tech expert.

'This is Mick Dunwoody,' Tibbett said, introducing Tessa to a young man with a shaved head, dressed in a faded checked shirt and jeans. 'He's with the Garda tech squad. The commissioner kindly asked him to consult on this case, and he's been able to access the *Dolphin*'s logs via the cloud.'

'Pleased to meet you,' Dunwoody said.

'You don't look like a nerd,' Tessa said, grinning.

He laughed. 'Don't be fooled – we come in all shapes and sizes.'

They took seats around Tibbett's desk. The tech expert had an untidy bundle of papers in front of him, the disorder standing out starkly amid the military precision of Tibbett's office.

'You've seen the captain's private journal too?' Tessa asked.

'I have.'

'Do the logs contain a similar... writing style?'

'Um... I'll let you decide. According to the logs, the journey went perfectly normally for the first fifteen hours. They were on their charted course through the North Sea when they sailed into a storm. The bad weather was expected, and while it was very heavy, a ship of the *Dolphin*'s size and scale is equipped to deal with it. The captain wrote, and I'm quoting here...'

Dunwoody shuffled through some papers until he found the one he was looking for. 'This was posted at 8 p.m. five days ago: *"Storm hit us at 15.46 hrs. Force 11 winds on the BWFS."'*

'What does that mean?' Tessa asked.

'The Beaufort Wind Force scale,' Tibbett explained. 'It's the measurement sailors use to express the severity of winds at sea.'

'Thanks,' Tessa said and nodded for Dunwoody to continue.

'*"Winds of 103–117 kilometres per hour, waves fourteen–sixteen metres in height. Head office had prepared us, and the ship was battened down and the crew all below decks. We sailed through her in four hours, and it was rough but tolerable. The pilot had already reduced engines to a minimal thrust before signing off his watch, and I sustained a low throttle until we were through the worst of it. Plan is to increase speed to make our deadline in Rosslare."'*

'All sounds very normal,' Tessa mused.

'It does, but that's the last "normal" entry,' Dunwoody said, making inverted commas in the air with his fingers. 'This was posted at 10.13 that same night: *"The pilot Mike is missing, as is the cook, Derek. Derek failed to call out during the routine rough-weather check, and Mike went to look for him before going to his quarters. I'd expected Mike to contact me to say he'd found him, but when he didn't, I assumed he'd found the man and simply gone to have his rest. I will admit I was distracted by the storm and didn't think to check until just now. His cabin is empty, and I've searched the ship but to no avail. Derek is known to take too much alcohol and find quiet places about the ship to sleep it off, but I've also been unable to find him. I've roused all hands, and we're currently conducting a thorough search, but so far neither man has been found."'*

'He seems anxious but not out of his mind,' Tessa said. 'I mean, losing two of your crew during a storm must be a nightmare, but he sounds like he's handling it, doing the right thing.'

'He adds these words to that log posting,' Dunwoody said. *"'I should also record that the radio comms went out during the storm, and I've been unable to get them back online. We all have our mobile phones, but while the mast remains standing, some part of it must have been damaged in the high water, as none of us has any signal. I hope someone is receiving these posts. We're powering along on course, but the ship doesn't feel right."'*

'So we're seeing the beginnings of the mechanical and electrical difficulties,' Tessa said.

'Yes. The next post comes at 4.02 a.m. *"Both the radar and the ARPA system have shut down. I remained on watch after the events of today and have been at the helm ever since. Ten minutes ago, both displays lit up as if someone was shining a strong torch behind them and then went completely blank. In all my years of shipping, I've never seen anything like this. Luckily all other systems remain online. It seems the storm did more damage than any of us knew."'*

'And so it continues,' Tessa observed.

'This at 05.27 a.m. *"Roy has just come to the bridge in a high level of distress. Kieran and Robbie are, he informs me, missing. He wasn't making sense, speaking about the ship being cursed among other things, referencing old sailing superstitions. I checked the men's quarters and their stations on the ship, and as they weren't in either location, I've once again called on the remaining crew to search for them. The wind is currently Force 6, with large but manageable waves."'*

'The crew has now lost half its complement,' Tessa said.

'Yes. And he adds: *"When I returned to the bridge, the auto-*

matic tracking aid, the echo sounder and the GPS receiver were all dead."'

'I presume that's really bad?' Tessa asked.

'He's now left without almost all his navigation systems and no radio or mobile network to call for help,' Tibbett said. 'In the middle of the North Sea, that's about as bad as it gets.'

'He signs off this entry with: "*Kieran and Robbie are not on the ship.*"'

'If I were him, I'd bring everyone onto the bridge at this stage,' Tessa said. 'He has to know the crew disappearances are no longer storm related.'

'He does just that,' Dunwoody said. 'It's the last log entry, at 6 a.m. "*I've called the remaining crewmen to the bridge. Roy and Peter both believe we have someone on board, someone who isn't a crewmember, who's killing my men and endangering the ship. Roy maintains he's seen this person, but I posted watches and scoured the* Dolphin *myself and have found no one. In the meantime, we're still five hours from Rosslare if we can sustain power. Even without electronic and satellite navigation I have the stars and the sun and my training, and experience won't let me down. If anyone is getting these entries, pray for us.*"'

'That's the last of the logs,' Dunwoody said. 'We have to assume the computer went down shortly afterwards.'

'And the journal?' Tessa asked. 'I read a bit of it, but does it shed any more light on what happened?'

'The journal is... interesting,' Dunwoody said. 'It seems to have been written all in one go, and I would surmise he began it after the computers went out. It's... it's the work of a man under tremendous stress.

'"*The sun is coming up on the horizon,*"' he began. '"*I haven't slept in a day and a night, and I doubt I'll see any rest until we make landfall. If we make it. Simon, Roy and Peter have barricaded both doors to the bridge, but Roy keeps saying, in a voice that's close to hysteria, that nothing will keep the creature out if it wants to get in. 'And it wants to,' he keeps saying. 'It's come for us and it won't stop.' I've told him I'll have him locked up in one of the cabins if he isn't silent, but in truth I don't dare separate us until I know we're safe.*

"'Simon just screamed. He says he saw someone outside. I looked but all I saw was a shadow that could have been caused by a squall breaking over the deck or a bird taking off. I'm trying to remain calm and contained for the men.

"'I saw it this time. A figure standing on the deck amidships. Small and dark. Hooded. One moment it was there, and the next it was gone. I would say I was hallucinating from exhaustion, but the others saw it too. The sight was enough to drive Roy over the edge and he tore the desk away from the door to the deck and flung it open. Peter tried to stop him from rushing outside, but Roy had the strength of the insane and broke free. I don't expect we'll see him again.

"'I just led the men in a prayer. When I finished the simple seaman's epistle and opened my eyes, I saw her, clear as day, standing right at the window, inches from my face. I saw her pale skin and lank hair. I saw the water dripping from the rim of her hood and I knew we were all dead men.

"'The Dolphin *is already a ghost ship. There might be three of us left alive, but the end is drawing nigh."*

'That's all there is,' Dunwoody said.

'It's enough,' Tessa replied quietly.

'The security footage we have cuts out after twenty hours of the voyage,' Tibbett said. 'We've got fifteen instances of the woman across those twenty hours. She's seen in almost every part of the ship, always alone. We have no clear image of her face, but using some measurements from the *Dolphin* itself, we've been able to assess she's five feet four, and allowing for the size of the jacket, we'd estimate she's about seven stone – maybe one hundred pounds – give or take.'

'But it would seem one hundred deadly pounds for all that,'

Tessa said. 'I know small people can still be dangerous, but what you've just read seems to be a little too... hysterical. I'm not sure I'm a hundred per cent convinced.'

'Sailors can be superstitious,' Tibbett said.

'I get that,' Tessa said, 'but these men weren't shrinking violets. Unless we're dealing with some form of mass hysteria, or perhaps the captain had some kind of psychotic episode, I don't think I'm going to take the journal as concrete evidence of what occurred.'

'The woman *is* real though,' Tibbett said. 'We have camera footage of her. She was on the *Dolphin*, of that we can be certain.'

'I'm not denying that,' Tessa said. 'I'd like to know how she's connected to the children. Speaking of which, did they appear on any of the later footage?'

'No,' Tibbett replied, an exasperated expression on his face. 'I mean, how the hell did they get on the ship? We have footage of every crew member boarding. But none of this woman or of the three kids.'

'Which means they must have been there well in advance of sailing,' Tessa said. 'Or they got on by some route that's hidden from the cameras.'

'Like where?'

'Most people who work in places for a long time get to know the security cameras' blind spots,' Tessa said. 'I'll bet the *Dolphin* has them.'

'But the dark lady there doesn't seem to care about being spotted during the voyage,' Dunwoody offered.

'Because by then it was too late for anyone to do anything about it,' Tessa said.

'So where does this leave us?' the sergeant asked her.

'We have two things,' Tessa replied. 'The log tells us the ship suffered a series of technological malfunctions after they hit the storm, and crew members began to disappear. That all has a ring of truth to it. Then we have the journal, which doesn't. What we know is that things began to go wrong shortly after the ship left port. Whether or not our stowaway had anything to do with it, I'm still not certain. Why she was there and why she's taken one of those children from the hospital is still a mystery.'

'I'm just as confused as I was before we read the logs,' Tibbett said.

'I'm starting to have some suspicions,' Tessa said. 'I just need a bit more information before I can confirm them.'

'Cryptic,' Dunwoody said.

'No,' Tessa said. 'Just not completely certain yet.'

19

Maggie Doolan arranged for lunch to be brought to the playroom, and with the kids' help, she set the sandwiches, juice, a cappuccino for herself and a few cupcakes for dessert out on a few towels on the floor, as if they were having a picnic. She placed some dolls and soft toys here and there too, the ones the children had shown an interest in, as if they were joining in with the meal.

She put some water in a bowl for Pavlov and laid a few dog biscuits that she carried with her beside it. Pav sniffed them (which always puzzled Maggie, as he knew exactly what they were, seeing as he ate them every single day), then sat down and began to crunch one merrily.

'I don't know what you ate when you were on board the ship,' she said as she tucked into a chicken salad sandwich, 'but I doubt it was as good as this.'

Two sets of eyes looked at her, but no answer came. Nor did either of them pick up any food.

'Please, eat,' Maggie said, motioning to the feast laid out before them. 'I know you're worried about your brother, but starving yourselves won't bring him back.'

As usual, it was Sofie who made the first move – tentatively reaching over and grabbing a very impressive-looking cupcake with pink icing and multi-coloured sprinkles.

'I had my eye on that one,' Maggie said in mock sadness.

The little girl paused, and the family liaison officer winked at her to put her at her ease.

The ice broken, the two children each grabbed a cake and began munching.

'My mammy used to take me on picnics when I was little,' Maggie said after they'd eaten in companionable silence for a few moments. 'I spent a lot of time in hospitals and special schools when I was a kid – do you know what I mean? A hospital, like this one, only I was on a ward for children with disabilities.'

Once again those eyes bored into her, but this time Noa nodded.

'You know what I mean, Noa?'

Sofie shot a look at her brother, but he nodded again.

Unbidden, Pavlov rose and trotted over to the lad, sitting beside him and laying his head in the boy's lap.

'Well, as you can see, I live with a condition called cerebral palsy, which makes walking difficult and sometimes impossible. My mammy and daddy wanted me to get as much help as I could with my movement, but nothing really helped much. But I was sent to a *lot* of places, in the hope I might get better. When I was at home though, Mammy always tried to give me days out and treats. She made the *best* cakes and sandwiches.'

Maggie hadn't relived this memory with anyone except Tessa, whom she considered to be her best friend after Pavlov. She didn't try to hide the emotions it brought up for her, and real tears welled momentarily in her eyes as she thought about that simple demonstration of love her mother had shown her.

She wiped the tears away quickly and cleared her throat. But she knew the two kids had seen them, and she didn't mind.

She wasn't trying to manipulate them. Just show them that feelings like these – happiness, affection, love and loss – were real, valuable and should be acknowledged.

Noa was rubbing Pavlov's head with one hand and holding his cake with the other. But Maggie thought she could see a slight tremor in his lower lip.

'My daddy died a few years ago,' Maggie continued. 'My mammy is still alive, but she's old now and in a nursing home, where she can get the care she needs. I visit her all the time though. I miss her when I don't get to see her.'

She paused, looking at the two kids, both of whom were now watching her very closely.

'Do you guys miss your mammy and daddy? I bet you're worried about your brother too.'

Neither of them responded for what felt like a long time, but then Sofie sniffed a very loud sniff, and large tears started streaming down her face.

'I miss Mammy,' she said in a quavering voice that sounded hoarse from lack of use. 'I miss Mammy so much. And now I miss my brother too.'

What struck Maggie right away was one remarkable fact: the child was speaking in an Irish accent!

The family liaison officer had no time to call the fact in however. Instead, she hand-walked around the food and was beside the little girl in a moment, wrapping an arm around her shoulders. Noa remained stoically silent, watching his sibling with an expression that seemed to Maggie to speak of exhaustion.

He sat a little apart as Maggie and Pavlov tried to comfort his sister.

20

Danny was interviewing a young man who had regularly helped unload goods from the *Dolphin*, but who admitted he was only on nodding terms with the crew, when his phone buzzed.

'Is this DS Murphy?'

'It is, yes.'

'This is Garda Alan Wilmott. I'm coordinating the search for the fugitive who abducted the young boy.'

'Hello, Garda. What can I do for you?'

'I was told you were the person to contact today if we found anything.'

'Yes, I'm in the field today. Do you have something?'

'I don't know. Maybe you should just come and have a look. I'm texting you a location.'

'Okay,' Danny said. 'I'm on my way.'

He put the location into Google Maps, and his phone took him to Wexford town's quayside, where teetering buildings, many of which looked as if they were leaning against one another for comfort and support, overlooked a harbour in which colourful fishing boats of all sizes were tied up. The crowds moving up and down a wide and well-maintained boardwalk were catered for by coffee pods, ice-cream stands and a fish-and-chip stall. At the woodenworks' end, a bridge leapfrogged over the River Slaney, giving cars and pedestrians access to either the Dublin road or the meandering beach that ran from Ferrybank to Ardcavan and the Slobs and salt marshes beyond.

Danny found a cluster of patrol cars parked midway up the quay and pulled up behind the last one. He was barely out of the Golf when a uniformed officer appeared from a doorway, beckoning him inside.

'Garda Wilmott,' the detective said, taking the proffered hand.

The officer was in his early thirties, his head shaved to the point of stubble, a goatee beard adorning his chin.

'Thanks for coming. I don't know what to make of this, and our sergeant advised bringing you in right away.'

The door, which was painted red and had the number sixty-three hung on it at eye level in black metal, was situated between a pub and an amusement arcade. It had one of those intercom/buzzer systems, but Wilmott had obviously obtained a key from somewhere, because he produced it and stepped back to allow Danny to enter.

The door opened onto a flight of stairs, which ran up to a landing, and then on to another door, this one with a glass panel upon which was a sign for *Murray/Cole Accounting*.

Two other uniformed officers, one male, one female, were standing on either side of the door.

'Do you know the people who work here?' Danny asked as he and Wilmott climbed the stairs.

'To be honest, no. I've been stationed in Wexford for three years, and I never even knew this business existed.'

The Garda opened the door. Inside was a small office space,

in the centre of which sat a desk smothered with papers and files. The walls were lined with shelves, similarly laden with ledgers, folders and bundles of accounts. A window behind the desk offered a view of an overgrown garden and the rear of more buildings.

There was an elderly man seated behind the desk, slumped backwards in his chair, with a red hole in the centre of his forehead. The old man was wearing a grey cardigan over a blue shirt and red tie, the tie slightly askew and the top button of his shirt open. He was bald on top, but white hair sprouted out of the sides of his head in a frizz, and he had a bristly moustache that covered his mouth and was stained yellow from nicotine – an overflowing ashtray sat at his elbow. The acrid smell of tobacco smoke pervaded the room, though Danny could still discern the tang of cordite just below it.

The lower pane of the window, which was directly behind him, was spattered with blood, bone and chunks of brain matter.

'Mr Murray or Mr Cole?' Danny asked.

'Murray. Cole died more than a decade ago. I don't know why the name was never changed.'

Danny tentatively picked his way around the desk and had a look at the dead man.

'A single shot,' he observed.

'Yes.'

'There's some powder burn. Whoever did it was very close. Probably sitting in that guest chair.'

'It's what we figure, yes.'

Danny looked at Wilmott. 'What does this have to do with the woman and the missing child?'

'Take a gander at this,' Wilmott said.

A metallic case with the words *Garda Síochána Loch Garman* (Wexford Guardian of the Peace) was sitting on the floor below the desk. Wilmott reached down and placed it on the edge of the cluttered workspace, then opened it to reveal a laptop.

'An amber alert was put out for the woman and child, so bulletins were broadcast on South East Radio, our local station, every hour, so most people would have heard a description and been on the lookout,' the guard explained. 'At 11.15 this morning, a call came into the station that a woman and child who matched the details given were seen entering these premises. Luckily, there are lots of security cameras on the quay. And we were able to pull this from one of them.'

He punched a couple of keys, and a video opened. It looked as if it had been taken from just across the street and showed a short dark figure (almost certainly the same one Danny had seen on the security tapes from the *Dolphin*) leading a small, red-haired child by the hand along the footpath he'd just parked on. The arcade was clearly visible, as was the red door.

The pair stopped at the door, and the woman pressed a button on the intercom panel Danny had noticed and spoke into it. She waited, the door opened, and she and the child went inside.

'Ten minutes goes by, then' – Wilmott said, causing the tape to scroll forward quickly – 'out they come.'

The door opened, and the pair stepped out and walked back the way they came.

'You think she killed Mr Murray?'

'We've been back over the tapes for the entire morning. Other than these two, he was the only one who entered the building. It can't be accessed from the rear.'

'Why kill an accountant?' Danny wondered aloud.

'That's what we hoped you might know,' Wilmott said.

'What kind of accounts did Murray and Cole do?'

'That,' Wilmott said, 'is something we're very anxious to find out.'

21

While Danny pondered this new mystery, Tessa was sitting in her beloved Ford Capri, which was parked outside Gorey station, a travel mug of tea cradled in her lap, Metallica's *Master of Puppets* album playing loudly from the stereo. She was aware many would find the musical stylings of James Hetfield and his associates less than restful, but she had always found their compositions soothing.

And right now, she needed to relax and allow her mind to sort through a thousand rushing thoughts and ideas. The case was a clashing maelstrom of direction and misdirection, and everywhere she looked there was something else to distract and lead her down yet another rabbit hole that, she was sure, was as likely to come to nothing as it was to bring her to a resolution.

She was intensely aware that her main priority had to be the children, and at that time the retrieval of Isaac was paramount. Her team had been formed to take on cases involving kids caught up in the criminal justice system, young people whose voices could so easily be overlooked as prosecutors and detectives alike sought a conviction. It would be easy for her to focus solely on finding Sofie, Isaac and Noa's parents and then let

Sheils and the coastguard address what had happened to the crew.

But Tessa wasn't built that way, and she believed, even more so after having heard the details of the log entries, that the plight of the children and the murder of the crew were related. The children were aware of the person the captain had indicated was the killer; they even had a name for her: Merrow. But who was she, and why was she on board in the first place?

And why had the children been spared? Had this strange woman looked after them during the fateful voyage? And if so, why had she abandoned them at the last minute? And how the hell had she made it to shore unseen?

Something wasn't adding up.

Tessa's experience, first in the Irish military and more recently in the police force, had taught her to trust her instincts, and her first thought, which she'd voiced to Danny the previous night, had been that the crew were smugglers, hiding some sort of contraband among their legally declared cargo.

And the contraband that had come to Tessa's mind first was people.

The behaviour of Eric Stafford during his examination of the ship had only confirmed her belief all wasn't as it seemed – she was sure he was also looking for signs of something among the hold that he hadn't declared to her and Danny. If there was something like drugs or firearms, Tessa reasoned, he would have comported himself differently. He'd have tried to have the bales of clothes and computers moved to one of the company hangers in Dublin. He hadn't even attempted to open them (despite being told he couldn't touch them, Tessa judged him as not being beyond 'accidentally' falling against a bundle and ripping the wrapping as he did so); he'd just gone by the numbers of items listed on each crate and had seemed satisfied with that.

But he'd surreptitiously glanced about behind each stack, had made a point of standing back in the corners and far reaches of the holds, as if to better survey the cargo, yet Tessa had noticed him glancing here and there about all the negative spaces on each level, as if something might be there.

Had he been looking for signs people might have been kept in those locations during the voyage? And how could she test this hypothesis?

Finally she shut off the music and reached for her mobile, scrolling through her contacts until she found the one she was looking for.

'Del, it's Tessa,' she said when the call was picked up.

'I know,' the voice at the other end said. 'What I don't know is why I answered the fucking phone. What do you want?'

Del Finnegan had met Tessa when they were placed in a care home together during their mid-teens. While they were housemates, Tessa and Del hadn't exactly been friends, but on one occasion, she'd prevented a staff member (a man who was subsequently removed from his job and prosecuted) from beating him, and he'd repaid her by getting her books, mostly crime thrillers and some military histories she enjoyed. They'd kept in touch to start with, but once she was on the force, Tessa had heard he'd become involved in petty crime and had even served some time. He'd always had a fascination for criminality in all its incarnations though, so had an encyclopaedic knowledge of its workings and machinations, and made it his business to know who the major players were and what they were up to. If anyone knew the inside track on what was going on in the south-east of Ireland, it would be him.

'I'm in Wexford,' Tessa told her old associate.

'Leave then. I'd feel more comfortable if you weren't on my doorstep.'

Del lived in a house his mother had left him in Wexford town.

'A ship was washed ashore here, minus all hands.'

'Why are you involved in a case like that? You weren't in the fucking navy.'

'Someone killed them all.'

'How do you know that?'

'We found one body. But there was security footage. The captain's logs. And the fact they're all gone.'

'Case closed then. Go and arrest the culprit and get back to Dublin where you're comfortable.'

'If only it were so simple. The logs hint at something fishy going on aboard the ship long before it was hit.'

'Something fishy. On a boat. Good one.'

'I'm leaning towards smuggling. Do you know of anything like that going on in this neck of the woods?'

The line went silent for a few moments as Del thought about the question. 'The ship was bound for Rosslare?'

'Yes. But it ran aground in Ballymoney. I'm wondering now if that wasn't an accident.'

'That's a big leap of logic.'

'Just work with me. Why would someone want to divert the boat from one port to another?'

'Rosslare is one of the main transport hubs in and out of Ireland. So is there smuggling going on there? Of course there bloody well is. Loads of it. Maybe whoever did the diverting was afraid that, if it reached its planned destination, whatever was being smuggled would still be picked up by whoever was supposed to get it. They wanted to make sure that didn't happen.'

'What kind of goods are passing through Rosslare illegally?'

'Well... everything you could imagine. Think of something people want but would prefer to pay less for, and you've got your answer. Luxury items: cigarettes, booze, drugs, gadgets of all kinds, labour...'

'Labour? What kind of labour are you talking about?'

'The shit no one else wants to do for wages most Irish people don't want to work for.'

'For example?'

'A very large number of farms and hotels employ individuals who were brought to Ireland by gangs and forced into what amounts to slavery.'

'I thought that kind of thing went out of practice 200 years ago. Wouldn't revenue work out the staff aren't being paid their wages?'

'Of course wages are paid. They just don't go to the actual workers. The poor fuckers arrive here already in debt, owing the price of their passage to the gangsters who brought them in. A big chunk of their salary goes on that to begin with. Then they're fixed up with accommodation in flats and houses owned by the gang, who charge exorbitant rent for the hovels they're leasing. Three quarters of these poor buggers simply agree to have their wages paid directly into bank accounts that belong to their traffickers and never see a penny of it. They eat at the hotels, steal odds and ends of food for their children if they have any, and live a twilight existence.'

'That's sickening.'

'It is, but it's a shockingly common story.'

'And you say Rosslare is a hub for this type of trafficking?'

'So is Dublin. Cork. Belfast. Anywhere with an active docklands basically.'

'There were three children on the ship when it was found.'

Del paused then admitted, 'Kids are trafficked as much as adults. They can fetch a high price if you can find the right buyer. It's grim, but there you go. What you've stumbled into might be part of a gang war – one faction trying to destroy the business of another.'

Tessa gritted her teeth and tried to quell the surge of anger those words stirred in her. 'Why were the children left on board then? Or left alive while everyone else was killed? If someone wanted to sabotage the transportation of the kids, why not just kill them too?'

'Well, a competitor could have wanted to send a message so hired an assassin to kill the crew, but said killer probably didn't have the stomach to do the kids. Most assassins are psychos, but even they have lines they'd prefer not to cross.'

Tessa considered that and decided it made a certain kind of sense. 'Is the trafficking you're talking about done by private operators or could it be run by the shipping company itself?'

'Both are possible. Some large freight companies aren't above a bit of illegal trading to sweeten the pot for themselves. But on the other hand, your crew might have been approached by a gang to transport the human traffic, and the gang then found out they were taking a bigger slice of the profits than they were supposed to, or they may have missed an order, or they allowed one of their passengers to escape. Any of these scenarios are enough that the gang might have decided to kill them for it. The owners of the ship could be completely in the dark about the whole thing.'

'Could the company themselves be working with a gang?'

'Absolutely. Business is business. Tessa, some companies basically *are* gangs. They're just the socially acceptable face of criminality.'

'Do you know anyone I could talk to down here? Someone who might be able to shed some light on the trafficking infrastructure?'

Del Finnegan heaved a sigh. 'Let me think about it. I'll call you back.'

'Don't take too long. This one won't wait.'

22

The forensics team arrived at Wexford General at 3 p.m. and took DNA samples from the children, as well as their clothes and shoes, which had been sealed in plastic evidence bags the previous day, to be combed over closely, with a view to discovering fibres or particles that might give some indication about where the children had come from if their DNA drew a blank.

They also dusted and combed over the doorway where the intruder had hidden, taking some small particles and a single strand of hair from it, and did the same in the children's room. Maggie hoped these might yield some results.

When they'd finished, Maggie went back to the playroom to find Sofie busily drawing and Noa sitting on one of the windowsills, gazing out as if there was something deeply interesting going on in the car park.

'What are you drawing?' she gently asked Sofie.

It was a house, set in a large garden with a fountain out front and what Maggie thought at first were people but then realised were statues dotted here and there, and a path of what looked to be blue and red crazy paving snaking its way up to the front door. The house itself had four storeys, and Maggie counted twenty windows.

'This is beautiful,' she said to Sofie. 'It looks like a house on a TV show a lot of people watch called *Downton Abbey*. Would you like to live in a house like that?'

'Home,' the little girl said, tapping the page.

'You would like to? Me too,' Maggie said, smiling. 'That would be a *lot* of garden for Pavlov to dig holes, wouldn't it?'

'Home,' Sofie said, more urgently this time.

'She's telling you that was our home,' a voice behind Maggie said in tones heavy with irritation.

Turning in her chair, Maggie found Noa gazing at her intently. 'You live in a house like that?'

'We *lived* in a house like that,' the boy said. 'But I don't think we'll ever go back to it.'

And he wouldn't utter another word, no matter how hard Maggie tried to coax one out of him.

Later, Maggie called a friend of hers from the Organised Crime Unit.

'Hey, Luca, it's Maggie.'

'Hi, Maggie, what can I do for you?'

Luca Bodahn had helped the Burns Unit on a previous case, and he and Maggie had kept in touch.

'Does the name Merrow mean anything to you?'

There was silence at the other end of the line.

'Luca, are you there?'

'Yeah, I'm here. Is it a woman you're talking about?'

'It is.'

'Okay. This isn't much, alright? But it might help.'

'I'll take any and all assistance I can get.'

'Fair enough. I was working a case maybe three years ago – I'd have to check to be sure – where a group of asylum seekers were being smuggled into Ireland in a shipping container. Poor fuckers had paid their life savings to get into Ireland, but they were still forced to travel from the Middle East in a metal box with barely enough food and water to do them the journey, and buckets to use as toilets, which of course they couldn't empty until they got to the other side.'

'Sounds awful,' Maggie agreed.

'The container was picked up in Dublin port and brought by truck to Swords, where it was unloaded in the yard of the trucking company. The group contained mostly women and children. They were to be directed into agricultural labour and cleaning jobs in hotels. Now these were mothers with their kids, but what they didn't know was that there was no plan to keep them together: the kids were all bound for the border region to work on fruit picking and mushroom farming. The women were to be brought into Dublin and dispersed through the hotels in the city. Of course all wages were going directly to the gang who smuggled them in – they weren't going to see a cent of it.'

'Where does the Merrow come in?'

'I'm getting to that. We'd been tipped off that these people had been brought in and we knew which freight company was involved. So when that container was opened, we were there, secreted in the yard, ready to arrest those involved.'

'And the Merrow was one of them?'

'She was. She was going to transport the kids to their destinations in Monaghan and Fermanagh and Roscommon.'

'What can you tell me about her?' Maggie asked.

'Not much, to be honest. She had no previous arrests on the system. Her DNA came up blank. She refused to give us any name other than Merrow, and she also refused a lawyer or to say anything at all.'

'How did she come across to you?'

'I remember a tiny woman dressed in a black parka and dark jeans. She was wearing some kind of fancy boots, like hillwalkers might use. I remember her eyes seemed to be almost black.'

'Is that all?'

'Oh, well, I remember that she caused me a mountain of paperwork.'

'Why?'

'She escaped from HQ. Fashioned a rope from strips of her own clothing and climbed out a second-floor window.'

NOA

Sofie was in bed napping with Pavlov nestled beside her. Maggie was reading her book again, and he was gazing at the ceiling, wondering what was coming next for him, his sister and missing brother.

'Do you want me to put on the TV?'

He pushed himself up on an elbow and saw that Maggie was smiling at him.

'I don't want to wake them up.' He motioned with his head to the bed beside his own. It was only the second time he'd let himself speak to her – he was beginning to believe he could trust her, though, and it seemed to him he would need to start communicating if he and his siblings were to get out of the mess they were in.

'I think they're in a very deep sleep. It'd take more than a TV to waken them. Pavlov likes his shut-eye, and Sofie seems to sleep like a log.'

'I'll be okay. Thank you though.'

The woman nodded and went back to her reading.

'You said you don't think you'll be going home again,' she said after a while.

Noa sighed. He wanted to tell her to leave him alone, but he was feeling sad and lonely, and at that moment he didn't have very much fight left in him.

'Yeah.'

'If your parents have a lot of money, which from that picture it seems they do, I have to imagine they've got people looking for you right now. Once we get the results of the DNA tests back we'll know who they are and we can let them know we have you. You'll be going home, Noa.'

'Maybe.'

'Don't you think Isaac is dreaming about being at home right now?'

Noa shrugged.

'Sofie misses your mother. Won't it be nice for her to see her again?'

He considered turning over and pretending to take a nap himself, but maybe it was time to give this kind woman a little more knowledge of his family.

'Mammy's not always well,' he said, trying to find the right words.

Maggie put her book down and trundled over so she was beside his bed.

'You mean not well like she's always getting colds and the flu, or not well like she gets sad a lot?'

Noa looked at Maggie, and suddenly he found tears had come to his eyes and he couldn't stop them.

'The last one,' he said. 'There are days when she's a good mammy, and she plays with us and takes us out, and she seems happy. But then there are days she can't get out of bed and she's crying all the time, and on those days we're told to stay with Grainne, our nanny, and not disturb Mammy at all.'

Maggie nodded and reached over and squeezed the boy's shoulder. 'Do you know the word depression, Noa? It's hard for me to tell, but I think that's what your mammy has.'

'Sometimes, even when she's happy, she's not... not really well.'

'Could you explain that to me?'

'There was one day when she took us out for ice cream,' Noa said, tears flowing freely now. 'When we got to the café she asked us what we wanted, but when we told her, she said that wasn't enough. She said she wanted us to have all the ice cream in the shop. The girl started to put some in our bowls, and Mammy kept on saying "more, more, more" and the bowls were getting fuller and fuller and fuller. At first it was funny, but then the ice cream was spilling out over the sides and melting, and everyone in the café was looking at us, but Mammy didn't care. In the end, Sofie and Isaac were getting scared, so I went out to our driver and told him we needed to go home, but when he came in, Mammy wouldn't get in the car. The driver had to half-carry, half-drag her out, and she started screaming and shouting. She said terrible things.'

'It sounds like your mammy has something called bipolar disorder,' Maggie said. 'It can be very scary to watch someone you care about get so upset. It can be treated with medicine though, and a lot of people live a good life once the right medicine for them is found.'

'My daddy doesn't like medicine,' Noa said.

'That doesn't really matter,' Maggie said, taking a tissue from her pocket and handing it to him. 'Your mammy needs it. And a lot of help and support, from all of you.'

'We hardly ever see Mammy anymore,' Noa said. 'When she got really bad, Daddy sent us away to school.'

'Maybe he thought that was best for you.'

'No,' Noa said, and he felt very tired then, despite the fact it was the middle of the day, and rolled over so his back was to Maggie. 'He did it because it was best for him.'

And then he did fall asleep.

PART THREE

SMUGGLERS COVE

23

Del Finnegan called Tessa an hour after their conversation about trafficking, and gave her a name and address.

'Let me be very fucking blunt,' he said with genuine anxiety in his voice, 'you did not get this from me. The individual you're determined to question is a very bad man indeed, and while I'm aware of his existence, I sleep better at night knowing that he's blissfully unaware of mine. Go and talk to him by all means, but leave me the fuck out of it. Do we have a deal?'

'You know we do. Is there anything I should keep in mind when I call on Mr Andrew O'Dowd?'

'My best advice is to put him *out* of your mind and don't go anywhere near him, but that doesn't seem likely.'

'Is that the best you can do?'

'Once you've met him, you'll see I was right.'

Tessa ran the name and address Del gave her through the system and learned that Andrew O'Dowd was seventy-one, and had been arrested three times: once in 1983 for aggravated assault, when he'd beaten a man almost to death in what was described in the report as a barfight; again in 1999 when he was found in possession of five grams of cocaine; and finally in 2007 when he'd been caught trying to come into Ireland through Cork Airport with €50,000, believed to be 'profits from organised crime'.

Interestingly, O'Dowd had served no more than five years in prison from the combined sentences of these three prosecutions so he must have been able to afford a very good lawyer.

Some notes attached to the file on O'Dowd informed Tessa that he was believed to be associated with two major crime families: one, the McCardles, were based in Limerick and had gained a fearsome reputation through dealing in drugs and guns and killing anyone who got in their way (often members of their own organisation) in brutal but imaginative ways. The other group, the Doorleys, were entrenched in various criminal enterprises on the east coast and were equally feared. One of their main sources of income, Tessa couldn't help but notice, was people trafficking.

She was sitting at a desk in the squad room of the Gorey station as she read O'Dowd's records. It was approaching four o'clock in the afternoon, and she suddenly realised she was starving. She got up and pulled on her parka, and was making for the door when Jim Sheils strode in.

'My mate, the electrician I told you about, is up to his armpits in the bridge controls,' he told her. 'He says it looks as if someone caused a series of timed power surges that overwhelmed the circuit breakers and shut down the equipment individually, one piece at a time.'

'How would a person set about doing that?'

'Any piece of electrical equipment will cause a surge really,' Sheils said. 'Every time you switch on a hairdryer, you set off a mild one. What's happened here though is that the surges were so severe, they fried the navigation desk's circuits. And they were focused – whoever did this knew exactly which circuits they wanted to fry. I've never seen anything like it. My friend is currently taking the desk apart to see if he can work out exactly how it was done.'

'Thanks, Jim. I appreciate it.'

'No problem. As soon as I hear anything, I'll let you know.'

'Actually, while I've got you, have you ever come across an Andrew O'Dowd.'

Sheils' face took on a grim cast. 'I'm sad to say that I have.'

'I take it you two aren't pals then?'

'No. Not exactly.'

Tessa looked at the coastguard, feeling that sense of giddy nervousness again in the pit of her stomach. 'I... um... that is to say... me... I mean...'

Sheils looked at her curiously. 'Are you alright?'

'Yes. It's just that... I was on my way to get something to eat. If you had time, maybe you could join me and tell me a bit about Mr O'Dowd?'

Sheils grinned. 'I could do that.'

Tessa felt relief flooding over her. 'Brilliant! I mean, yes, that's good. I could... I could use some info on this guy.'

'Lead on, then. There's a lot to tell, so I hope you're hungry.'

They went to a gastropub called The Coach House which was at the northern end of Gorey's main street. The place was busy, even on a weeknight, all polished wood and low lighting, decorated (as the name might suggest) with bridles, horseshoes and paintings of jockeys, horses and carriages, and red-jacketed hunters leaping ditches on their mounts. They both ordered steak – Tessa's medium rare with garlic butter and fries, Sheils' rare with pepper sauce and a baked potato.

'So here's what we've got so far,' Tessa said. 'The *Dolphin*, a vessel owned by a shipping company named Farnogue Freight, washes up on Ballymoney strand, all the crew missing except the captain, who's dead on the bridge, showing signs of a beating and with his throat cut. The only living people on board are three unaccompanied children. CCTV shows the captain having a row with his ship's cook and subsequently murdering him with an axe, but the security footage also shows a strange woman wandering about the boat, who we know isn't one of the crew, and isn't one of their wives or girlfriends either. The ship's logs, and the captain's journal, suggest the crew believed this woman somehow came on board during a storm at sea and was sabotaging the ship's navigation and communication systems and killing the crew – they refer to her as a merrow, which is some kind of homicidal mermaid. We know that the cook, whom the captain killed, had a criminal record and was possibly involved with gangs – the biggest gangster in the south-east being your old pal Andrew O'Dowd. And in the middle of all of that the woman, mermaid or not, breaks into the hospital, has a scuffle with one of my team and escapes with Isaac, the middle child, with whom she's still currently at large. In the company of Isaac, she visits an accountancy office on the quays in Wexford town, then murders the old guy who works there before making good her escape.'

'I feel dizzy just listening to the whole saga,' Sheils said.

Tessa laughed. 'How do you think I feel?'

'So where do you go with it all next?'

'We need to get Isaac back,' Tessa said. 'That's our primary concern. He's been with that woman for sixteen hours now. CCTV on the quays picked her up on her way to the accountants, so I'm hoping they can show us where she went afterwards, which gives us somewhere to look.'

'That's a start,' Sheils agreed.

'We have the first names of the children now, thanks to Maggie, so that should help us find out who they are, and even if that doesn't work, DNA samples have been taken for testing. If we know who they are, that might give us a strong clue as to why they've been taken.'

'You'd think,' Sheils said. 'And you think O'Dowd is involved with what happened on the *Dolphin*?'

A waitress came and brought them water and cutlery, and when she was gone Tessa said: 'Someone who knows about such things tells me O'Dowd is the main guy in this part of the country when it comes to smuggling, particularly where that involves the movement of people. So it seems reasonable to talk to him.'

'Andrew O'Dowd isn't someone you just go and talk to.'

'Why not?'

'Because people who piss him off have a tendency to turn up deceased shortly afterwards. And it strikes me that your line of questioning won't please him much.'

Tessa smiled in spite of herself. 'Probably not,' she said, 'but I'm sort of hard to kill.'

'I believe you. But please believe *me*, this man is lethal.'

'He's more than seventy years old,' Tessa scoffed. 'How deadly can he be?'

'Don't be fooled by his age. O'Dowd may be due for retirement, but he's a long way from taking up gardening or writing his memoirs. He's fully active in every aspect of his business, and even though we haven't been able to catch him for anything serious yet, it's widely known that he is the captain of the Doorley gang.'

'He's O'Dowd though.'

'He's some kind of cousin of the family. Working out the connections is always complicated with crews like that. The last guv'nor was Terry Doorley, but good old Andrew got rid of him and took over in the early 2000s.'

'Power struggles are a part of the day-to-day workings of gangs,' Tessa observed.

'Not like this. O'Dowd didn't just kill Terry. He wiped out every member of the collective who was still loyal to him.'

'Charming.'

'There was nothing charming about it,' Sheils said, his voice dropping so she had to lean in to hear. 'The way drugs used to be smuggled in in those days was that small boats would drop them in barrels a few miles off the coast, then gang members would row out, often in dinghies or inflatables, to pick them up – it's how I've had dealings with him. The coastguard has intercepted quite a few of these small boats, either on their way to pick up the barrels or heading back in to shore with them. Usually this was done by the lowest soldiers in the group, but O'Dowd informed the crew that a major shipment was being dropped, so it was going to take a lot more men than usual. Of course, he hand-picked all the Doorley loyalists, got them to row out to collect this large shipment. They never rowed back in again.'

'He had them killed?'

'Specifically, he had them nailed to life buoys and set adrift. Eight men. If they didn't drown, they died of exposure. It was two months before we found the last poor bastard. They were all bad guys, but no one deserves to die like that. I heard from one of our informants that O'Dowd did the dirty work himself, pounded in every single nail.'

'I can see how people might respond to that with some trepidation,' Tessa admitted.

'Andrew O'Dowd is an animal. I presume you're not going alone.'

'My team consists of three people and one dog,' Tessa said. 'Danny's following up that death in Wexford town, and Maggie's with the two kids, which means so is Pavlov, her dog. That leaves me. So yes, I'll be going to see O'Dowd alone.'

Their food arrived at that point, and the conversation stopped while plates were placed on the table, pepper offered and applied, and their glasses replenished.

'You won't be going alone,' Sheils said when the waitress left them to their meals. 'I'm going with you.'

Tessa looked at the man and decided there and then that she liked him. Really liked him.

'Best eat up then,' she replied. 'I'm on a deadline, and that means Mr O'Dowd will be having the pleasure of our company tonight.'

24

Forensic Science Ireland arrived on the Wexford Quays as soon as they were finished with the kids in the hospital.

'Is there anything you can tell me at this stage?' Danny asked the team.

'The gun was probably a .22. You'll notice there's blood and brains on the window, but the glass isn't broken. The bullet is, in fact, on the carpet three inches from the wall – it used up most of its velocity just getting through Mr Murray's skull,' Mildred, a young blonde forensic technician told him.

'The captain of the *Dolphin* had his throat cut, most likely with a kitchen knife,' Danny said. 'If she had a gun on the ship, why didn't she use it?'

'She might have been afraid to fire in case it damaged the integrity of the ship. Or perhaps she's acquired this weapon since. Who knows?'

'Where would she get a gun though?' Danny shot back. 'She's operating alone, from what we can tell.'

'There are lots of places if you know where to look. Did you notice the open drawer on the vic's side of the desk?'

'I didn't hang around there long,' Danny said honestly. 'I didn't want to contaminate the scene any more than I had to.'

'There's a drawer on the right of his seat,' Mildred said. 'It's open, as if he was trying to take something out of it just before he was shot.'

Danny thought about that. 'Was she looking for a file on someone?'

'I'm more thinking that Mr Murray was going for a firearm,' Mildred said.

'This old guy?'

As they spoke, uniformed officers were removing the files and folders from their shelves and placing them in evidence boxes.

'Why not?'

'He just doesn't look the type.'

'Why do you think she would have come here?' she asked in reply. 'A woman who was at the scene of eight murders and has abducted a child decides to visit an ancient accounting firm on a busy thoroughfare in a town where she had to know she would be under scrutiny? It was one hell of a risk to take.'

'Maybe she knew him,' Danny said, thinking aloud.

'Oh, I'd say that's a certainty.'

'An uncle maybe?'

'She shot him dead,' Mildred replied. 'If they were related, familial bonds must have been strained.'

'I'm really worried for that little lad,' Danny said, shaking his head. 'To have been taken in the middle of the night and then forced to watch a man being murdered...'

'I don't think the kid was in the room,' she told him. 'I've been examining the carpet, and I can just make out footprints. They're all adult sized. My guess is the kid stayed outside, at the top of the stairs.'

'Why would she do that?' Danny wondered. 'Surely she must have been worried the kid would bolt.'

'Maybe she knew it would go down this way?'

'She didn't want the little fella to see,' Danny replied, his voice little more than a whisper. 'She *is* trying to protect the children.'

'Maybe from herself as much as anyone else,' Mildred said.

Danny was halfway back to his car when he realised he was being followed.

He'd had to move the Golf so the local boys could park a van outside the accountancy firm to load up the files and had ended up in a large parking facility at the south end of the quay.

He hadn't realised the two men were following him until he'd stopped to check his phone and spotted that they'd stopped too, pretending to gaze in a shop window. He watched them in his peripheral vision: both were a little over six feet and looked like rugby players gone to seed, each wearing tracksuits and expensive trainers. One sported a baseball hat with an enormous brim turned up so high it would never offer him any shade; the other had longish dark hair, pulled into a bun on top of his head, and tattoos snaking up his neck.

Danny continued to fiddle with his phone for thirty more seconds then broke into a run and crossed the street rapidly, dodging in and out of the cars until he was on the quayside again, where he slowed slightly and jogged through the dogwalkers and sightseers. The big detective kept in shape, visiting the gym as regularly as his job permitted, and the run didn't even cause him to breathe heavily. He covered 500 metres in a little over ten seconds, then turned and saw his two shadows – they were a good distance behind but were now running awkwardly in a bid to catch up.

He slowed even more, wanting to give them a chance to narrow the gap, then when they were close enough to see the whites of his eyes, he took off at a full sprint, eating up another 100 metres of the waterside promenade before veering right and crossing the road yet again. This time, however, he didn't continue along the pavement but dove into an alleyway, keeping his swift pace until he reached a stack of beer crates, which he lunged behind, pressing himself against the wall.

Danny remained there, feeling loose limbed and full of oxygen. He knew his two followers had seen where he'd gone – he'd made sure they would – and it would only be a matter of minutes before he heard their footsteps.

He waited.

The narrow passage smelled of urine, rubbish and stale alcohol. Voices echoed as people went past, on their way to get dinner or have a drink or visit friends. Car engines roared, and horns honked. Herring gulls called to one another, and a little further up the alley, an urban fox, common in Wexford, stuck its head out from under a pile of rubbish bags, sniffed the air and decided to duck back under cover.

Danny was beginning to think he'd inadvertently lost the two men and was about to make for his car when he heard a slow tread and knew they'd arrived. He let them cover half the distance, then stepped out.

Peaked Cap and Man Bun froze. Danny noted both were flushed and breathing laboriously. Sweat soaked through their tracksuit tops.

'What do you want?' he asked without preamble.

'To send you a... a message...' Man Bun said, forcing the words out between gulped breaths. He had an accent Danny didn't recognise – somewhere from the southern end of Ireland. West Cork possibly.

'I'm all ears.'

'Let the kids be taken into care. Close the case,' Peaked Cap said.

He was bent almost double, his hands on his knees. He took

a couple of breaths and continued. 'If you don't, people you care about will be hurt. Hurt bad, like.'

Same accent, Danny thought.

'Are you two aware you're threatening a police detective?' he asked.

'Don't matter,' Man Bun said. 'You don't know who you're fucking with or what you're messed up in. Now back off and tell anyone else involved in the case to do the same. If you don't, bad things are gonna happen.'

Danny laughed. 'Are you two going to be the ones to do it? Because I have to tell you, I'm not scared.'

Peaked Cap straightened up and took a phone from his pocket. He opened a screen and held it up to Danny. 'Recognise the house?' he asked.

Danny didn't have to step any closer to see the man was showing him a photograph of a red-bricked detached property in a small housing estate in Bray, a coastal town in Wicklow, where he'd spent most of his childhood. The couple who lived there had fostered him, and while Danny had always known they weren't his blood relatives, they'd treated him as if they were. He still called them Mam and Dad, spoke to them on the phone several times a week and visited whenever he could. He looked at the image on the phone and felt something detonate somewhere deep in his consciousness.

The big detective had a temper which he usually kept in check, but hearing a threat against the people he loved most in the world made him want to shake the man until his teeth rattled.

'I suspect you know I do,' he said, his voice steady even though his vision was beginning to take on a reddish tinge.

'It won't be us who visits them,' Man Bun said. 'It'll be people much worse.'

What happened next occurred so quickly Danny only experienced snapshots of it.

One moment he was standing in the alleyway, staring at the photo of the place he called home. The next he was on the ground, Man Bun spread-eagled beneath him, nose bloodied and broken. Peaked Cap had his arm around Danny's neck, trying to put a sleeper hold on him, but the detective was so riled up, he couldn't get it locked in.

Reality tilted again, and then Danny was standing, holding Peaked Cap by the neck of his tracksuit top and slamming him into the wall: once, twice, three times, more.

'*Who sent you?*' a voice was saying, each word punctuated by a thud as the man hit the wall with ferocious force. '*Who sent you?*'

The phrase was repeated five, six times before Danny realised it was him saying it. Actually, he was screaming it.

'I can't fuckin' tell you,' Peaked Cap whined. 'You can kill me if you want, but I ain't gonna tell you!'

'Okay,' the voice that was Danny's but wasn't said, and hands he wasn't controlling anymore clasped Peaked Cap about the face and drove his head into the wall with a hollow thump that made the part of the detective that was still vaguely in control feel sick.

The man sagged for a moment, and Danny was sure he'd killed him, but then his eyes snapped open and he started to struggle, and Danny drew the head back for another blow.

'Alright, alright, no more! For God's sake no more!'

Danny, his breath rasping in and out, paused, still cradling his prisoner's head in grimy, sweaty hands.

'It was my boss, but he was only doin' it as a favour to someone else.'

'Who's your boss?'

'He'll fuckin' kill me if he knows I told you!'

'I'll kill you right now,' Danny said, his face so close to the other man's they were nose to nose. 'And you know I'm not bluffing.'

'Don't let him know I told you! Promise me!'

'You just threatened to hurt my family,' Danny said, his voice little more than a growl. 'If I don't have to bring you into it, I won't. But if I need to in order to find out what I want to know, I'll sell you down the river without a second thought. So you'd better just hope it doesn't come to that.'

Peaked Cap looked into Danny Murphy's eyes and saw the truth in them, and then he started to talk. And Danny didn't want to believe what he told him.

25

Andrew O'Dowd lived in a cottage on the Rosslare road, five miles outside Wexford town. It was hidden behind a high hedge, and Tessa almost missed the place.

A small gate barely allowed room for one person to pass through at a time, so closely did the vegetation press in on both sides, so Tessa went first and Sheils followed. The gate opened (if that was the right word) onto a narrow path, cracked and subsided, reeds and meadow grass poking through the rough concrete here and there.

The walkway led to a small, single-storey building, which looked to be in as bad repair as the approach to it. A light shone in one of the windows, and Tessa didn't pause but rapped smartly on the front door, which was of dark varnished wood that had a thin covering of green moss which almost obscured the original finish entirely.

They heard the knock echoing through the cottage's interior. Above them, the moon cast a dim glow through a small gap in the cloud cover. The clouds had also obscured most of the stars, and a wind that chilled them both to the bone whistled through the gap in the hedge, making the bramble, elderflower and sloe bushes rustle eerily. The sound of cars and trucks thundering by on the nearby road reminded Tessa that as isolated as the dwelling seemed, they were actually only yards from civilisation.

Although they might as well be on another continent for all the help that would bring if things turned bad.

'I don't think anyone's coming,' Sheils said. 'I don't see any cars either. Maybe we should try another time.'

Tessa gave him a look that was all the answer he needed and struck the door with the full weight of her fist. 'Police! We'd like to talk to you please. This is an urgent matter. Open up!'

She continued to bang, and finally they heard the sound of approaching footsteps followed by someone unlocking something on the other side. The door opened a crack, and Tessa held out her ID to the eyes that peered forth.

'I'm Detective Inspector Tessa Burns; this is my colleague Chief Officer Jim Sheils of the Wexford coastguard. We'd like to have a word with Mr Andrew O'Dowd, who according to our files is living at this address.'

'He's not home,' a gruff male voice said.

'We'll wait for him.'

'You're welcome to wait in your car,' the voice shot back.

'That's not very hospitable. We're looking for Mr O'Dowd's help with something. Wouldn't it be to his benefit to have done the Gardai a favour? I'd have thought after all this time, he'd be interested in earning some brownie points.'

The eyes narrowed for a moment.

'Wait here,' the man said then disappeared, the door closing with a click followed by the rattle of the locking mechanism as he secured the cottage once more.

'Interesting approach to gaining entry,' Sheils said.

Tessa grinned. 'You catch more flies with honey than with vinegar.'

'I have to tell you that's not been my experience in my dealings with Andrew O'Dowd or his people,' Sheils said grimly.

A couple of minutes passed then the door opened again, fully this time, and a tall, slim man who looked to be in his forties, dressed in a black T-shirt and jeans, his hair long and greasy, his feet shod in biker boots, stood back to allow them entrance.

'Andy is in his office,' the doorman said.

A short, dark hallway opened onto a sparsely furnished living room on the right, opposite which was a closed door. The hall led to what Tessa figured must be a kitchen, and through the open door, she counted three more men, all long-haired, tattooed and sullen. She made a mental note that there could be more standing beyond her line of vision, which was a good reason to keep their interaction as calm and civil as possible.

The man who'd shown them in knocked on the closed door and said in raised tones: 'Andy, those coppers for you.'

'Bring 'em in,' a voice responded, and the man opened the door and gestured with his head.

Tessa and Sheils went in.

The room was small, the walls rough stone painted white, the floorboards bare and treated with a light varnish. Large paintings had been hung on every wall: on the right, above a hearth, in which a fire was blazing, was a field of corn beneath a sky full of storm clouds; on the left a rendering of Wexford town seen from across what the locals still called the 'new' bridge, although it had been completed in 1959. And in front, above where Andrew O'Dowd sat behind a large desk, was a ship tossed on a stormy sea.

'What brings two officers of the law to my home on a dark evening such as this?' the old man asked.

For he *was* old. Tessa could see every day of his seventy-odd years writ on the man's lined face, but there was about him an energy and charisma that told her he was far from feeble, and, pensionable age or not, would be a formidable adversary.

What hair he had left was still dark and gelled back on a finely domed skull, his brown eyes were dark and flashing, and the crisp white shirt he wore was fitted, showing a musculature many far younger men would be proud of.

'My name is Detective Inspector Tessa Burns; this is Coast-guard Chief Officer James Sheils. We're working a case, and your name came up as someone who might have some... *insight*... into the nature of what happened.'

'Are you accusing me of something?' O'Dowd was smiling as he said the words, but there was an undercurrent to his voice that was anything but friendly.

'Not at all. Maybe the best way to look at this is that we're consulting with you.'

O'Dowd pushed his chair back and stood in one fluid motion, stretching his arms above his head as if he'd been sitting in the same position for too long and had become stiff.

'You, Detective Burns, I do not know. Chief Sheils and I, though, have had occasion to cross each other's paths from time to time. So I'm certain he informed you that I'm not the kind of man who usually consults with an Garda Síochána.'

'This might be the time to make an exception,' Tessa said jovially, but under her veneer she was on high alert.

'Do you think?'

'Why not?'

O'Dowd gave the two law enforcement officers a wry look and moved around so he could sit on the edge of his desk. There were no seats in the room other than the one the gangster had just vacated – it was a management tactic Tessa had encoun-tered before, one designed to make employees and underlings feel nervous and ill at ease.

And it was working.

'Do you know how I have managed to achieve the grand old age I have in this business?'

'What business might that be?' Tessa asked.

O'Dowd laughed at that. 'Very good, but I'm not going to bite. You wouldn't be here if you didn't know.'

'I'm going to go out on a limb and say charm?'

'I've survived so long by establishing a strict code of... ethics, for want of a better word... which governs how I behave: what I am prepared to do and what I will absolutely *not* do. I adhere to this set of standards rigidly, and they've served me well.'

'That's great,' Tessa said, nodding, her expression one of calm interest.

'Yes, I think it is,' O'Dowd agreed. 'Not exactly at the top of that list, but close enough as doesn't matter, is the proviso that I do not, under any circumstances, collude with the guards on any topic. Collude, consult – I think it boils down to the same thing.'

'I'd owe you a favour,' Tessa offered.

'What could you possibly do for me?'

'I work directly for the police commissioner. I expect you can think of one or two things she could do for you.'

That caused O'Dowd to pause for a moment.

'She's telling the truth, Andy,' Sheils said. 'She's part of a special task force.'

'Specialising in what?'

'We work cases that involve children,' Tessa said, and told him about the *Dolphin* and its strange passengers, including the fact that one had been abducted.

'Why come to me about that?' O'Dowd asked, seeming genuinely incredulous. 'I don't know anything about children. I've never had any of my own and have nothing to do with other people's.'

'We're investigating whether or not these children might be

the victims of trafficking,' Tessa said. 'And I've heard you *do* know something about that.'

'Who told you I did? This bollix?'

O'Dowd glared at Sheils, any semblance of hail-fellow-well-met gone in the blink of an eye.

'Not at all. We have our sources. To be clear, I'm not accusing you of having anything to do with this, but I would like to get an insight into how the trafficking networks operate on the east coast of Ireland. My main goal is to get Isaac back to his brother and sister, and after that reunite them all with their family.'

'And bring the traffickers to justice, no doubt, and solve the murders while you're at it.'

'The kids are my main priority,' Tessa repeated.

'I have nothing to say to you, Detective Burns.'

'I'd appreciate any information you can share. I won't divulge that you've assisted us. This will be purely confidential. Unless it does turn out you were involved of course.'

'You're asking me to be an informant? A fucking grass?'

'I wouldn't call it that...'

'What would you call it? A consultant? You're insulting me, Detective, and that is a very dangerous thing to do.'

O'Dowd rose from the edge of the desk to his full height, which was perhaps an inch taller than Sheils and probably a foot above the top of Tessa's head.

'I'm asking you to leave my home, both of you. I'll ask politely once. You don't want to see me when I'm being impolite.'

Tessa gazed up at the older man and took a step towards him. 'Mr O'Dowd, *I've* been polite too. Do you think I give a damn about your code of ethics, which is a laughable title to give anything associated with the toxic line of work you've thrived in? I don't know whether or not you're responsible for those children being on that boat, but I do know that nothing goes on along the Wexford coast that you *don't* know about. So why don't you cut the crap and tell me what you know before Jim and I sit down and cook up a reason to come back here with a warrant, after which we'll search every inch of the place, and I'm pretty damn sure we'll find one or two things that will give us ample reason to bring you down to the station, where I can ask you the same questions all over again.'

O'Dowd peered down at Tessa, his dark eyes flashing. 'What makes you think you'd make it out of this room, never mind this house?'

'Let's just say I'm a confident woman.'

'I'd call it foolhardy,' O'Dowd sneered, and suddenly he had her by the throat with both hands.

Without any apparent effort, he lifted her from the ground, and Tessa felt her windpipe compress, and then she couldn't breathe. Instinctively, she went for the gun in its holster under her left arm, but as she did, O'Dowd let go of her throat with his right hand and clamped his gnarled fist about her wrist, squeezing and twisting, and the SIG Sauer P226 fell from her hand and skittered under the desk.

As the world began to fade before Tessa's eyes, she thought she heard Sheils shout something. A phone started to ring somewhere, but then everything became very still and very quiet, and then there was nothing.

26

As soon as he was back in his car, Danny called Tessa. Her phone rang out, so he tried again. Figuring she must be otherwise engaged, he tried the commissioner.

She also didn't answer at first, and he sat, sweating and grimy, his breathing heavy as he nervously watched the crowds pass by on the footpath. Deciding it was too dangerous to stay where he was, he turned the ignition and pulled out into traffic.

As soon as he did, he realised he didn't know where to go and decided to simply drive until a destination presented itself. As he piloted the Golf, he dialled the number for Ciaran, his foster father. This time, he was answered after one ring.

'Daniel! How are you? Your mam and me were just talkin' about you!'

'Dad, I'm good, but I need you to listen to me. This is really, really important.'

'Okay. Are you alright, lad? You don't sound great.'

'Yes, I'm fine. Dad, you and Mam need to get out of the house for a while. I want you to go to Aunty Maureen's right away. I'm going to arrange someone to pick you both up there, and they'll take you to a safe house.'

'What? Danny, you're not making sense. Is this a joke? If it is, it's not funny.'

'It's no joke, Dad. I need you to go now.'

'You're serious?'

'I'm deadly serious, Dad.'

Danny's father paused for a moment. 'What are you mixed up in, Danny?'

'I don't know yet. All you need to know is you're not safe, and I'm getting you somewhere where you will be. Go now, Dad. Pack nothing, take nothing, just get in the car and leave. Everything you need will be got for you.'

'Your mam won't be happy about that.'

'I know and I'm sorry. She can give me a hard time later. For the moment, just get her out of there. I'll call you with a description of the person who'll be coming to pick you up. Answer the door to *no one* but him. That's really important, Dad. *No one* but him, even if they say they're guards. Do you understand?'

'Yes. I think so.'

'Okay, good. Now go. I'll be in touch as soon as I can. I love you, Dad.'

'I love you too, son.'

And they hung up.

He was about to cross Wexford Bridge when his phone rang in its cradle, and the words 'THE COMMISH' flashed across the screen.

'What can I do for you tonight, Danny?' It was Dawn Wilson, her northern tones echoing around the car's interior.

'My parents have been threatened and... well, there's stuff I've learned I'm not comfortable saying over the phone.'

'Okay. Where are you?'

'In the car driving over Wexford Bridge. I... I don't know where I should go. I don't want to lead anyone to the kids or to Maggie. I can't get hold of Tessa... I... I...'

'Go to your hotel. I'll be down as soon as I can, and we'll get this sorted. I presume you've told your folks to get out of the house ASAP?'

'Yes. They've gone to my aunt's place.'

'Good. Keep checking on them. They should be okay for a couple of hours though.'

'Thanks, boss.'

'I'm on my way. See you in an hour.'

Dawn knocked on his hotel-room door fifteen minutes after he got there. The Irish police commissioner was six feet two, with a strong, muscular build, a striking, handsome face set off by green eyes that showed a razor-sharp intelligence, and long red hair which this evening hung about her shoulders, still wet from the shower.

Danny was used to seeing her either in a business suit or the blue, red-trimmed uniform of her rank, but just then she was wearing a Green Lantern T-shirt under a leather jacket, paired with scuffed blue jeans. Her feet were shod in green Converse high-tops.

'Come in,' he said. 'Do you want tea, coffee or something stronger?'

'I'll take a whiskey, if you've got one.'

'I bought this in an off-licence on the way,' Danny said, producing a bottle of Writers' Tears Irish whiskey.

'Nice to see you thinking ahead,' the commissioner said and sat down in one of the room's chairs while he poured them both a glass. 'Now let's get your folks to safety. What's your aunt's address?'

He told her, and she rang a number.

'Bob, I want you to pick up two people for me, the parents of a detective who works on one of my task forces. I want them brought to the safe house in Athlone. This is need-to-know, and the only people who need to know are me, your relief and their son, do you understand? This is top priority.' She paused, listening. 'Good. You stay with them. I'll send along your second within twenty-four hours, but that's going to be it. I don't want to make this a big operation. Right, I'm texting you their current location. Let me know when you have them locked down.'

She hung up.

'I need a description of Bob so my father will know he's safe to go with when he arrives.'

Dawn fiddled with her phone. 'I've just sent you his ID photo. Text it on to your old man.'

Danny did, and while he was still texting, Dawn commented: 'You say the two boyos who came for you were from Cork?'

'I think so, yes.'

'And you let them go. Why?'

'I wanted them to take back a message to their employer.'

'Arresting the fuckers might have sent a stronger message,' Dawn said tersely.

'How long could we hold them? They'd produce a hotshot lawyer who would have them claim police brutality and they'd be out before we had a chance to even question them properly. I... I know I lost my temper, boss. I'm sorry about that. I really am.'

'They threatened your family,' Dawn replied, her tone milder now. 'I'd have given them a hiding too probably. What message did you ask them to carry back?'

'That Tessa, Maggie and me aren't going to be scared off. No matter who's trying to do it.'

'Any thoughts on who that might be?'

'Oh, one of them told me who sent them. I... I put the fear of God in him. I don't think he'd have broken confidentiality otherwise.'

'Feel like telling me who it was?'

'That's the main reason we're here,' Danny said. 'He told me they'd been sent by a man called Graeme Clohessy.'

Dawn shrugged. 'Means nothing to me.'

'According to the lad I roughed up, Clohessy is only a messenger boy. He does the running and fetching for his own boss.'

'And his boss is?'

'Damien Forde.'

'Damien Forde... *the Junior Minister for Foreign Affairs?*'

'The very same.'

'Who happens to be of this very constituency?'

'Yes. He's an independent TD for Wexford.'

Dawn gave a dry chuckle and downed the contents of her glass before pouring another. Danny took a breath and did the same, holding out his tumbler with only a tiny tremble in his hand as she offered the bottle.

'What are we going to do, boss?'

'Let's you and me see if we can't work that out,' Dawn said, sitting back. 'Will we order some food?'

27

'Let her go now!'

Sheils grabbed at O'Dowd's arm, but he might as well have been grasping an iron bar for all the good it did. The older man turned to look at him for a moment, and all the coastguard saw in his eyes was rage and murder, but then those dark orbs were turned back on Tessa, who'd begun to turn an alarming shade of blue.

'I. Said. Let. Her. Go!'

Sheils punctuated each word with a punch – to the kidney, the ribs, the stomach, the groin, then another there for good measure. If he hurt the man, there was no sign of it. In desperation, Sheils flung himself onto the floor and reached under the desk to retrieve Tessa's gun, cursing the fact that Irish coastguard officers were forbidden to carry weapons.

For a second, he couldn't find the SIG, but then his hand fell on something hard, and a second later he felt the comfortable weight of the weapon in his hand. He hauled it out and rolled onto his back, the weapon now held in the two-handed shooter's stance he'd learned in the Irish navy.

'Let her go or I will shoot you in the back of the head, you ugly fucker!'

O'Dowd, who had his back to Sheils, threw the now semi-conscious Tessa across the room and turned with savage speed. Suddenly the old man had a gun in his own hand, and Sheils (who'd never shot anyone before in his life) felt a cold sweat break out on his forehead as he tightened his finger on the trigger.

At that moment, the door to the room opened behind them. Someone stepped inside, and a mellifluous voice with hints of western Ireland said, 'Mr O'Dowd, may I invite you to put your weapon down? I think it pertinent you know I have a gun trained on you, so I believe I have the advantage, and I will not hesitate to shoot if I deem it necessary.'

As if to prove the truth of these words, the sound of a cartridge being jacked into the chamber of some kind of shotgun cracked through the tension-filled room.

O'Dowd didn't move. Sheils, trying to keep his hands steady despite the terror threatening to consume him, couldn't see the person who was speaking, as the large form of the gangster still blocked his view. But he thought he recognised the voice now.

'You'll never get out of this house alive,' the older man said.

'I'm afraid I must contradict you on that point,' the voice responded calmly. 'You'll find the men who were bivouacked in your kitchen are all unconscious. They should recover, although I did have to strike the one with the red hair four times before he had the good grace to lie down. He may need some stitches. And perhaps some painkillers – he'll have quite the headache when he awakens.'

Sheils observed a flurry of expressions pass across O'Dowd's face: rage followed by disbelief followed by a brief something that might have been fear but which was replaced by cunning and an overwhelming desire to survive.

The gun clattered to the ground, and the old man half-raised his hands. 'What do you want?'

'A conversation. Nothing more.'

'So talk.'

'First, I would be appreciative if our friend Chief Officer Sheils could check on the well-being of DI Burns. You were less than gentle in your remonstration of her.'

Sheils didn't move. He was frozen to the spot, Tessa's gun still pointed at the centre of O'Dowd's mass.

'Chief Officer Sheils, would you be so kind?'

The voice addressed him directly this time, and with a huge effort of will, he lowered the weapon, rolled to his feet and went to Tessa, who was lying prone against the wall.

It was only then that he was able to confirm the identity of their rescuer. The grey-suited, grey-haired form of Eric Stafford, Farnogue Freight's fixer, was standing just inside the doorway, a pump-action Heckler & Koch shotgun held nonchalantly in his hands. Sheils noted, somewhere in the back of his mind, that the man seemed remarkably calm and contained, despite the situation in which they were currently embroiled.

Tessa had fallen on her side by the wall to the right of the doorway. Blood ran from a cut on her forehead, just above her left eyebrow, and livid bruises were already coming up on her throat, but to his relief, she was breathing, and when he checked her pulse, it was strong. His touch seemed to bring her back to awareness: she moaned and rolled onto her back, but then it was as if memory kicked in and she sat bolt upright, her hand going to her shoulder holster, which was of course empty.

'I think you're looking for this,' Sheils said, handing her the SIG.

'Welcome back to the party, DI Burns,' Stafford said. 'I'm glad to see you're not too badly injured.'

Tessa looked askance at their surprise visitor then back at Sheils.

'Don't ask me,' the coastguard said. 'I'm as surprised as you are.'

Tessa accepted Sheils' hand and rose stiffly to her feet.

'Hello, Mr Stafford,' she said, nodding at the fixer.

The grey-clad man smiled. 'Good evening.'

'Is that gun licensed?'

Stafford feigned a hurt expression. 'If you wish to examine my work permit, you'll see that it affords me the use of certain... tools of my trade. Firearms up to and including automatic weapons are among those devices.'

'That sounds like the kind of permit a soldier or police officer might have,' Tessa observed.

'Well. My job is, at times, not dissimilar.'

'I'd say there are lots of differences, but that's a conversation for another day,' Tessa replied, touching the wound on her forehead and wincing before shaking her head to clear it.

'I'm inclined to agree.'

'Why are you here?'

'I wager for the same reason you are. I wished to discuss the trafficking of people with Mr O'Dowd, who I'm reliably informed is something of an expert on such matters.'

O'Dowd grimaced at this statement. 'I already told this pair, I know nothin' about your boat.'

'The *Dolphin* is a *ship*, Mr O'Dowd,' Stafford said, sounding mildly offended. 'I'm considering the hypothesis that it was intentionally run aground but that a person – or persons – was supposed to row out and rendezvous with the vessel for the purpose of picking up the children before the grounding occurred. I'm told that you do *not* generally trade in children, Mr O'Dowd, though I've been advised it's for pragmatic reasons rather than moral ones. But I think you know who does in this part of Ireland.'

O'Dowd eyed Stafford, and Sheils could almost see the cogs turning.

'There's a man locally who does that kind of work,' he said, after a long moment had passed. 'But if he was meant to send people out, he'd have sent them. Why were these kids not picked up?'

'That I don't yet know,' Stafford said. 'But if you would be so kind as to furnish me with a name, I'll bother your home no more and will take my inquiries elsewhere.'

'His name is Finnegan,' the gangster said. 'Del Finnegan.'

Sheils noticed a flash of anger on Tessa's face before she forced it away. She obviously knew the name.

'Thank you kindly,' the fixer said. 'I take it you have no further questions, DI Burns? Chief Officer Sheils?'

'No,' Tessa said. 'I think that about wraps things up.'

'Then we shall take our leave. Goodnight to you, Mr O'Dowd. As I said, I shan't bother you again.'

Stafford motioned with his head, and Sheils and Tessa fell in behind him as he began to walk backwards out the door, still covering the older man with his shotgun.

'I might bother you though,' O'Dowd seethed. 'You think I can have you waltz in here, get the better of my men and I do nothing about it? That's bad for business.'

Stafford made a sound Sheils assumed was a laugh.

'Mr O'Dowd, you're most welcome to try. But might I remind you that I subdued eight of your personal bodyguards without firing a single shot. The next time I won't be so subtle. And I give you my most solemn promise – I will shoot you on sight.'

O'Dowd said nothing, just glared at the smartly dressed fixer.

Then they were in the short hallway, where Tessa opened the front door, and the three of them ran down the cracked path as fast as the uneven footing allowed.

28

Tessa and Sheils followed Stafford's Volvo into Wexford town.

On the way, Tessa called Maggie after noting she had two missed calls from Danny.

'Can you run a name through PULSE for me?'

'Of course. Who are we looking into?'

'Del Finnegan. I don't know whether Del is short for Derek or Delbert or something else entirely. Or if it's his given name, which seems unlikely, but who am I to judge?'

She could hear keys clattering.

'I thought I knew this guy,' she said, more to herself than to Maggie. 'But I'm starting to think I haven't kept as close an eye on him as I'd believed.'

'Delbert Finnegan, forty-three, with an address on Skeffington Street in Wexford town. He's been arrested once for drunk and disorderly, twice for assault and has also clocked up a successful prosecution for the sexual molestation of a minor – an eight-year-old girl, to be precise. That got him a stint in Wheatfield Prison and his name on the sex offenders register.'

'Seriously?' Tessa asked, genuinely shocked. 'I... I don't believe it. So he's grown into a proper scumbag then.'

'To put it mildly, yes,' Maggie said. 'You know him?'

'We were in care together. I knew he was bad, just not that bad.'

'I'm sure there's a sob story there about a rough childhood, but you, me and Danny can all claim that. It doesn't excuse him exploiting a child.'

'He may still be exploiting kids,' Tessa said. 'He's been named as a possible trafficker. I'll keep you posted. Any word on Isaac yet?'

'Danny's been trying to get hold of you. I'll let him fill you in.'

'And Noa and Sofie?'

'They're both as well as can be expected. I'll let you know as soon as the DNA results come through.'

Tessa hung up and rang Danny, who filled her in on the events of the day as well as his unsettling altercation with the two men and their threats to his family and, by extension, everyone else on the team's.

'The local boys are going through the paperwork they took from the late Mr Murray's office,' Danny said. 'Until then we can only guess as to why the Merrow broke cover to kill this old man.'

'Well, you never know,' Tessa said. 'There might be one or two clues to be found.'

'Tessa, why is a local politician trying to stop us looking into this case?'

'I don't know, but we're damn sure going to find out.'

'We will, won't we?' the big detective said.

'Give my best to Dawn. I'll see you soon.'

Tessa, Sheils and Stafford convened in a pub called The Sky and the Ground on Wexford's South Main Street.

The bar was decorated in traditional old-world fashion: dim lighting, an open fire and lots of vintage advertisements for cigarettes, whiskey and soap, though the draught beers were mostly recently created micro-brews and craft ales, which Tessa and Sheils were very happy to sample, while their rescuer was content to sip a sturdy white mug of black coffee.

The bar was busy but not overly full, and they found a quiet table near the back door.

'We owe you a word of thanks,' Tessa said to the fixer. 'Jim has filled me in, and it's likely things would have gone very differently if you hadn't arrived when you did.'

'You're most welcome. It was chance I happened along. I'm glad our paths converged at a moment when I could be useful.'

'It really was a stroke of luck,' Tessa said. 'Almost too lucky, when you think about it.'

'Whatever do you mean?' Stafford asked, although his facial expression suggested he knew exactly what she was hinting at.

'A person might think you were following us.'

'That would be a suspicious person indeed.'

'Wouldn't it though?'

Eric Stafford took an appreciative sip of his coffee and sat back, smoothing out a wrinkle in the trousers of his suit.

'Let us just say that my employers have an active interest in the case, and on their behalf I'm pursuing various lines of inquiry. If one or two of these cross over with yours, well then so be it. Perhaps we can be of assistance to each other.'

'Why are you suddenly interested in the children? Last time we spoke, you didn't seem to care much.'

'If rumours began to abound that my employers were involved in the trafficking of people, particularly children, it would seriously damage their reputation, which has been established over years of successful trading in good faith with their clients. My goal is to suppress any such Chinese whispers.'

'How can you be sure they're *not* behind the kids being on board?'

Stafford tutted quietly. 'My employers have no reason to lie to me. If they told me the children were on the *Dolphin* at their behest, but they wanted word of their presence hushed up, I would follow those orders without question. If they informed me their crews were trafficking people alongside their standard freight, with their explicit permission, I wouldn't be overly enamoured of the fact, but I've followed orders I didn't personally approve of before. It is, as the saying goes, the cost of doing business. I would still do my job and do it to the best of my ability.'

'And to clarify, Farnogue Freight have indicated they had no knowledge of the children or the woman who seems to be behind the death of the accountant, Mr Murray, and possibly the captain of the *Dolphin*?'

'They have stated so, yes.'

Tessa took a sip of her beer. Her head had settled into a dull pounding throb, and her neck felt as if a car had driven over it. Talking caused her pain, yet she had no choice other than to persevere.

'Mr Stafford, I had the impression when you were examining the cargo on the *Dolphin* that you were expecting to find something other than computers and clothes.'

The man shrugged. 'Perhaps I was. Just because my employers weren't responsible for something illegal going on aboard their vessels doesn't mean there was no illegality. Let's just say I've had my suspicions about certain crewmembers for a little while. That a tragedy such as this occurred isn't a happy turn of events, but neither is it wholly surprising to me.'

'Funny,' Tessa said. 'You never told me about these suspicions.'

'You didn't ask.'

'You're not a copper,' Sheils said. 'You don't need evidence to shut this down, whatever it is that's going on. You can just pay people off to remain quiet, or...'

'Chief Officer, all I wish to do is ensure my employers' reputation remains intact. Thus far, I've committed no crimes, and you and I are all on good terms.' He turned to Tessa. 'Is that not so, Detective?'

She sighed. 'I could probably charge you for assaulting O'Dowd's bodyguards, but I'm not sure why I would. I mean, what good would it do?'

'And I only did that to come to your aid.'

'How did you know we were in trouble?'

'I may have accidentally seen how things were developing through the window of Mr O'Dowd's office.'

Tessa couldn't help but laugh, though it hurt when she did.

'What a happy accident,' she said.

'Sometimes life is kind,' Stafford demurred. 'Might I furnish you both with fresh beverages?'

'Yeah, go on,' Tessa said. 'I think I'll see if I can't get a room in Wexford tonight rather than driving back to Gorey, so another drink would be very welcome.'

'I've got a spare room,' Sheils said. 'You can crash at mine if you like.'

Tessa felt a surge of excitement but tried to keep it from showing on her face, though she felt her cheeks heating up and knew she was blushing in spite of herself.

'That's great, Jim, thanks. Your... your family won't mind?'

'I'm divorced and my kids are both away at college. So no, no one's going to complain about a house guest.'

'Oh. That's... that's fantastic.'

Stafford, who'd been eyeing them both during this exchange, stood up. 'I'll remove myself from this uncomfortable juncture in the conversation and get you both pint glasses of the same?'

'I'll have a short this time,' Sheils replied. 'Double Bushmills please.'

'I'll take a large Teachers if they have one,' Tessa said. 'If not, some other Scotch with a bit of peat in it.'

Stafford nodded and went to the bar. As he did, the coastguard gallantly rescued Tessa from any more embarrassment by asking: 'What does that guy actually do for the shipping company?'

'He says he's a fixer,' she replied. 'But if I'm honest, he seems more like an enforcer, like the old-school gangs used to have.'

'Why would a freight company need someone like that?'

'These days, most large, successful companies probably employ someone like Stafford. Business can be dangerous, I suppose.'

'You think he's ex-army?'

'I do. My best guess is he's a former Ranger. I don't know many men who could take out eight armed thugs without breaking a sweat, and the ones I know who could are all either Irish Rangers or British SAS.'

'He doesn't look like much, but there's something about him,' Sheils agreed.

They noted that Stafford had their drinks and hushed as he returned to their table, another mug of coffee purchased for himself.

'You a teetotaller?' Sheils asked.

'No, I partake of alcohol on occasion. I just prefer to abstain while I'm on a case. Perhaps we can imbibe together once this job is concluded.'

Sheils raised his glass. 'You're on.'

'I'll look forward to it.'

'So what do we think about Del Finnegan?' Tessa asked when they'd all had a drink.

'I've never heard of him,' Sheils said. 'If he has been smuggling people, he's managed to do so under the coastguard's radar.'

'PULSE has him for assault and drunk and disorderly, as well as sexual abuse of a minor,' Tessa shared. 'I thought I knew him, but I've been badly wrong. There's something going on here, and it seems Del is involved in it up to his neck. I'm kicking myself, to be honest. I don't know how I missed it.'

'I made some calls while we were driving in from Mr O'Dowd's residence,' Stafford said. 'Some of my contacts know of him – they tell me he is assuredly a paedophile but as a trafficker he's a small operator.'

'The movement of children is a highly specialised area,' Tessa said. 'The fact he hasn't come to the attention of the authorities in a major way could just mean he's exceptionally good at what he does.'

'Which makes him doubly dangerous,' Sheils said.

'Wait till he gets a load of us,' Tessa replied.

29

Jim Sheils lived in a bungalow situated two miles into the Dublin side of Wexford's not-so-new bridge. Stafford dropped them off a little after eleven – Tessa left her Ford in the car park behind the pub.

'I'm sure I'll be seeing you both again very soon,' he said as they got out.

'I'll let you know if we learn anything from Del Finnegan tomorrow,' Tessa said. 'But after that we're even, okay?'

'DI Burns, I'm not the kind of man who expects anything in return for the kind act of saving your life. So consider us even right now, as we speak.'

'Perhaps, but I *am* the kind of person who repays my debts,' Tessa said firmly. 'You did me a solid, so I'll do you one in return. But after that the slate is wiped clean, and we go our separate ways.'

'That thought saddens me, but if it's what you wish, I shall continue my efforts without recourse to you.'

'It is my wish,' Tessa confirmed. 'And don't get in the way of my investigation with whatever efforts you're considering!'

'I will proceed with discretion.'

'See that you do.'

Stafford executed what Tessa would have called a bow, even though he was sitting behind the wheel of the big car, then performed a U-turn and sped back towards the lights of Wexford town.

'He could be a big help you know,' Sheils said as they walked to his front door.

'He's not a copper,' Tessa replied. 'He's not even a private investigator. Eric Stafford is essentially paid muscle, and I can't have some industrialist's pet thug co-working a case with me.'

'Even if he's going to be working it parallel to you anyway?'

'Even then.'

'You're a tough cookie, Tessa Burns.'

'And don't you forget it.'

Sheils' home, to Tessa's surprise, was impeccably tidy and well maintained, the interior painted in various shades of white, which gave the small one-storey house a greater sense of space than it possessed. The living room, into which he showed her, had a cream couch as its centrepiece, set in front of a large wood-burning stove in which a fire had been set though not lit. One wall was covered in shelves that were laden with books, and there was a large vintage-looking stereo system, the speakers of which had been hung from each of the four corners of the room at ceiling level, angled so the listener experienced the full effect. For a moment Tessa couldn't work out what was missing, but then she pegged it.

'No TV?'

The coastguard, who was busying himself lighting the stove, paused in what he was doing. 'What? Oh, no. I had one up to about a year ago, and there are sets in both of the kids' rooms, but I don't really watch the thing, so I got rid of it from the spaces I use in the house. When I'm home evenings, I read and listen to music.'

'What do you like to listen to?'

Kindling crackled in the stove, and Tessa felt a blast of warmth as the flames rose. Sheils watched them for a moment then closed the door on the conflagration and motioned at the couch.

'Take a load off. Can I offer you one more drink before bed?'

'Yeah, why not?'

'I don't have any Scotch, but there's a bottle of twenty-five-year-aged Bushmills if you'd like to sample some.'

'I'll risk it.'

'Great. Find something to listen to. My vinyl collection is in the cupboard underneath the stereo. I'll get the drinks and be right with you.'

He left to get their whiskeys, and Tessa opened the unit he'd indicated.

Within seconds, she realised this might be more of a challenge than she'd expected, as Sheils didn't appear to like any of the music she did. While Tessa was a huge devotee of rock and heavy metal of the seventies, eighties and nineties, the coastguard seemed to favour Irish folk and trad, a genre of which she knew almost nothing. When Sheils returned, she was holding an album that had an intriguing cover image: an elderly man on his hands and knees building a rickety bridge out into what looked to be an enormous lake, placing one board on the surface at a time, the previous pieces creating an unstable-looking path behind him, much as the water seemed to stretch into infinity in front.

'What's this one?' she asked, holding up the sleeve. 'There's no name on it.'

'Ah, now that is something special,' he said. 'Have you ever heard of The Gloaming?'

'Jim, I like AC/DC and Led Zeppelin. I'm embarrassed to say that your collection is *all* new to me.'

'Then prepare to be wowed. You won't want to come within an ass's roar of an electric guitar once you listen to this.'

Tessa laughed. 'I sincerely doubt that.'

'Don't knock it till you've tried it,' Sheils said, nodding sagely. 'Here's your drink. Sit down and let's see if I can't convert you.'

She took the glass and settled on the couch while he took out the disc, carefully wiped it with a shammy retrieved from a shelf behind the stereo, then placed it reverently on the turntable.

'I defy you not to be moved by this,' he said, lowering the stylus.

The music began and he sat beside her.

'The first track has the rather uncatchy title of "Song 44",' her host said. 'But don't let that put you off.'

The song opened with the sound of fiddles being plucked in short staccato bursts, followed by a male voice stretching to reach a falsetto note. The voice was singing words in a language Tessa didn't at first recognise, then she realised it was Irish.

'Is the whole album *as Gaeilge?*' she asked, mildly irritated at the prospect.

'It is, but even if you've no Irish at all, the music and the way he sings tells you all you need to know.'

A plaintive piano gently added its resonance, and as Tessa listened, she had to admit the sound the musicians created was haunting. The singer's voice was full of pain and loss, and even though she couldn't understand a single word, she knew this was a song about grief.

'Do you speak Irish, Jim?' she asked, suddenly realising she was exhausted but also that the few drinks had numbed the pain from her head and throat, so she was, for that moment at least, not experiencing any great discomfort.

'I do.'

'I only know the words they barked when they were drilling us in the army. And even then, I learned what the commands indicated I had to do – march this way, shoulder your weapon and so on – but I don't think I ever really understood what the words themselves meant.'

'I get you. My dad was from Clare, so we grew up speaking it.'

'Are you close with him?'

'I was, but he passed when I was a kid.'

'I'm sorry to hear that,' Tessa said gently. 'My parents both died when I was ten. So I know the hole it leaves in your life.'

Tessa was surprised at the sudden surge of sadness she felt as she articulated that truth. Not a day passed where she didn't think of her father at some point.

Deciding this wasn't the time to ponder such sad memories however, Tessa forced the thoughts from her mind and turned her attention back to the gorgeous music and the handsome man seated close enough beside her that she could feel his warmth and smell his cologne, both of which were very pleasant indeed.

'What's he actually saying? The singer?' she asked, not just to break the silence; she was genuinely interested.

'The song tells about a man waking from a dream in which the ghost of the girl he once loved visited him,' Sheils said. 'As he realises it was just a dream, he begins to feel like he's become a ghost himself.'

'That's sad,' Tessa said sleepily.

'Sad but beautiful,' Sheils agreed.

They sat quietly, the music washing over them. Somewhere towards the end of the song, he reached over and placed his hand on hers, and Tessa felt a tingle run through her.

'I thought I'd lost you in that awful fucking house,' Sheils said.

'I thought I *was* lost,' Tessa agreed.

'I'm glad you weren't.'

She turned to look at him and saw that he was gazing at her.

'Did you invite me here to try and have your way with me, Jim Sheils?' she asked, her voice little more than a whisper.

'I don't know,' he replied. 'Maybe I kind of hoped you'd want me to.'

'Maybe I do,' she said.

And he leaned over and kissed her, and even though the record remained playing, neither of them was listening to the music anymore.

30

Tessa's phone buzzed at six thirty the following morning, and she rolled over and answered it without realising where she was. She'd already said, 'Yeah, Tessa Burns here,' before experiencing a brief moment of disorientation – then the memory of the previous night came flooding back, and she looked to her left, and there was the sleeping (and delightfully naked) figure of Jim Sheils snoring lightly, his arm still resting in the spot she'd just vacated as she sat up to get her phone.

'Hey, Tessa. The DNA results are through,' Maggie's voice said into her ear. 'I thought you'd want to know right away.'

'Yeah, thanks, Maggie. So what's the story? Did we get lucky?'

She almost laughed at her own (completely unintentional) choice of words but kept the mirth to herself. She may tell Maggie about her and Jim (the family liaison officer was her best friend after all), but then there may be nothing to tell after today. But she couldn't dwell on such considerations now – there were more important issues afoot.

'We got a hit,' Maggie was saying. 'But I'm not sure how much it's going to help us.'

'Why not?'

'It's complicated. Can you come in?'

'Why wouldn't I be able to come in?'

'I don't know. I just thought you might be busy.'

'Busy doing what?'

The other end of the line went silent for a moment. Then Maggie retorted in an irritated voice: 'With work stuff. Weren't you planning to look into Del Finnegan today?'

'Yes.'

'Exactly. What's up with you, Tessa? You're acting as if you've got a bug up your ass!'

'Nothing. Sorry, Maggie. I'm still half-asleep. I'll be there as soon as I can.'

'Good. The commish and Danny are on their way. They should be here by seven thirty.'

'I'll aim for the same. See you in a bit.'

She put the phone back on the bedside locker and gazed down at the man whose bed she'd shared. Every fibre of her being wanted to lie back beside him and spend the morning on round two of their nocturnal activities. Instead, she got up and padded naked into the shower before slipping quietly out the front door and making the thirty-minute walk to her car.

31

'They're the children of a super-rich Wexford family, the Bolgers,' Maggie said.

Pavlov was perched on her knee, watching everyone intently with an expression that suggested he thought he was chairing the meeting.

They were all seated in a conference room on the third floor of Wexford General. It was a simple, utilitarian space with white walls and a carpet which, from the pervasive smell in the room, was newly laid and so bright a shade of blue it was uncomfortable to look at.

'John Bolger runs a major export company, dealing mostly in electronics, and he funds several fairly right-wing political parties: Identity Ireland and the Irish National Party are just two he's bankrolled over the years. His wife, Matilda Bolger, is involved in charity work and sits on the boards of the Wexford branch of Amnesty International. She seems to have been quiet lately, but there's plenty about her online.'

'Is she a bit less right-wing than her husband?' Tessa asked.

'Hard to tell,' Maggie said. 'Most of the charities she's involved with are church related, so it's anyone's guess.'

'Could the fact they're rich be behind the kids being apparently abducted?' Danny wondered. 'Not to mention Isaac being taken a second time?'

'That's what I thought too,' Maggie replied. 'Except for one very important point.'

'Which is?' Dawn asked.

'The children haven't been reported missing.'

'Seriously?' Danny spluttered. 'We're tying ourselves up in knots here and those fuckers haven't even reported that their kids have disappeared?'

'Maybe they didn't want the police involved,' Maggie suggested. 'The rich do have a tendency towards going privately – paying for their own services, if you get my meaning. Maybe they've hired a private investigator or a mercenary group to look for the children.'

'Is it possible they don't know they're missing?' Tessa wondered. 'I mean, if they're supposed to be visiting relatives or staying with friends?'

Danny considered that. 'I dunno, Tessa. It doesn't seem likely. Do we know if they're in boarding school, Maggie?'

'No idea. I've contacted our equivalent task force in Norway. The fact they were on the ship means they must have been there to begin with, so it's possible.'

'There's another issue I haven't mentioned yet,' Dawn said. 'I just had the pleasure of speaking to a lady called Ella Carling. She works for Tusla and, according to what I've been able to dig up online, is about two steps down from the Minister for Children and Families.'

'She's what, a civil servant then?'

'Yes, but a high-profile one.'

'And what did Ms Carling have to say?'

'That they're sending a social worker here to take those weans into care.'

'What?' Maggie asked incredulously. 'But why? They're

still under medical observation, and more to the point, they're here under *our* care.'

'Apparently a complaint has been made by someone from the locality in which you currently reside suggesting that the children are being used as a tool in your investigation. According to Ms Carling, the complainant is convinced they're already traumatised from their experiences, and keeping them in a hospital for the sheer purpose of getting them to open up is emotionally and psychologically abusive.'

'And being put in care would be better?'

'Ms Carling put it to me the children might not even be Irish.'

Tessa snorted. 'Well that's moot now.'

'And they landed on Irish soil!' Danny said indignantly.

'The issue is the fact that the kids stayed on the ship and you took them off. Which is classified as *wrecking*, which is the term used for stealing goods off a wrecked vessel and it is, needless to say, highly illegal.'

'They're children – we couldn't very well leave them there!' Maggie spluttered.

'Ms Carling states that, until we can ascertain who they are and which jurisdiction they rightfully belong to, they're wards of the state,' Dawn said. 'Well, as of this morning, we know who they are, which means as of right now, social services can fuck right off. They've no claim on these kids. As to why they weren't called in as missing, I reckon we'll hear that story soon enough. In the meantime, there's no point in playing guessing games.'

'It's weird though, isn't it?' Maggie said, almost to herself.

'Yes, it is very feckin' weird,' Dawn agreed. 'Right, Danny, do you want to talk about your recent adventures?'

Danny nodded and began with his conversation with Tom Doran from Rosslare's Port Authority, then what he'd learned from Seamus Quigley about Derek Sherlock, the *Dolphin*'s cook, the fact he had served prison time and was a member of a gang at one time, and the death of the accountant.

'Thoughts on the murder of Mr Murray?' Dawn asked him.

'Forensic accountants are going through his books as we speak,' Danny said. 'The theory we're going on is that he's in some way involved in the financial side of whichever gang – or individual, I suppose – is behind all of this.'

'So we wait on their findings and then follow up the leads, I suppose,' Tessa said.

'Maggie, I thought you might be able to run down what those tattoos Derek had represent,' Danny said. 'I know they're all like badges of honour to some gang members.'

'They're a kind of code, yes,' Maggie said, nodding as she typed rapidly on her laptop. 'I've made a note of them.'

'So to be clear, this guy, Derek, hinted that he was being forced to do something he didn't agree with?' Tessa asked.

'It's hard to be sure,' Danny replied. 'You could explain it away by saying he was carrying a lot of guilt over things he'd done in his past. But I don't think so. In light of everything we know happened on the *Dolphin*, I'm starting to lean towards Derek's past coming back to bite him on the arse. Either the gang as a whole or someone within that world coerced him into doing things that didn't sit well with him.'

'Stafford, Farnogue Freight's fixer or enforcer or whatever he is, apparently had his own doubts about the goings on aboard the *Dolphin* and had suspicions about certain crew members.'

'Did he suspect this Derek lad?' Dawn asked.

'He wasn't specific,' Tessa said. 'But from what I know of Mr Stafford, he'll have known who was likely to be up to no good. He seems to be a few steps ahead of all of us.'

'So are we looking at the company then?'

'Stafford says no, and that they've no reason to lie to him about it.'

'He would say that though, wouldn't he?' Dawn said tersely.

'His job is to clean up their mess. Part of which is making sure they're not incriminated.'

'Possibly,' Tessa said. 'He seems like a straight shooter though.'

Dawn raised an eyebrow at that but said nothing.

'So you reckon the cook was being pressured into doing something he wasn't happy about?' Tessa asked Danny.

'I do,' Danny retorted. 'Quigley said Derek mentioned a debt he was being forced to repay. But I think it runs even deeper than that,' he said and retold the story of the two men who'd followed him, of the altercation in the alley and the threat against his family.

'And this guy claimed he was sent by a government minister?' Tessa asked, incredulous.

Danny nodded. 'Damien Forde – Junior Minister for Foreign Affairs.'

'And you think this is credible, boss?'

Dawn sighed and sat forward in her chair. 'Many years ago, when I was still in uniform, I was involved, very peripherally, in a case where a truck was held up with a view to robbing the goods it was carrying – fertilizer the robbers intended to use to create explosives which they were going to sell to various factions of the political and sectarian divide in the North. When these gentlemen opened up the truck's container, they found more than compost. Five hundred automatic weapons had been hidden in the fertilizer. I was on the checkpoint where these boyos were caught trying to get their ill-gotten gains over the border into the six counties.'

'Were they gangsters?' Tessa wanted to know.

'Not at all. The eejits were from a small village in Wexford and had hit on the idea of making some big money fast. No, what's interesting here is the company who owned the truck. It was owned by Damien Forde, who, according to the chap you were forced to subdue, sent them to warn us off the case.'

'I'll bet he claimed he had no knowledge of the guns,' Maggie said.

'Of course he did. But he wouldn't be the first Irish politician to get involved in gunrunning, and to be honest, no one involved in the investigation believed him. We just couldn't find any proof that he knew the guns were there.'

'What you're saying is that he has form,' Tessa said.

'I surely am. I've kept an eye on him over the years. His company, Forde Trucking International, has skirted the borders of some dodgy dealings, but there's never been anything you could put your finger on. But now, his name pops up in connection with something very strange and very dark. Oh, he has form, Tessa. And I wouldn't be one bit surprised if we found out he's in this right up to his neck.'

'So where do we go with that?' she asked.

'The first thing we do is make sure that anyone connected with you is moved to safety,' Dawn said.

'I've no one outside this room,' Tessa replied.

'My mother is in a nursing home,' Maggie said. 'Unless they're planning on breaking in and hurting her...'

'I'll have a couple of uniforms placed at her door,' Dawn said.

'Thanks, boss.'

'After that, the obvious thing to do is have a chat to Graeme Clohessy, the PA who was named.'

'I'd like to do that,' Danny said.

'I might just go along with you,' Tessa said.

Danny grinned. 'I'd appreciate that.'

They were all quiet for a moment.

'Do we have any further knowledge of the woman who has Isaac?' the commissioner asked. 'He's been missing for twenty-nine hours now. It'd be good to know who has the lad.'

'The children have said nothing much relating to her,' Maggie said. 'But it's clear from their artwork that they knew her, and the name Sofie wrote on her painting, Merrow, refers to an ancient Irish legend.'

Dawn made a 'please go on' gesture.

'The merrow were a violent species of mermaid who protected Ireland's shores against invaders.'

'The captain and crew seemed to believe they'd picked up a mermaid during a storm they passed through,' Tessa said.

'Yeah, but this lassie was on board long before the storm,' Dawn said. 'And we all know there's no such fucking thing as mermaids.'

'We know she has some kind of experience with ropes and mountaineering,' Danny said. 'She never would have been able to get in and out of the kids' room without it, never mind do so while carrying a child.'

'I spoke to Luca in Organised Crime,' Maggie said. 'He told me they had a woman who matches the description and went by the name Merrow in custody a couple of years back, and she escaped Harcourt Street by making a rope from her own clothes and climbing out through a second-floor window.'

'So the mountaineering thing is an avenue we might explore,' Dawn said.

'I was thinking the same thing,' Maggie replied.

'Do we think she was there to make sure the children arrived safely in Ireland?' Tessa asked. 'Most minors who are trafficked have a minder with them until they're handed over to whoever is taking possession of them at the destination point.'

'Maybe,' Maggie said. 'I do believe she was here to check on the kids – she was in their room. And her having taken Isaac, and her behaviour towards him since then, all points to a feeling of protectiveness.'

'If we could just find her and Isaac now, I'd sleep a lot easier,' Danny said, 'not that any of us have been doing much sleeping.'

Tessa tried not to look uncomfortable at this comment.

'We believe she's travelling in a blue 2008 Ford Focus,' Dawn said. 'One was stolen near the hospital the night before last, and we got a shot of it going through a set of traffic cameras on the Enniscorthy road, and the driver looks to be our woman.'

'Just the one shot?' Danny asked.

'She was cute enough to turn off the main road and take to country lanes and byroads. The tech guys have set up a system where an alarm will sound the second that registration number is captured on any traffic cam, but if she's as smart as we think she is, she'll have had the good sense to change it, so I'm not sure how much good it will do.'

'The fact no alarm was sounded when she drove into the middle of Wexford town, with Isaac in tow, to kill an elderly accountant suggests you're right,' Tessa said.

'Sadly it does,' Dawn agreed. 'We've combed all the CCTV footage available from this morning, and while we have close to twenty blue Ford Focuses, our girl and the wee lad aren't captured either getting into or out of any of them.'

'She parked somewhere far away from cameras,' Danny said.

'That she did,' Dawn sighed. 'I have our boys scanning shots of every car of that model leaving Wexford around the time that fits then tracing them to wherever they're going. We've had no luck so far.'

'Could be she never left,' Tessa suggested.

'That would be a bold move,' Dawn said, mulling it over. 'I wouldn't rule it out, but I've not come across a fugitive yet who'd have the balls to do it.'

'What have you got for us, Tessa?' Danny asked.

She told the group about her visit to Andrew O'Dowd's, about Stafford's timely intervention and finished with what she'd learned about Del Finnegan.

'Will your pal the coastguard go along to that interview with you?' Dawn asked.

Tessa blushed. 'I can ask him.'

'Do – please. I don't think any of you should be alone right now. Maggie, you liaise with the Norwegian police about the kids possibly being in school there. The uniforms from the Wexford station are still here, and I've asked for them to stay on with you until I give the word they're not needed. For now we are in a *code red*. Hopefully we can find out what's behind it, but until we do, we tread very carefully. Do you all understand?'

Pavlov barked once, to show he did.

'Good. Now, do they do a decent breakfast in this place? I'm feckin' famished.'

PART FOUR

SOMETHING IN THE WATER

32

A representative from Child and Adolescent Psychiatry was with the kids, so they drove into Wexford town and had a hearty breakfast in a café called Joanne's, a big, bustling, old-school establishment with chequered tablecloths that smelled of freshly baked bread and good coffee. To add to its appeal, the staff were happy to have Pavlov gnaw a bone under Tessa's chair.

The team, it seemed, shared Dawn's appetite, because little was said as they tucked into full Irish breakfasts, and for a brief moment the danger they were in was put out of their minds and they simply enjoyed the excellent food and one another's company.

When everyone was full and sitting back enjoying tea or coffee according to their liking, Dawn looked about the group.

'This has been traumatic for all of you,' she began. 'Losing the wee lad has knocked you all – I can see it. But you have to keep your heads straight if you're going to get him back and untangle the mess this case is.'

The group all nodded.

'We hear you, boss,' Tessa said. 'We'll work this the right way until it's done.'

'I know you will,' Dawn replied, smiling reassuringly. 'I'm not the team leader, but I'm going to insist you proceed with caution. The whole business has gone beyond a standard criminal case. Tessa, I'm not gazumping you, but with respect, you're not a politician and you've no experience dealing with the kind of shite we're about to find ourselves up to our arses in. You need to be on your toes when you're dealing with these people.'

'No argument here, boss,' Tessa said. 'Although I should add that if Damien Forde, TD or not, did send those thugs to try and scare us off, he's just as much a common criminal as anyone else I've dealt with and should be treated the exact same.'

'I couldn't agree with you more,' Dawn said. 'But we all know it's not going to be that easy. Even if his underling admits sourcing the strong-arm crew that braced young Daniel, Forde will deny having any knowledge of it. And even if that underling agreed to swear to it, Forde can afford lawyers that will have us tied up in knots for decades, and the department would know that right off the bat and simply refuse to pursue it. We'd be finished before we even started. We're going to have to be subtle on this one. Tread carefully.'

'I'm not really known for being subtle,' Danny said ruefully.

'You can say that again,' Tessa and Maggie said in unison, and the four of them collapsed into laughter.

It had been a long time since they'd all shared a joke, as silly and misplaced as this one was, and Tessa had to admit it felt good.

'Luckily I've enough subtlety for all of us,' she said when their mirth had subsided.

'On a more serious note,' Dawn cut in, 'by interviewing Clohessy and Forde, you'll be letting them know we know what they did, which of course incriminates them both, which means whoever they're involved with will know.'

'Meaning they'll send tougher guys and more of them next time,' Tessa said.

'Exactly. For all we know, the woman on the ship is in their employ. And she doesn't strike me as any kind of amateur.'

'I've never seen anything like her,' Maggie agreed.

'So we go carefully, we stay in touch and we think before we jump. We still have no idea what exactly is going on, but I'm hoping that, once the parents of those kiddies arrive, things will become clearer,' Dawn replied. 'Right, does everyone have their assignments?'

'I'll go and talk to the local boys about Del Finnegan, see what they can tell me about his activities now,' Tessa said, 'then Jim and I can have a cordial chat with him.'

Dawn looked at her. 'I know you feel this guy has let you down in some way, but put the emotion aside, okay?'

'I will,' Tessa said. 'I want to kick the living shit out of him, and out of myself for not seeing what he was... is. But the self-recrimination can wait.'

'Good,' Dawn said. 'Remember why you're talking to him. He may be able to throw this whole business wide open for us.'

'Pav and I will go back to Wexford General and await the arrival of Mom and Pop Bolger,' Maggie said. 'And while I'm waiting, I'll see if letting the kids know we're now fully aware of who they are and where they're from might encourage them to share a bit more information.'

'I'll look into Clohessy and see what I can learn before Tessa and I go and chat with him,' Danny said. 'No harm in being prepared.'

'Can we agree to check in every two hours?' Tessa asked. 'Just a quick text so we all know we're okay?'

Each member of the group nodded their assent.

'Okay then,' Dawn said. 'Let's go to work.'

33

'You are Sofie and Noa Bolger,' Maggie said to the two children, who were sitting on Noa's bed, gazing at her blankly, Pavlov lying across their knees having his belly rubbed. 'You're from right here in Wexford, and I've been told your parents, who were in Amsterdam on business, are on their way here and should arrive by six o'clock this evening.'

The children looked very different to the waifs Maggie had met only a couple of days ago: their old-fashioned haircuts had been styled into more modern coiffures by one of the nurses, and they were wearing hoodies, jeans and trainers now, which gave the impression they were ordinary kids from any town in Ireland.

Which of course they weren't.

Sofie seemed utterly unmoved by the family liaison officer's news, but Noa scowled. His sister leaned over and whispered something to him, and her older brother responded in similar hushed tones. Maggie had pulled them up on whispering before, pointing out that it was a bit rude, and decided to call them on it again. If they were going to exclude her, she might as well let them know she was aware of the fact.

'You know I'm sitting right here, don't you, guys?'

Noa gave her a hard look. 'Sofie is afraid.'

'Mammy and Daddy are coming?' the little girl asked.

'I think so, yes.'

'Will they be cross with us?'

'Why would they be cross with you? You've not done anything wrong. I should think they'll be very happy to see you.'

'You don't know our parents,' Noa said.

'No, I don't,' Maggie agreed. 'And I don't know what happened to you to end up on that ship to begin with. If you could tell me, I think this would all be much easier.'

'We can't tell,' Sofie said, tears springing to her eyes. 'We promised not to speak to anyone about it.'

'Who did you make that promise to?' Maggie asked, rolling closer and putting a hand on the little girl's shoulder. 'No one should have asked you to keep a promise like that. It's not a fair thing to force you to do.'

Noa looked utterly dejected as he watched his sister sobbing. '*She* told us not to talk about it.'

'The woman who was on the boat with you?'

He nodded.

'And who was here the other night and took Isaac?'

He nodded again. 'The Merrow,' he said.

'She told you that's her name?'

'She said it's what people call her.'

'Merrow,' Sofie said, seeming to perk up at the mention.

'Did she care for you on the boat?'

'Yes, she gave us food and water and let us watch films on her laptop.'

'Did she take you from your home?'

Noa went deathly pale and his breathing became rapid.

'If this is too hard, we can stop,' Maggie said. 'I want to know but not so badly I'd want you upset.'

'We were at our school in Norway,' Noa said. 'One night I

was woken by someone shaking me. It was her – the Merrow. I don't know how she got in, but she told me that Daddy wanted us all to go with her on a trip.'

'So you went with her,' Maggie said.

'Yes. Daddy has a lot of helpers. One of them always picks me up from school to bring me home for the holidays.'

'So even though this isn't holiday time, you didn't think anything of it?'

'No. She gave me some clothes, and I went to pack more, but she said we would have everything we needed. So I got dressed and went with her. She had a car, and Sofie and Isaac were already in it. I didn't begin to wonder if she'd lied until we got to the boat. It didn't look like the kind of ship Daddy would have had us travel on.'

'You must have been very frightened,' Maggie said.

'I didn't want to scare Isaac and Sofie, so I didn't say anything about it. And the Merrow was kind to us. When I saw that she wasn't bad, I was less afraid.'

'But she told you not to tell anyone about her.'

'Yes,' Noa said. 'She said she would be in trouble, and it would put our parents in danger.'

'Did she ever tell you what you were coming back to Ireland for?'

'I didn't know where we were going,' Noa said. 'She told us there would be people to meet us when we got there, and that we'd be looked after.'

'Did she say your parents would be here too?'

Noa shook his head. 'She told us they didn't want to see us anymore,' he said, and this time his voice broke. 'She said we would have new families, and that it was for the best.'

Maggie opened her arms, and both of the children came in for a hug.

'I'm sorry she told you that. You know it's a lie, don't you?'

'You don't know our parents,' Noa said again through his

tears. 'When she said it, I believed her. And I... I thought things might be better for us without them.'

And Maggie didn't know what to say to that.

The kids and Pavlov were watching a show called *The Adventures of Jimmy Neutron, Boy Genius* on Nickelodeon, and Maggie used the time to fire up her laptop and Google mountaineering in the south-east.

The problem was, she didn't know what she was looking for.

One of the comments Dawn had made had stuck in her head though – the idea that perhaps the Merrow, and by extension Isaac, hadn't left Wexford town at all. Was there somewhere locally where this woman's skillset might come in particularly useful and enable her to hide right under their noses until the heat died down?

There were a number of mountains around County Wexford – Mount Leinster in the north of the county being the highest – and Forth Mountain, which was really more of a hill, was situated about nine kilometres to the south of the town. But to access these, the Merrow would have to pass numerous traffic cameras, which at this stage it seemed she hadn't.

Going back to a more rigorous search of the town itself, Maggie happened upon a site for a place known as The Rocks – a hilly and mountainous area on the outskirts of Wexford town, characterised by rocky outcrops and skirted by walking trails, trees, grass and wild plants. There was also a historical significance to the region, as Oliver Cromwell had used Trespan Rock, the area's highest point, to bombard the town during his siege of Wexford in 1649.

Maggie pulled up some images and a map.

The walking trails – one long one which ran around the perimeter of a landscaped area and another shorter one that formed a loop inside it – were in only one part of the region known as The Rocks, but Trespan Rock itself was in the middle of acres of wilderness that stretched for several kilometres out of the town, and Maggie could see several caves and alcoves that might be accessible to a person with rock-climbing skills.

Looking at the map – which showed Wexford town and the surrounding area – the family liaison officer caught her breath. The Rocks was right next door to – in fact, the land they occupied actually adjoined – Wexford Garda station.

Could the Merrow be so bold as to hide herself and the child she'd abducted right under the noses of the people who were looking for her?

Maggie was starting to believe that she was.

She composed a rapid email containing the information and links to what she'd just read online then sent it to Danny and Tessa.

34

'Del Finnegan is dangerous, for sure,' Garda Josh Feeney said.

He and Tessa were in Wexford station. The squad room was a maze of desks and filing cabinets, alive with the sound of phones ringing and barked conversations. Tessa had spent a good deal of her life in spaces just like this and felt right at home.

Feeney was thirty years old, fair-haired, tall and well built, the blue stab vest of his uniform doing nothing to hide his physique.

'Dangerous how?' Tessa asked.

'He's an inveterate abuser of children,' Feeney said. 'There were complaints about him for years before we had enough to put him away.'

'What were the circumstances of his arrest on the abuse charges?' Tessa inquired. 'I know he has a couple of other convictions, but...'

'Yeah, they're tuppenny/ha'penny stuff in comparison. He was literally caught in the act. That's all you need to know, believe me.'

Tessa nodded. It *was* all she needed to know. Anger coursed through her again, but she shoved it aside. 'How long did he get?'

'Not long enough. You know how tough it is to score a long-term conviction in Ireland. He was sent down for a couple of years and served fourteen months. The judge offered the chance of therapy when he was inside, but Del refused it, as so many of them do. He's out but is in no way rehabilitated, and I have to tell you, he's utterly without remorse.'

'You're in charge of monitoring him?'

'For my sins, yeah. There are currently forty-three people on the sex offenders register here in the Wexford Urban district and environs. I had forty-five up to three weeks ago, but the majority are only on the books for ten years, and two timed out last month.'

'The majority?'

'In rare instances some judges place offenders on the register for longer. Twenty years or even for life.'

'Why not just keep them locked up?'

'I don't want to sound cynical,' Feeney said, 'but that comes down to the cost. It's cheaper on the taxpayer to have someone like me check in on these guys every week or so than it is to keep paying their bed and board in Portlaoise or Wheatfield or Shelton Abbey.'

'Even if they still pose a risk?'

'Even then.'

'How long will Finnegan be on the register?'

'The standard decade, which means another seven-and-a-half years. There wasn't enough to establish a pattern of consistent risk.'

'But you believe our Mr Finnegan will offend again, given the opportunity?'

'Without a doubt. He's smart and knows damn well I wouldn't trust him around a fucking budgerigar, but even with that knowledge, he likes to play games with me. The conditions of his release are that he can't be within one hundred yards of a school, a children's playground or anywhere kids will congregate, but there have been reports of him hanging about close to locations he shouldn't.'

'Send him back inside then.'

'I'd love to. Problem is, the bollix has measured one hundred yards from every school gate in town, and makes sure that's where he stands, right at the hundred-yard mark. The same with the parks and playgrounds. And a couple of preschools.'

'Surely that's grounds...'

'Nope. He's keeping to the letter of the conditions he agreed to on his reinstatement into society.'

Tessa shook her head. 'Though not exactly the spirit of them.'

'I wish "the spirit of the law" was important,' Feeney said with regret. 'But unfortunately it isn't. Not upholding the ethical implications of your release isn't something I can bring before a judge.'

Tessa couldn't disagree with that, so instead she said, 'He's pretty much a loner from what I can see. That said, I can't attest to what he does when I'm not keeping an eye on him.'

Feeney sat back in his chair and looked at Tessa searchingly. 'What do you think Del is involved in? I know you're investigating that ship that ran aground in the north of the county, but I don't see how Del Finnegan could have anything to do with that.'

'He was named as a child trafficker by an individual who's very prominent in the criminal community in this part of the world.'

Feeney's eyes widened. 'Seriously?'

'Deadly serious. I'm going to talk to him today, so if I learn anything, I'll let you know.'

'Do – please. I just don't see how though. His online activity is monitored, and we keep tabs on his phone records too.'

'I know a few eight-year-olds who could get around that kind of surveillance,' Tessa said. 'So if he's as smart as you say he is – and once bitten...'

'True. Well, keep me posted. You know where to find him?'

'I have his address. Google Maps will get me there.'

35

When the children were finished watching the latest episode of their TV show, Maggie decided to revisit the topic of their parents once more.

'Can you tell me why you think it would be good not to see your parents again?' Maggie asked. 'I know about your mammy being sick, and I know you've been through a tough time these past few days, but if there's something else going on, maybe I can help with it.'

The children looked at one another and then at Maggie. Noa said something in a hiss just above a whisper to Sofie, but it was so quick the family liaison officer couldn't catch it.

Sofie turned to Noa and hissed back.

Noa nodded and said, 'Daddy's angry with us. He told us he prefers us not to be around. It's why he sent us away to school.'

'He said this to you?'

'Yes. He's said it loads of times.'

'Did he say what he's angry about?'

'He blames us for Mammy being sick.'

Maggie shook her head. 'If he did say that, it's not true.

What your mammy has was probably handed down to her from her own parents, or even another member of her family. You guys had nothing to do with it.'

'Daddy says she didn't start to get sick until she had me,' Noa replied.

Maggie nodded then said, choosing her words carefully, 'I'm not disrespecting your dad when I say this, but anyone who knows how the mind works would never say that. A lot of women get sad after having babies, and some can get really ill, but that's not the babies' fault. You should never have been made to think you were to blame for how your mammy is.'

'I don't think Daddy likes us,' Sofie said. 'When he's with us, he's always angry, even if he isn't speaking.'

'Daddy's always angry,' Noa agreed.

'Well when he gets here, maybe I'll have a chat with him about that,' Maggie replied.

The kids looked at her in disbelief.

'No one tells Daddy what to do,' Noa said. 'Everyone's afraid of him.'

'Well, Noa lad, there's something very important you need to remember,' Maggie said, putting her arm around the boy and pulling him into a side-hug. 'I bet everyone your father deals with on a day-to-day basis works for him. Am I right?'

Noa thought for a moment then nodded.

'Well I don't. If your dad gets mad at me, what's the worst he can do? Shout? Say some mean things to me? I'm not afraid of that. I can shout back just as loud, and words don't hurt me. Over the years, lots of people have said terribly mean things to me, and do you know what? None of them made any difference because they weren't true.'

Noa hugged Maggie back.

'I know you'll stick up for us,' he said, 'but I don't think Daddy will change.'

'Everyone can change,' Maggie said. 'If they want to.' She paused, then said: 'You must miss Isaac terribly.'

Both children nodded.

'It's strange him not being here,' Noa said. 'I keep wanting to say something to him, and then I look and he's not there.'

'He always makes me laugh,' Sofie said. 'I wish he was here so he could do that. Are you going to bring him back, Maggie? You and your friends?'

'We're trying our hardest,' Maggie replied.

Noa nodded at her when she said that, but in her heart, Maggie knew he didn't believe her for a second.

An hour later, the kids went for play therapy. Maggie got a cup of tea and bought a pack of digestive biscuits in the hospital shop before going back to the room. She put some water in a bowl for Pavlov, broke up three of the biscuits for him and left them on a plate, then opened her laptop and began to research tattoos and Irish gangs to try to determine the significance of Derek's ink.

She already knew that for members of many criminal gangs, a stay in prison was a mark of honour, and the harder the time served, the better, as it showed a gang member's resilience. And that it had been the prison community that had cemented the tradition of using tattoos to tell one's story.

Maggie found several online resources that listed the various meanings of Irish gang tattoos, many of which managed to be both beautiful and terrible in equal measure. The Madonna and Child meant that Derek had been forced to become a criminal at an early age and had probably served his first prison sentence when he was still a child; it marked him as a 'child of the prison' and was supposed to act as a talisman, to ward off evil and bad luck.

Well that didn't work too well, Maggie mused.

The ship indicated that Derek was on the run, perhaps having escaped prison at some point, or maybe he was fleeing a gang to whom he owed something – which made sense given what Danny said he'd told Quigley about being forced to pay a debt.

A crown suggested Derek had risen to the rank of gang captain or had been placed in a position of authority – though the fact he'd ended up on the *Dolphin* in the role of cook indicated he hadn't been able to maintain that status.

By the time the kids got back from their therapy, Maggie had no doubt that Derek Sherlock was a man with the experience, the connections and the skills to facilitate the movement of the Bolgers' children. And the presence of such a man on the *Dolphin* was too much of a coincidence to be ignored.

She put what she'd learned in an email and sent it to each member of the team. Which was just as well, as things turned out – they wouldn't get a chance to be together as a group until it was all over.

36

Danny sat at the window of the bar in the Riverbank House Hotel, just across the bridge from Wexford town, watching the River Slaney meander past on its way to the Irish Sea.

The large bar, pleasantly lit and decorated like an old-school hotel in light wood, the walls bedecked with paintings of schooners and fishing boats, was already filling with people looking for a late breakfast or an early lunch, both of which the kitchen catered for with consummate ease.

A scruffy-looking man wearing a long trench coat that had seen better days came in through the door that led from the beer garden, cast about for a moment, spotted Danny and made a beeline for him.

'You're the detective that called to speak to me?' he asked as Danny shook his hand.

'Yes. DS Danny Murphy.'

'I'm Patrick Moran. I'm not sure why the National Bureau of Criminal Investigation wants to speak to a journalist from a local newspaper.'

'The name of one of your local politicians has come up in an investigation, and I'd like to know a little about him before I go and talk to him. Get some... I dunno, some insider knowledge.'

'Who's the politician?'

'Damien Forde.'

Moran was about fifty, and his hair, which was mostly still dark, looked like it hadn't seen a comb in a month. He had bright, quick-moving blue eyes and pronounced cheekbones, and the lower part of his face was obscured by a thick, unruly beard that looked more like wire than whiskers.

Beneath the trench coat he wore a rumpled brown suit.

'Let's move to the beer garden,' the journalist said. 'It's mostly empty in this weather, and I'm going to want to smoke anyway.'

Danny followed him outside, where ten tables had been arranged into a square under a Perspex roof, trellises draped with vines and creepers forming the walls.

'What do you want to know about Junior Minister Forde?' the journalist asked once he was seated in the far corner, a Benson & Hedges cigarette smouldering in his mouth.

'Whatever you can tell me.'

'He's from a political dynasty,' Moran said.

'He's a junior minister now?'

'Yes. The Foreign Affairs brief.'

'Is he any good?'

Moran laughed cynically and stubbed out his smoke. 'Damien Forde doesn't give a rat's ass about anything. He wanted to look honourable in advance of mounting a bid for the leadership.'

'That's very calculating,' Danny agreed.

'Damien Forde is nothing if not that,' Moran said. 'Don't get me wrong, he's brilliant, a gifted politician – sure, hasn't he been bred to it? But the causes he throws himself into are all carefully chosen to make himself look good.'

'Is he popular locally?'

'Hugely so. His followers and supporters treat him like JFK, just in Leinster House rather than the White House. I have no doubt he'll be Taoiseach one day.'

'He's a businessman too?'

'Oh yes. His brothers run the company for him, mostly importing materials to agri-business and construction abroad. He lost a lot of money during Covid, and took a hit during the 2008/2009 economic crash. I would say he's making ends meet right now, but I'd wager he's glad of the ministerial wage he's receiving.'

'Are there any rumours about the legality of his business dealings?'

'Loads. And I'd believe most of them. The family have links to paramilitaries in the North, gangs in the thirty-two counties and have been accused of doctoring their accounts to raise share prices on more than one occasion.'

'This leadership bid,' Danny said. 'Will he need a war chest to get it going?'

'To be sure he will.'

'So a big payoff on some kind of deal would be beneficial?'

'Very.'

'What about his assistant – Clohessy?'

Moran laughed. 'Have you ever seen *The Simpsons*?'

Danny nodded.

'Do you remember Mr Smithers, assistant and toady to Mr Burns? Well that's as close an approximation as I can think of for Graeme Clohessy. He lives to serve Damien Forde. He'd do anything he could to help his boss, and I'd guess it would take a lot for him to say or do anything that would incriminate him.'

'Anything else I should know?'

'I don't think he's the brightest light bulb in the pack. I'd be surprised if he so much as wipes his arse without Forde instructing him to do so.'

Danny nodded and thought about the money that might be

earned from three foreign adoptions to wealthy US or Canadian families. And about how Forde's political machine might well have been used to secure that money.

It was high time he had a conversation with Damien Forde and his people.

37

Graeme Clohessy, personal assistant to the Junior Minister for Foreign Affairs, was half an inch below six feet, and Danny estimated he weighed only a shade over ten stone, 140 pounds. He looked to be in his late twenties, but the blonde hair that adorned his small head was already receding, and he'd gelled it back so it formed a pronounced widow's peak. That day he was dressed in a tailored pale-blue suit with a pink shirt and grey-and-white striped tie, held in place with a silver pin. His shoes, which were also grey, seemed to be suede.

Danny and Clohessy met in Wexford's county council offices in Ferrybank, half a mile from where he'd met Moran. If the visit unnerved the skinny man, he hid his discomfort well.

'Could I get you tea or coffee?' he asked as they sat down in the sparse meeting room, which had blue carpet tiles on the floor and a print of Irish politicians going back to the foundation of the state on the walls.

'No thank you, I'm good,' Danny said.

'Very well. How can I help you?'

Clohessy folded himself into a chair, and Danny thought for a moment that he looked like some kind of insect – a praying mantis or maybe one of those ones that seemed for all the world to be made of sticks.

'I was hoping you might be able to point me in the direction of some information.'

'Of course. I'd be delighted to help you if I can.' The ministerial aide's larynx bounced and bobbed as he spoke, as if it had a life of its own.

'That's good to know.'

The man smiled, or, Danny thought, perhaps simpered was a better word.

'I'm sorry to tell you I was assaulted while returning from a crime scene yesterday evening.'

'Really. Well that is bad news. I trust you're not too severely hurt, DS Murphy.'

'I'm fine.'

'I'm glad to hear it. Did you apprehend the culprit?'

'Unfortunately, they got away.'

'They?'

'Yes, there were two of them. I got a good look at them though. I would definitely recognise them if I saw them again.'

'I'm glad to hear it.'

'When I'm done here, I may sit down with one of our sketch artists. It's amazing what those lads can do. Toddy, who works with the National Bureau of Criminal Investigation, can produce photo-realistic images with that pencil of his.'

'Remarkable,' Clohessy said. 'Might I ask as to what any of this has to do with me?'

'Of course, Graeme – is it alright if I call you Graeme by the way?'

'Yes, of course.'

'Fantastic. Well, Graeme, the thing is this: I can be an extremely persuasive individual, especially when my blood is up.'

'I could see how you might be,' Clohessy agreed.

'Well one of these lads who attacked me, he threatened my family. Showed me a photo of my parents' house and made *very* explicit threats.'

'My goodness, that's just... it's beyond the pale!' the skinny man said, trying to look irate but only managing to achieve slight bewilderment.

'*Completely* beyond the pale,' Danny agreed.

'What was the reason behind the threat?' Clohessy asked. 'Did they tell you?'

'Oh, they surely did,' Danny went on. 'They wanted me and my team to step away from a case we're working.'

'What case might that be?'

'I'm not at liberty to share that information,' Danny said, feigning a crestfallen expression. 'But what I can say is that my team would never bow to intimidation. What kind of a police force would we be if a couple of yobs can scare us?'

'Yes, but there's no point sacrificing the safety of your parents—'

'We know how to look after our own, Graeme!'

'I'm certain you do, Detective, but...'

'Anyway, as I was saying, I managed to get one of the fellas who attacked me to talk.'

'Surely nothing he says can be taken as fact though?'

'I don't know about that. He was pretty scared.'

'Probably unreliable though...'

'He said Graeme Clohessy, personal assistant to the Junior Minister for Foreign Affairs, had sent him to warn me off, and that I was to pass that message on to my team mates too.'

Clohessy was opening and closing his mouth by then, but no sound was coming out, and his Adam's apple was performing a veritable ballet.

'Why would I do such a thing?' he managed to hiss finally.

'I asked myself that very question,' Danny said. 'And I spoke to a few people about you too. Do you know what I found out?'

The PA looked terrified but nodded.

'I learned that you're a very loyal man. Loyal to a fault perhaps. And that *nothing* – and I mean *nothing* – you do occurs to you out of your own head. You follow orders. Minister Damien Forde, your boss, issues instructions, and you carry them out.'

'That's my job,' Clohessy said, the words coming out almost as a whisper.

'Exactly,' Danny said. 'So the question I now have is: why the hell did Damien Forde want us to back off from a case involving a grounded ship, a dead crew and three lost children?'

'I... I don't know.'

'Now that, Mr Clohessy, might be the first thing you've said this afternoon that wasn't a lie.'

Danny stood up. 'I want you to think about today's visit,' he said. 'If you decide there's something you want to tell me about all of this, you'll get through to me at this number.' He passed him his card. 'If I don't hear from you within the next twenty-four hours, I'm going to assume you were behind the whole thing and I'll arrest you for conspiracy to pervert the course of justice. Are we clear?'

Clohessy nodded.

'Very good. I'll be on my way.'

Danny covered the ground between him and Clohessy in a single step, and leaned down so he was looming over the man. 'No one,' he said through clenched teeth, 'and I mean *no one* threatens my parents and just walks away. I don't know if you were told to get those lads to do it, or if they came up with that trick all by themselves, but I want you to put the word out that when I find out who gave the word, I'll be coming for them. I'm giving fair warning.'

Then he stalked out, leaving the minister's PA trembling in his seat.

38

Sheils met Tessa outside Dunnes Stores in Wexford's Redmond Square, which was a two-minute walk from Del Finnegan's house.

Wexford was an old Viking town, and while the buildings had altered with the passage of time, the streets themselves retained the narrow, winding design the Norsemen had first conceived. Redmond Square was a wide, green area with a cenotaph in the middle, flanked by the railway station on one side and the large Dunnes Stores on the other, and from there, you could easily walk down to Selskar Street, a bustling mixture of second-hand book shops, tiny artisan cafés, art galleries and vintage-clothes boutiques.

'Last night was... well, it was great,' Sheils said as they strolled onto the busy thoroughfare.

'Yeah,' Tessa agreed. 'It really was.'

'I... um... if you were interested, I'd like the chance to take you out properly and... like... you know... maybe have a date with you or something like that.'

Tessa laughed. 'So you don't classify both of us being attacked by a gangster as a date?'

'Well no, I have to say I don't.'

She stopped and put her hand on his arm. 'I'd love to go out with you. And when all this is over, maybe we will. But for now, we both need to focus, yeah?'

Sheils nodded. 'What are we expecting?'

'I'm still not sure,' Tessa said, steering him onto the footpath to avoid a kid who was zipping through the crowd on an electric scooter. 'I knew Del a long time ago. My dealings with him in the intervening years have been brief and few. Feeney, the uniformed officer I spoke to, doesn't have much good to say about him, but he thought it unlikely Del could've got involved with something like that without him knowing.'

'What do you reckon?'

'Feeney doesn't strike me as someone who lets a lot get past him, so I'm not sure how much of what O'Dowd told us wasn't just red herrings meant to slow us down.'

They took a left onto Skeffington Street, short and lined on each side by Edwardian three-storey houses, leading down to the quay. Most had freshly painted doors, polished knockers and windowsills replete with flower boxes. Del Finnegan's home, which was number six, did not. In fact, if Tessa hadn't known this was his address and that Josh Feeney visited regularly, she would have assumed the house unoccupied.

'Clearly not a dab hand at decorating,' Sheils observed.

Tessa muttered agreement and rapped smartly on the door. At first there was nothing, but then she spotted a curtain twitch, and moments later, the door opened, revealing a small, unshaven man with greasy hair that somehow managed to be sparse yet untidy at the same time, wearing a moth-eaten jumper that might have been three sizes too large. His jaw was covered in dark stubble, and the baggy jeans that adorned his bottom half were stained and filthy. From where Tessa was standing, she could discern the strong aroma of unwashed humanity emanating from him.

'Del Finnegan,' she said, holding out her ID, despite the fact the little man knew she was a guard.

The little man squinted at the card, and then up at Tessa. 'I told you not to come near me. You'll get me fucking killed!'

He spoke in a dense Wexford town accent, drawling the words a little.

'This is my colleague from the Irish coastguard, Chief Officer James Sheils,' Tessa said, ignoring her former house-mate's anxious tones. 'We'd like to ask you a few questions. The subject matter is perhaps more suited for an *indoor* conversation, if you catch my drift.'

Del eyed them both with unveiled distaste. 'Now isn't a good time.'

'It is for us. We won't keep you very long.'

In a movement so rapid Tessa was completely blindsided, Del slammed the door closed, shouting: 'Come back later. I might be free then!'

Unfortunately for the filthy little man, Sheils was quicker off the mark than his colleague, and got his booted foot into the gap between the door and its frame just in time to prevent Del from completing his evasive manoeuvre.

'You're not being very polite, Del,' he said, hitting the door with his shoulder, forcing it back open and knocking the diminutive man several steps down the dust-choked hallway. 'The lady asked nicely. Now let us in and answer a few questions, then you can get back to your activities, which seem to be very important to you, whatever they are.'

Del scowled, visibly shaking with temper. 'I don't have to let you into my home. You obviously don't have a warrant.'

'Under the conditions of your release, you're obligated to cooperate with the police if requested to do so,' Tessa said. 'If you're determined not to, I can let Garda Feeney know, but I imagine it will have a disastrous impact on your current state of freedom.'

Del made a noise that sounded like he was being strangled but which seemed in fact to be an expression of impotent rage. He stamped one of his tiny feet – both of which were clad in what had once been socks, but were now so full of holes they qualified better as fishnet stockings – in fury and balled his fists. 'I helped you!' he spat. 'You guards are all the same! Thugs and bullies.'

'You're going to hurt our feelings,' Tessa said. 'Now where do you want to do this? The hallway is as good as anywhere, but we'd probably be more comfortable if we were sitting down.'

He led them through a door on their left, into a room Tessa took to be a lounge or sitting area, but which was so cluttered with detritus – dirty plates, half-empty teacups (most of which sported a crown of mould), crumpled drink cans of both the soft and alcoholic variety, pizza boxes, paper from fish-and-chip shops, magazines and newspapers – the entire room looked like an active rubbish dump and smelled about as pleasant. There were large windows that looked out onto the street, but they were so grimy very little light came in, giving the whole scene an even darker hue than it already had.

A couch and two armchairs were beneath the garbage; Del swept some junk off the chair closest to the door and plonked himself down into it. Tessa perched gingerly on the arm of the couch, and Sheils rested against the windowsill, his arms folded across his chest.

'Del, your name has come up during an investigation into child trafficking,' Tessa opened the conversation.

'I don't know anything about it,' he spat. His voice was slightly high-pitched, as if it had never fully broken during puberty.

'No one said you're actively involved,' Tessa replied. 'If I had evidence you were, you'd already be arrested. Someone who has knowledge of such things told us you have some expert insights into child trafficking and you might be able to help us.'

'Who told you that?'

'Like I said, someone who would know.'

Del thought for a moment then said, 'I already told you everything I know about the movement of goods in and out of Rosslare. Those goods might be cigarettes, or booze, or adults or kiddies. I've been away for a stretch, and if you talked to Garda Feeney about me, he'd be able to tell you I've gone straight. I might have taken an interest in things like that once upon a time, but not anymore.'

Tessa stared at the grimy little man. It was taking all of her willpower not to shake him until his teeth rattled.

'I'd like to help,' Del went on, as if he was pondering the gravity of the situation. 'And maybe I could...'

'Go on,' Sheils said grimly.

'If you were to see to it that certain restrictions on my actions were lifted, I might feel more inclined to remember some names.'

'Let me get this straight,' Sheils said. 'You want us to have a restraining order removed so you can more easily access children in parks or preschools?'

'Don't think of it like that,' Del said. 'Think of it more as re-establishing my freedom of movement. It's a basic civil right really.'

'Hold on, Jim,' Tessa said, feeling nauseous from even pretending to support Del's request. 'Del, why don't you tell us what you know and I'll see if it's worth trading for?'

She knew he loved to bargain for things, particularly when he thought he had something the person on the other end badly needed.

'You mean it?' Del asked, perking up.

'Try me,' Tessa said. 'Maybe we can strike a deal.'

'Okay. Well I told you I don't know who brought your children into the country, so it stands to reason I don't know who they were to be sold to. But maybe I know something I could share with you.'

'Go on,' Tessa prompted him.

'The kids would have been picked up at Rosslare by at least one but maybe two handlers.'

'Handlers?'

'People who take custody of the children and bring them to whoever they're being handed over to.'

'So these are people who are good with kids?' Tessa asked. 'Know how to keep them calm and happy while the financial end of the deal is done?'

A look passed across Del's face, something furtive and deeply unpleasant. It was only there for a moment, but it was long enough. Tessa had seen it.

'I suppose you could describe it like that, yes.'

'And do you know any of these handlers?' Tessa asked. 'Or are you one yourself?'

Del jumped up from his seat. 'Look, all I know is that your three kids would have been held somewhere local for a week or so while the exchange was set up. That's it. And even with that I've said too much.'

Tessa smiled. 'Do you want to take it from here, Jim?'

The coastguard grinned back. 'No, you go right ahead.'

'What?' Del asked, sensing the change of atmosphere.

'Oh, just a small thing,' the detective said, leaning forward conspiratorially.

'I don't know what you're talking about.'

Tessa smiled. 'Neither of us told you how many kids we're talking about in this case.' It was a detail they'd managed to keep out of the news reports. 'Yet you just commented that there were three.'

All the colour drained from Del's face. 'I... I...'

'You'll be accompanying us back to the station, Del, where we can sit in a much more hygienic and comfortable environment, and you can cut the shite and tell us what you *really* know.'

They were just putting Del into Sheils' jeep when Danny called, letting her know he was on his way to see Damien Forde. Sheils agreed to take Del to the station, and Tessa went to her own car to drive the short distance to the politician's office at the other end of the Main Street.

39

'So we have motive,' Tessa said – she'd parked up and Danny had got into her car. 'I'm still not convinced though. I mean, children who get abducted are usually the children of the poor, right? Why pick kids from one of the richest men in the country if there's no ransom demand?'

They were parked at the end of Bride Street, a narrow, curving hill that ran from the first of Wexford's twin churches down to the Main Street and would, during Viking days, have terminated on the waterfront. The last hundred yards of that route today consisted of an alley between a photographer's studio and a Turkish barber.

On Wexford's North Main Street, one could still smell and – on quiet nights when the wind was just right – hear the sea.

'It's another part of the case that doesn't gel,' Danny agreed. 'But let's face it, nothing fits together in this. All we can do is follow the clues and see where they lead us.'

'What we do know is that Forde is crooked,' Tessa said. 'We might not know what his logic is, but if he'll traffic guns and explosives to terrorists, is selling three kids into foreign adoptions to fund a political coup such a huge ethical leap?'

Danny shook his head. 'No. Tessa, I'm really worried about Isaac. It's been so long, and we're no closer to finding him.'

'We know he's alive.'

'We know he *was* alive yesterday. What if the Merrow's made the drop and he's gone? I don't think Maggie could cope with that. I don't know if *I* could either.'

'Danny, we're doing all we can,' Tessa said, gently but firmly. 'The entire county is being combed, and we're doing our part by leaving no stone unturned, no matter how bizarre the clues may be.'

'I hear you. It's just, well, that wee lad was in our care. Once they're with us, they're meant to be safe. One of us should have been with Maggie.'

Tessa thought about that. It hadn't been strictly necessary for both she and Danny to have been at the *Dolphin* that night. But then, how could they have guessed the Merrow, whom they believed to be on the run, would have returned to snatch one of the children from a second-floor room, abseiling to the ground on a piece of old rope she'd found in a skip somewhere?

It was another impossible turn of events in a seemingly impossible case.

'Maybe,' Tessa said finally. 'All we can do now is keep working to find him. For now, let's go and see what Forde can tell us, shall we?'

'Let's do that.'

Wexford's South Main Street was much wider and more open than the north end, less densely packed with shops and therefore less crowded with shoppers and tourists. As Tessa and Danny came within view of the junior minister's office, Damien Forde, the man they'd come to see, strode onto the pavement through its front door, surrounded by a group of two men and three women.

Forde was a bulky, overweight man in his late forties, his

ample frame clad in a well-tailored suit. He had hair so dark the colour clearly came from a bottle, and his dimpled face always wore the expression of a man who was singularly pleased with himself. He and his retinue turned right, as if they were heading for the town's main shopping area, and Danny and Tessa broke into a run and came up behind Forde and his associates as they rounded the corner, just in time to see a small dark figure striding down Peter Street, resplendent with eighteenth-century three-storey houses and abandoned grain stores. The figure, dressed in a black parka and jeans, had their right arm extended and looked to be gripping a Glock 19 handgun.

The Merrow didn't pause in her stride; she continued to advance on Forde, the gun trained directly on him.

* * *

Things happened rapidly after that, yet everything seemed to occur in slow motion.

Tessa threw herself at the politician, tackling him like a rugby player and knocking him to the ground. As she did so, by some kind of unspoken understanding, Danny drew his own sidearm and shot the woman in the left shoulder.

The impact caused her to stagger back, though she still held the gun aloft.

'Drop the weapon or I'll put another one in you!' Danny called sharply.

The Merrow had stopped and was swaying slightly. All around her people were running and screaming, and Forde's team had all dropped low – Danny noted one of the men who were with the politician throwing his arms over him and Tessa, as if Tessa's body wasn't enough to protect such a valuable personage as the junior minister.

'I said drop your weapon!' Danny called again.

'You don't understand,' the Merrow replied in little more than a whisper.

Her voice was tremulous, and Danny knew she was going into shock. He could see beads of sweat forming on the pale face beneath the hood.

'You're right,' the big man said, quietly this time. 'I don't understand even a quarter of what's going on. But that doesn't matter. You can explain it to me. But lose the gun. I won't ask again.'

The mass of civilians had dissipated. Now, it seemed to be just Danny and the Merrow, gazing at one another over the prostrate forms of Forde's people and Tessa.

'You're not taking me in,' she said.

'I'm afraid I am.'

'I can't allow it.'

'Is Isaac alright?'

'He's better now than he ever was.'

'Away from his brother and sister?'

'At least he's safe.'

'Who's he with now?'

She shook her head.

'One final time, and this really is the last time: drop the weapon and lie face down on the ground.'

Danny saw something change in the woman and flung himself backwards as, without warning, she fired the Glock. He felt the heat of the bullet as it passed above him.

She would have hit me in the face, he thought in fury. *I went for her shoulder, and she aimed to shoot me in the face!*

He hit the ground with an explosion of breath and rolled over onto his stomach, the gun extended in front of him, in time to see her sprinting back up Peter Street. Danny was tempted to squeeze off a shot – she was in his line of vision for a good five seconds – but he was afraid of hitting someone coming down the hill towards them, unaware of the risk.

Angry and frustrated, he rolled onto his back and swore loudly and fluently at the sky.

He'd let the Merrow get away – and a chance of finding Isaac.

40

Dawn rang Maggie just after she'd finished lunch.

'I can't get through to either of your two sidekicks,' the commissioner said.

Maggie laughed. 'And here I was thinking you'd called me for a girlie chat.'

'The forensic accountants have come back with word on their initial sweep through the books taken from Murray/Cole's.'

'And?'

'It's pretty clear the place was being used as the nerve centre of O'Dowd's people trafficking business. CAB found records of very large funds being transferred from overseas into numbered deposit accounts in the Cayman Islands. There're also ledgers with the names of personnel assigned to various tasks, and the salaries they're paid for doing the jobs.'

'How'd they know that was what the list represented?'

'The Merrow is on it. The names are all aliases, nicknames: the Merrow, Beluga, Mr Spock and so on. But it's clear they're all employees of O'Dowd in some form or other. The book has a list of ships that are regularly used. The *Dolphin* is just one of many. There's a fucking fleet of them.'

'So why kill the old man?' Maggie asked.

'My guess is the Merrow wanted information which he wasn't prepared to hand over.'

'What information?'

'Most likely who ordered the sale of the kids, or who was buying them. Or both.'

'What difference would that make to her?'

'Maybe she intends to complete the job she started. I'm damned if I know, Maggie. This is why we're called "detectives". Now we have a clue, we follow it, and try and detect another one.'

'Thank you for the call, boss, complete with extra servings of sarcasm.'

'You're most welcome. Will you let the guys know?'

'I surely will.'

And Dawn hung up.

41

The Armed Response Unit were on the scene seemingly in minutes, and both Tessa and Danny answered the same questions again and again as they were interviewed and re-interviewed. Forde said not a single word to either of them the whole time they were there and was finally whisked away in a black Lexus without so much as a 'thank you for saving my life'.

When they got back to the Garda station, Danny had a ream of paperwork to fill out for discharging his weapon. He grabbed a desk in the squad room and got to work.

Del Finnegan had been stowed in a cell and left there to sweat in the hopes it might encourage him to talk when interviewed.

Sheils was on a call to his own supervisor, so the desk sergeant loaned Tessa his office (which was about the size of an airing cupboard and contained little more than a desk and one filing cabinet) so she could check in on Maggie and write up her own report on the afternoon's encounter. She was at the desk doing just that when the phone rang.

Assuming it was the desk sergeant, she cradled the receiver between her chin and shoulder and said: 'Yes, Sarge?'

'Tessa, I've got two people here from the governmental task force on human trafficking. They insist it can't wait.'

'Don't they always,' Tessa sighed. 'Can I use your office to talk to them?'

'You can of course. I'll send them down.'

Tessa continued to type until she heard a knock on the door.

The men from the task force weren't quite what she'd expected. One was tall and exquisitely groomed, sporting a neatly trimmed beard and silver-grey hair, expensively cut. His three-piece suit was charcoal grey, complete with an aquamarine pocket square. The other man was even taller, sporting a shaved head that glistened in the sunlight thrown from the window. The bald man looked as if he worked out and was dressed in a well-tailored black suit, complete with a starched white shirt and black tie.

Tessa knew immediately these two weren't from any government department. Rather, they were men whose job it was to instil fear by whatever means necessary. She could see the bulge of a firearm on the left side of the bald man's suit and wondered how the hell he'd made it through security.

This has happened way faster than I thought it would.

'Good afternoon, Detective Burns,' the first man said, sitting in the tiny office's only guest chair without being invited.

Baldy took up a position just inside the door, his hands crossed in front of him, as if in prayer, staring at a space midway up the opposite wall.

'Good afternoon to you. Who, might I ask, am I addressing?'

'You can call me Devlin, and this is Clarke.'

'What does Clarke do?'

'Security, among other things.'

'Why does someone who works for the governmental task force on human trafficking need a security detail?'

Devlin smiled. 'He's a... private acquisition.'

'So you've paid for him out of your own money?'

'I have, yes.'

'What can I help you with?'

'I decided to call over regarding this whole business with the children from the boat.'

'What about it?'

'I think our interests intersect, don't you?'

Tessa sat back. 'I'm all ears.'

'It's come to our attention that one of your team was asking about Minister Forde, and that indeed you saved his life this afternoon, though I believe that was more down to duty than admiration.'

Tessa shrugged. 'His name came up in our investigation.'

'Might I suggest that you've been hoodwinked by a smear campaign designed to discredit Minister Forde by association.'

'I see. And how exactly is this smear campaign supposed to work?'

'Some ruffians attack one of your lads and claim they were hired by the minister's aide-de-camps. The poor detective comes running back to you with the news, you pass it on to the Department of Justice and before it's time for evening drinks in the Horseshoe Bar, some pencil pusher in Harcourt Street has leaked it to the press.'

Tessa chewed her lower lip, thinking about this. 'That's a compelling story,' she admitted. 'On the face of it, it's quite convincing. But I think I can pick a couple of holes in it.'

'Go right ahead.'

'Number one, anyone who knows me knows I don't go telling tales to the justice department. Yes, I report to the commissioner, but the glorious thing about the Irish constitution is that it separates governance and the judiciary, to avoid corruption. I daresay someone has already checked my phone records, so you probably know I spoke with Danny Murphy at about ten minutes after ten. It's now' – she glanced at the clock on the laptop in front of her – 'quarter to three the following day and, as you're aware, I've not made a single call to anyone in the department.'

The man whose name probably wasn't Devlin and who certainly didn't work for the governmental task force on human trafficking, looked at her with a mild expression but didn't attempt to argue with her.

'If you or the people you're working for took the time to ask around about me, you'd have learned that my team and I deal with stuff like this by ourselves. We would see no cause to bring in any outsiders. Doing so would only put them at risk anyway.'

'I trust we can reach an agreement,' Devlin said, smiling warmly at her. 'There's really no need for you to deal with anything.'

'Wouldn't it be nice to think so,' Tessa said, smiling back. 'Number two, the case Danny and this team are supposed to step away from is a highly sensitive one, which we haven't gone to the press about. Very few people know we're working it. So for threats to be delivered and for you to come knocking, well, I'm considering one of two things: first off, is there someone in my own house who wants this case closed and reached out to the most unsavoury person they knew to get that job done – said unsavoury person being you or whoever you represent; or secondly, did the people responsible for those kids being on that boat realise my people weren't going to just stick the poor things in care and then walk away, so they decided they needed to bring some pressure to bear on us? And if they did, why did they go to a minister's aide to hire the muscle? There's only one obvious reason, and it's that the minister is up to his neck in this whole mess through extra-curricular business activities.'

Devlin smiled, an empty expression. 'It's an interesting theory, Detective, but just a theory, for all that.'

'My guess is that your organisation, whoever they are, freaked out when my team began asking questions, and you decided you needed to get us to stop. As Forde has the most to lose, you tasked him with sorting it out. You probably thought he'd use official lines, make it look as if resources were being redirected and just have my crew moved to a different case, but by then the Child and Family Agency were involved, not to mention the Department of Children and Youth Affairs, and it was turning into a proper shit-show, so he and his bumbling assistant had to resort to good old-fashioned strong-arm tactics.'

'Are you finished now, Detective Burns? Is it my turn to talk?'

'No, I'm not finished yet. You're in my house now, Mr Devlin or whatever the fuck you're really called, and you will treat me with some respect. Do you hear me?'

Devlin nodded sarcastically. 'Loud and clear.'

'I think Forde gave Clohessy the number of some leg-breakers he'd probably used before and thought they'd be enough to get the job done. It was two on one after all. But he hadn't reckoned with someone like Danny. And it never occurred to him that we'd just entrench ourselves even more tightly once Danny told us what had happened.'

Devlin sighed deeply and shifted in his chair. 'DI Burns, there are forces at play here you can't hope to comprehend. I'm asking you, as one professional to another, to withdraw your team and allow things with those children to simply... play out how they will. I mean, the case is virtually closed anyway, isn't it? You have a suspect for the killing of the crew. The children's parents have been identified and are on their way back to Ireland as we speak. The shipping company have recouped their lost cargo. What else is there for you to do here?'

Tessa laughed and waved a finger at the man. 'Do you know, I never really wanted to lead a team? I hate all the politicking and I-dotting that goes along with the role. What I like, Mr Devlin, is a nice, juicy mystery to get my teeth into. Once I've got one of those, I won't give up until it's solved and I know exactly what happened. I'm a regular Jessica Fletcher. Dogged, some might say.'

'So you won't walk away from this before people get hurt?'

'*Before* people get hurt? The crew of the *Dolphin* are dead. Those children are deeply traumatised by what happened to them, and one of them is missing. Your two thugs probably needed to be hospitalised after Danny was through, and I have to tell you, there have been some fisticuffs with the local hoodlums. The horse has bolted. First blood has long been drawn.'

Devlin shook his head, an expression of deep sadness on his rugged face. 'I implore you to reconsider. I don't want to have to unleash the dogs, so to speak, but I will if I have to, and if that happens, the only losers will be you and your task force.'

'There's nothing to reconsider,' Tessa said, and any good humour was gone from her voice now. 'I'm a detective with the Irish police force. It's my responsibility to protect the people of this island and to support my officers in every way I can. I took an *oath* to carry out those duties to the best of my abilities, and that is something I take very seriously. So unleash your dogs, and we'll see who comes off the better.'

Devlin sighed again and stood, straightening his suit. 'Have it your own way,' he said. 'I'll take my leave, but before I do, I'm going to need that laptop.'

'Fuck off,' Tessa said, not even attempting to keep the disdain from her voice.

'I know that in police stations laptops act as a security device, and I have no intention of leaving a recording of our conversation behind. Clarke, see to it, won't you?'

The shaven-headed man strode over to the desk and reached out for the device, but Tessa was ready. As the big man leaned in to grab the computer, she drove her elbow hard into his larynx, causing him to make a loud gulping sound and then fall back, grabbing his throat.

'I think your security officer could do with some extra training,' Tessa said, closing the laptop lid. 'He left himself wide open.'

Devlin was squatting down beside his bodyguard, who was struggling for breath, his face bright red.

'Have you killed him?' Devlin asked, the answer seemingly of only academic interest to him. There was no emotion in his voice, just idle curiosity.

'No. He'll be okay in a few moments. His windpipe will naturally expand.'

'That's good,' Devlin said, but then he was standing, and he had a Glock handgun pointed at Tessa. It seemed he'd taken it from his fallen colleague.

'I'm walking out of here,' he said. 'I'm aware you're no slouch with kung fu or whatever the hell it is you can do, but be in no doubt I will shoot you the second you move.'

Tessa grinned. 'People have been pointing guns at me and threatening me for most of my life,' she said. 'It doesn't scare me anymore.'

'Perhaps. But look into my eyes. You'll see that I'm not bluffing.'

'Oh, I know you're not.'

'Give me the laptop.'

'I didn't punch out your gorilla to stop him taking the laptop,' Tessa said. 'I did it because no fucker is going to walk into an office I'm occupying and waltz out with mine or anyone else's stuff. It'd do you no good anyway. If you'd done your research, you'd know that anything that's recorded on this laptop is automatically saved to the cloud. Now, I'm not really sure where that is, but I do know it means you can smash the machine to smithereens and nothing on it will be lost.'

Devlin's gun hand began to shake a little. 'You're bluffing.'

'Maybe I am and maybe I'm not, but listen closely, because I mean this: you're not leaving this room with that laptop. Or a coffee mug. Or so much as a paper clip.'

Devlin hung in indecision for a long moment, then swore, turned on his heel and fled.

Tessa picked up the phone on the desk and dialled the front desk. 'Sarge, a man has just exited your office, six foot two, longish grey hair, wearing a charcoal-grey suit. I want him apprehended, but be advised he's armed and dangerous. No. Seriously. I'm not joking.'

She then came around her desk and slipped handcuffs on the man she'd just felled.

ISAAC

The Merrow said she was going to be his new mammy.

They were sitting in the dark place, where he couldn't see much unless the fire was lit, eating ham sandwiches she'd just made for them, when she told him.

'But I have a mammy,' he said.

'When was the last time you saw her?' the Merrow asked.

Isaac didn't know. It had been a long time. When he was in school, he didn't get to go home until holiday time. His mammy used to come and visit him at school sometimes, but that hadn't happened in ages and ages.

'Daddy says Mammy is sick,' he told the Merrow. 'Are you sick?'

She looked ill. Her skin was always white, but now she made noises as if she had a pain somewhere, and when she got back to the dark place, she'd told him she needed to sleep, which she hadn't done before.

And she'd only taken one small bite of her sandwich.

'No, Isaac,' she said. 'I'm not sick. I hurt my shoulder, but it'll be okay.'

The Merrow was a grown-up, so if she told him she was okay, he believed her.

'Will I see my mammy again?'

She looked at him in the firelight. 'I don't think so.'

'Will I see Noa and Sofie again?'

She sighed. 'I don't know. I'd like to have them with us too, but it would be very difficult to get them.'

'Can you try?'

'I'm not going to lie to you, Isaac. I probably won't be able to.'

'So I won't never see them again?'

'I don't think so, love.'

And he cried to hear that.

42

Del Finnegan had been processed and photographed on his arrival at the station, but due to the afternoon's events, it was a few hours before Tessa and Sheils were able to interview him. Feeney, who came down to view the conversation, shook his head in disbelief.

'So he's really in on this awful business?'

They'd retired to the control room, which was little more than a cubbyhole that overlooked the room where Del was to be interviewed. It had a console with a microphone that fed through to speakers in the interview room itself, so the officers inside could be called out if new information came to light, or if another cop wished to be brought in for a time, to alter the dynamic or just give someone a break.

'To some degree, yes,' Tessa said. 'He certainly knows a hell of a lot more than he's saying. I'm hoping the prospect of a return to the delightful institution of Wheatfield Prison might loosen his tongue a bit.'

'Let's see what he has to say then,' Feeney said. 'Want me to come in as a familiar face?'

'Why not,' Tessa said. 'Jim, you keep a watch through the

one-way mirror. Call me out if you think there's something I've missed or if anything occurs to you.'

The coastguard nodded.

Tessa and Feeney went into the interview room and sat down. The room itself was small and square, consisting of a metal, Formica-topped table that was bolted to the floor and two uncomfortable seats on either side, similarly affixed to prevent them being used as weapons.

A camera, set into the corner of the ceiling, recorded each interview and was controlled by a remote control embedded in the top of the desk on the interviewer's side. The floors and ceiling were painted a muted magnolia.

Del was brought in by an officer who asked if anyone needed anything then took his leave.

The little man settled into his chair and scowled at the two cops. 'I knew I never should have let you in,' he said contemptuously to Tessa.

'You're too polite for your own good,' Tessa said, smiling.

'Interview with Del Finnegan. Present are Detective Inspector Tessa Burns and Garda in charge of the sex offenders register Josh Feeney. Interview is commencing at 4.45 p.m., Wednesday, 7 September 2022. Mr Finnegan, you've had your legal rights explained to you and the reason for your arrest this afternoon clearly outlined?'

'I have no clue why I'm here.'

'It was explained to you that, during an interview this morning at your home in Skeffington Street, you demonstrated knowledge of a criminal case involving the kidnap of three children and the murder of eight men.'

'I didn't express any such knowledge. That was just a lucky guess.'

'Mr Finnegan, are you aware that it was Andrew O'Dowd who named you as someone locally who's involved in child trafficking?'

A lot of the fight went out of Del at the mention of O'Dowd. 'I... I don't know why he would do that.'

'Do you know Andrew O'Dowd, Del?' Feeney asked.

'I wouldn't say I know him well.'

'But you are acquainted with him?'

'I know him to see, but that's all.'

'So why would he name you as a child trafficker?'

Del's face, blotchy though it was, was cycling through a variety of colours, from deathly white to tomato red as he fought the wave of feelings he was obviously experiencing.

'Del, there's no one more aware than you of the conditions of your release,' Feeney said. 'You're already looking at a term back inside while we put together a book of evidence. If you want to keep that term as short as possible, I'd advise you tell us what you know.'

'As of right now, the only person we have for this is you,' Tessa said. 'No one is suggesting you killed the crew personally, but I bet we could put together a case that has you ordering their deaths.'

Del began to make a gulping sound, and his face went from red to something closer to purple.

'Are you okay, Del? Do you need some water?'

The little man nodded, and Feeney got up and came back seconds later with a bottle. Del swallowed a couple of mouthfuls and sat back, rivulets running down his stubbled chin.

'I'm not going down for this,' he said. 'I'm not responsible for what happened, and I'm not going to take the fall for a fucker like Andrew O'Dowd.'

Tessa and Feeney exchanged a look.

'You're saying O'Dowd was the person those kids were being shipped to?' Tessa said.

'He was to take collection, yes. Well... I was to pick them up, hold on to them and make the drop on his behalf. But he was the money guy. He'd arranged it all.'

'And he was going to sell them on?' Feeney asked.

'He'd made the contacts. Found the three sets of adoptive parents. Two Americans and one Canadian, I think.'

'I thought he doesn't usually trade in kids,' Tessa said.

'He doesn't. This was a... a one-off thing. Special. I think he was doing a favour for someone.'

'And you don't know who?'

'No. I wouldn't be let in on that kind of information.'

'And that was your only role?' Feeney asked. 'Taking custody of the children at this end and caring for them until handover?'

Del nodded vigorously. 'I've told you what I know.'

'You're sure that's all?' Tessa pressed. 'As of right now, I could have you for accessory to the trafficking of three minors, and I could throw the kidnapping and conspiracy to murder in there for good measure. You're skating on very thin ice here, Del Boy, so I'll ask you again: was that your only involvement?'

Del put his head in his hands. He was trembling, and from the strange mewling sounds that were coming from him, it seemed he was crying too.

'I was called in as a consultant,' he said.

'What exactly does that mean?' Feeney wanted to know.

'Just giving advice and such. I didn't actually do anything. Just, if O'Dowd or his people had a question, they'd ask me.'

'And you had nothing whatsoever to do with the selection of the children you were so excitedly telling us about?' Tessa asked.

'Not at all,' Del said earnestly.

'You didn't advise on how the deal might be arranged? Or on the personnel involved?'

'Well... I told them the same type of stuff I told you. That's not a crime, is it?'

'Del, you knew a crime was being committed, that three children were about to be abducted, and your response was to advise the people trafficking them on how to run the show,' Tessa said, aghast. 'Yes, I would say that's a crime.'

'I just answered a few questions!' Del wailed. 'You don't want to be rude, particularly to someone like Andrew O'Dowd!'

'You're the model of good manners,' Tessa said darkly. 'And were you paid for this advice?'

'A man has to make a living,' Del spat back. 'Because of my prison record, there are fuck-all jobs I can do these days.'

'My heart bleeds for you,' Tessa replied. 'Through your communication with O'Dowd, do you have any idea about what went on during the sailing?'

'O'Dowd thinks someone in the crew found out the kids were on board and decided they wanted the money for themselves. Killed the others so they wouldn't have to share the profits.'

'Did you have a contact within the crew?'

'The cook.'

'So O'Dowd thinks someone else came across the kids and realised what they were there for?'

Del nodded.

'What about the woman who was on board?' Tessa pressed.

'The Merrow, yes. What about her?'

'You advised O'Dowd to use her to look after the children during the sailing?'

'She's well known in trafficking circles as a chaperone. Been doing it for years.'

'Where is she from?'

'I don't know,' Del said. 'She's Irish, as far as I can tell. She works for the gangs, spends the bulk of her time at sea, hence the name.'

'Is it possible she went mad and killed everyone?'

Del shook his head. 'I don't see it.'

'Why not?'

'There's a story about her... I don't know if it's true or not. Might just be gossip.'

'We're all ears,' Feeney said.

'Well, some say the Merrow was abducted herself as a kid, little more than a baby. She was supposed to be sold on, but the deal fell through, so the Doorleys kept her, brought her up in a cottage on Mount Leinster, where she was looked after by an old mountain ranger who taught her how to live up there in the rocky places.'

Tessa froze for a moment – could this be how the little woman had attained her prowess with ropes and climbing?

'When she was old enough, she was taken from the old ranger and set to work looking after kids while they were moved from place to place, for whatever reason: adoption, to work during the harvest, as companions to rich children in the Middle East. The Merrow isn't going to bite the hand that feeds her. It's all she knows.'

At that moment, Sheils' voice rang out over the intercom speakers. 'Tessa, can I have a word?'

'Interview concluded at 5.15 p.m.,' Tessa said and nodded at Feeney. 'Can you take him to his cell?'

'Of course.'

Sheils was waiting for her in the corridor.

'You're needed at the hospital,' he said. 'Something's happened.'

'What? Is it the kids?'

'No. It's your friend Maggie.'

'What about her?'

'She's been taken.'

43

Half an hour before Tessa and Feeney were sitting down to interview Del Finnegan, Maggie, Pavlov and the two Bolger children were packing up the few meagre possessions the kids had accumulated in their brief stay in the hospital. These amounted to a few clothes, most of which were from the lost-and-found or goodwill, and a collection of toys, the majority of which had come from nurses who'd taken pity on these strange, sad-eyed kids.

Maggie had bought a suitcase in Tesco and was helping the kids arrange everything inside it carefully.

'There's an art to packing, you know,' she said. 'Tessa used to be in the army, and she showed me how they do it. You roll rather than fold your clothes. That way, you fit more in.'

'We had servants who did stuff like this for us,' Noa said, though not in a condescending way – more as a statement of fact. 'They did everything, from picking out our clothes to deciding what we'd eat.'

'You never made a sandwich?' Maggie asked.

'No.'

'Would you like to?'

'Yes. I think I would.'

'I like chocolate-spread sandwiches!' Sofie said, giggling at the thought.

'I like salami!' Noa added.

Maggie laughed. 'Well that is an interesting combination. Chocolate and salami!'

They just managed to fit all the clothes and toys into the case, and when it was zipped up and sitting at the end of Noa's bed, Maggie said, 'How about we go to the nurses' kitchen and see if we can make ourselves some sandwiches?'

'Really?' Noa asked, blushing.

'Yes, really. Everyone, even the super-rich, should know how to make themselves something nice to eat. I'm sure the nurses won't mind. Let's go and ask them.'

They didn't mind at all. In fact, the ward sister called the canteen on their behalf and asked if some salami (which was the only ingredient the kids wanted that wasn't available in the nurses' kitchen) could be sent down.

The kitchen was long and narrow, with a counter that doubled as a prep station and a dining table, but no one minded the cramped space, and Maggie, Noa and Sofie spent a happy ten minutes making their favourite sandwiches. The family liaison officer was delighted to see how much joy the kids got out of such a simple thing as deciding whether or not to cut their creations into squares or triangles, and then showed them how, using a glass, they could make circular ones too (although that did leave some waste, which she stressed wasn't desirable unless they had a dog like Pav who was happy to rapidly consume the leftovers).

When they'd eaten what they'd made and were still hungry, they experimented with peanut butter and raspberry jam, ham, cheese and mayonnaise, and even Marmite, which neither of the kids had heard of before but, when paired with cheese, they decided they liked very much.

Maggie then showed them how to make a sweet French toast, which she liked to have for dessert every now and again – it was delicious with honey drizzled over the top – and the kids were fascinated by the idea of soaking bread in an egg-and-milk mixture and then frying it.

'So you're *cooking* the bread?' Sofie asked.

'Yes. When it's done, it's crispy on the outside but all gooey and nice in the middle. Then you sprinkle it with icing sugar and pour over your honey or syrup or even spread some jam on it. Or marmalade, if you're like Paddington Bear.'

'Well now. Is this the castaways I've heard so much about?'

Turning sharply, Maggie saw a man standing in the doorway to the kitchen. They'd been so caught up in what they'd been doing, he could have been there for ten minutes and they wouldn't have noticed. He was tall – not quite as tall as Danny but only slightly smaller – and while he was definitely old, he didn't look frail. In fact, he exuded a sense of power and menace. He was dressed in a dark suit with an open-necked white shirt, and his face was angular and hard. What little hair he had was gelled back on his head and still dark.

'Can I help you?' Maggie asked.

'I don't know,' the man said. 'Can you?'

'I'm with the Gardai. The children are in my care until their parents arrive later today.'

'You're a guard?' the man asked, his voice betraying a hint of derision. 'Well isn't that grand for you?'

'I didn't catch your name,' Maggie said, rolling towards the unwelcome visitor.

Pavlov, who'd been sitting on a high stool so he could watch the kids' culinary efforts, started to growl, a deep, rumbling sound in the back of his throat, and jumped from the stool onto the ground, positioning himself in front of the children.

'That's a cute dog you have there,' the man said. 'I hope he's not vicious. I can't abide a nippy mutt.'

'He's only aggressive when he needs to be,' Maggie said. 'Could you please identify yourself?'

'My name is Andrew O'Dowd.'

Maggie knew the name, and that the presence of this individual could only mean trouble.

'What business do you have here, Mr O'Dowd?'

'The same as yourself really,' O'Dowd answered. 'I have an interest in those kiddies. Quite a sizable interest, as it happens.'

'Be that as it may,' Maggie said, and then her baton was in her hand, and with one motion she whipped it to its full extension, 'I'm going to have to ask you to leave.'

'And I'm going to have to decline.'

O'Dowd lunged forward, and Maggie did the thing he probably least expected her to do – she gunned her chair at him at its top speed. She hoped she would run over his feet, which if done at just the right angle could break toes, but at the last moment, he sensed what she was planning and actually threw himself on top of her. The chair, with O'Dowd perched atop it and its pilot, sailed out the door and crashed into the wall opposite, then rebounded and did a kind of skid, and O'Dowd used the opportunity to hop off and deliver Maggie a crushing blow to the temple.

The last thing Maggie Doolan was aware of was powerful arms lifting her, and of Pavlov barking, though he seemed far away, but then darkness reached up to swallow her, and she was gone.

PART FIVE

HOSTAGE OF FORTUNE

'And yet to every bad there is a worse.'

— THOMAS HARDY

44

Tessa Burns was furious.

A uniformed officer named Blake, who was perhaps twenty-five, was standing opposite her in the hospital's conference room, his eyes lowered, hands crossed behind his back. Between the two of them was Maggie's empty wheelchair.

'We knew there was a chance someone was going to try and take a run at the kids,' Tessa said, her cheeks flushed and her voice coming out as a snarl. 'And we also knew the team were in danger. *You* were supposed to be her backup! You! How the hell did Wexford's number-one gangster manage to waltz in here and take my best friend? *I mean, where the fuck were you?*'

'I was posted outside the room where the kids sleep, ma'am.'

'Right. That's where you were told to stand.'

'Yes, ma'am.'

'And why were you instructed to stand there?'

'To keep the kids safe, ma'am.'

'Yes. And to keep Maggie safe. Remember her? She's kind of hard to miss being in that wheelchair and all – the one that's currently empty because Andrew O'Dowd took her out of it and made good his escape!'

'Ms Doolan told me to make the kids my priority,' the guard said meekly. 'I was informed she's able to take care of herself.'

'Oh, she is. She'd kick your arse from one end of this hospital to the next. The only thing is, she wasn't dealing with just any fucking villain, was she? She was up against a man it took two armed officers and one mercenary with an automatic weapon to subdue the last time I had dealings with him. You can still see the fucking marks of his fingers around my neck!'

Blake still had his eyes lowered.

'That means I want you to look!'

He lifted his gaze for a moment, registered the bruises and returned to staring at the floor.

'So I don't think it could be considered a fair fight, do you?'

'No, ma'am.'

'Did it not occur to you that guarding an empty room was a waste of your time?'

'It did, ma'am, but I also reasoned that if someone was going to try to abduct the children, they would probably look for them in their room first. So it would be wise to be there to take the opportunity to arrest them. I never thought anyone would go to the nurses' kitchen to look for the kids.'

'It's the first door you encounter when you come on the ward,' Tessa said, her tone betraying that she was running out of steam. 'The kids told me they were laughing and talking loudly. He heard them when he came in.'

'I believe so, ma'am. I'm... I'm sorry I let you down. And I'll do whatever I can to find Ms Doolan – I give you my word.'

'Oh fuck it. Your logic was probably sound. You remained at your post – you should be commended for that, not given a bollocking. I'm sorry. Maggie is my best friend, and I'm worried and pissed off. This case... every time I think we're making headway, something else comes along to screw it all up even worse.'

'No apology needed, ma'am. I've taken worse. If there's

anything I can do, please ask. I'll work in my own time if it will help get Ms Doolan back.'

'Did you see anything at all that might help us find her?'

'I was alerted to the incident by Noa. By the time I arrived on the scene, all I saw was the empty chair. The children were all very upset, and that dog...'

'Pavlov,' Tessa said. 'His name is Pavlov.'

'Yes, ma'am. Well Pavlov was barking loudly and running up and down the corridor. I took it that he was distressed over what had happened. He was always with Ms Doolan. I assumed he missed her.'

'It's more likely that, now you were on the scene, he wanted to leave the children in your protection while he went after O'Dowd,' Tessa said.

'Seriously?'

'Yes. Pavlov would give his life for Maggie, or me, or those children, without a second thought. The only reason he didn't go after her right away was because she'd told him to guard the kids any time she wasn't around.'

'That's quite an animal.'

'Don't let him hear you call him that.'

'I won't. I've been through the security footage,' the guard said. 'There was an empty wheelchair left outside the door of the children's ward. O'Dowd put Ms Doolan in that, took the elevator to the ground floor and took her out a delivery exit to the rear of the building. He had a car parked there and left the hospital by the gate that opens onto the Ferrycarrig road, which is a back road that joins up with the main Dublin road five kilometres to the north. From there, he could have travelled towards Enniscorthy, Dublin or turned back in for Wexford town or Rosslare.'

'Surely there are enough traffic cams to tell us where he did go?'

'The boys in the station are checking them as we speak.'

'I want her found. Right now.'

'I do too, ma'am.'

Tessa nodded and put a hand on the young man's shoulder. 'I know you do.'

'Ma'am, can I ask you why you think she was taken?'

Tessa looked Blake dead in the eye. 'That's an excellent question. My gut reaction was that he took her to get at me. I disrespected him. But then I got to thinking: it's just too audacious an act for that. The sensible response to a lack of respect is to put a bomb under my car, or set fire to my flat, or have some asshole claim I'd sexually assaulted him during questioning. But to abduct a police officer? In a public hospital? That's going thermonuclear.'

'So what are you saying?'

'Thirty seconds before I got the call that Maggie had been taken, I was informed Andrew O'Dowd was pivotal in the trafficking of the Bolger children. And there seem to be a few very big names mixed up in it all too. They've tried to warn us off, and we wouldn't budge. It looks like they're upping the ante.'

'What are you going to do?'

'I'm going to get my friend back. And then I'm going to tear the whole fucking thing down, along with every crooked politician and businessman who's a part of it.'

45

Tessa, Danny and Pavlov sat in the waiting area outside the children's ward. It was empty except for them.

No one said anything, until, finally, Tessa announced, 'This whole thing is fucked.'

Danny nodded. 'It is.'

'What are we going to do?'

Danny sighed and ran his fingers through his short dark hair. 'Isaac's been taken,' he said. 'Now Maggie's been taken. The only thing to do is go out and get them both back.'

'How do we do that?'

Danny pulled out his phone and tapped his email app. 'Have you seen the message she sent us this morning?'

'I only just read it.'

'It's possible she's on to something.'

Tessa sat up straight. 'Do you want to check it out?'

'I do.'

'Maggie says there are places there you'd need mountaineering skills to access.'

'Which is exactly where the Merrow is likely to be hiding.'

'Yes, but do *you* have the necessary skills to get there?'

Danny thought about that. 'I do wall climbing at the gym,' he offered.

'I doubt that's the same thing,' Tessa said ruefully.

'From the photos she sent, I don't think this is a situation that'll require an expert. I think I can handle it.'

'And get Isaac out?'

'I'll cross that bridge when I come to it,' Danny shot back.

Tessa looked at her partner. 'That doesn't exactly fill me with confidence, DS Murphy.'

'Me either,' Danny said. 'But time is running out.'

'Okay. You look after Isaac; I'll take care of Maggie.'

'What's the plan?'

Tessa looked at him sadly. 'I don't know yet. We might just have to wait for O'Dowd to call.'

'That's a killer,' Danny observed.

'Yes, but I don't think it's going to be a whole lot longer,' Tessa said. 'For now, you go and see if Maggie's hunch was right. I have the Bolgers arriving, and I need to interview that thug who tried to intimidate me earlier this afternoon. I have a few questions I want to ask them.'

Danny nodded and stood. 'You okay, Tessa? I know you and Maggie have known one another forever.'

'No, Danny,' the detective said. 'I'm very far from okay. But for now, we have work to do. I'll deal with my own stuff when this is over.'

Danny looked a bit uncomfortable. 'Tessa, you were there for me when I found things tough on the last case. I... I'm here if you need to talk is all I'm saying.'

She stood and put her arms around the big detective. 'I know you are, Danny, and that means the world to me. Now, go and find that little lad and bring him back to us.'

46

Tessa sat opposite Clarke, the man who'd come to her office under false pretences, in another interview room in Wexford Garda station. So identical was it, it could have been the same one she'd interviewed Del Finnegan in, except this one was at the other end of the station and was accessed by a different corridor.

Not that any of that mattered.

Tessa was seething with anger and was trying to keep it focused on the man in front of her.

'Who sent you?' she asked.

Clarke smiled and shook his head.

'We're running your fingerprints and your DNA,' the detective went on. 'We'll have your real name and your record, both here and overseas, very soon. Which will include a list of your associates. So if you help us now, that will make things a lot easier for you. All I need is a name. Who asked you and Mr Devlin to come here to try and scare me? That's it. One word. It's all I'm looking for.'

'You can look,' the man said, speaking for the first time. 'I have nothing to say to you.'

Tessa could discern a slight accent but couldn't place what it was.

'I don't know why you're remaining loyal,' Tessa continued. 'Devlin left you and saved his own skin. Do you know he shot and seriously wounded an officer as he left Garda HQ? Seeing as I don't have him in custody, I'm going to make sure that gets added to your list of crimes.'

'Good luck.'

'Think about it, Mr Clarke. Right now, we have you on accessing a government building under an alias, which doesn't carry much of a sentence – if I play it up, we could probably get you for a couple of months. I've also got you attempting to steal a police laptop – I'd guess a lawyer could argue that one down to virtually nothing. The biggest one is carrying a concealed firearm, which I'm pretty sure you don't have any paperwork for. That's a minimum of five years. You'd probably serve three. For a man like you, that's a very moderate sentence. Help me out, and I'll turn a blind eye completely. I have no interest in you, Mr Clarke. I want your employer.'

'I want to see my lawyer,' Clarke said.

'That's how you want to play it?'

'I want to see my lawyer.'

Tessa shook her head and stood. 'As you wish,' she said. 'But be warned: I have every intention of digging up every single charge I can find to bring against you. The maximum sentence for carrying that gun is fourteen years. I bet I can make a case that bringing it into my office presents a genuine threat. Might even be able to get it kicked up to carrying with intent to commit murder. That'll get you a maximum sentence of life. Think about that, Mr Clarke.'

She met Feeney at the door.

'He spilling yet?'

'He is not,' she said. 'Won't say a damn thing. He's looking for his lawyer now.'

'Has he nominated one?'

'Not that I know of.'

'Will I get the name of whoever he's using and give them a ring?'

'That'd be great, Josh. I'm gonna grab a sandwich. I haven't eaten since this morning.'

'Enjoy.'

Tessa was in the canteen twenty minutes later with a large mug of tea and a chicken-and-stuffing sandwich, an issue of *Ireland's Own* magazine open in front of her, when her phone rang. It was the desk sergeant.

'DI Burns, you're needed in interview room two.'

'Can I finish my sandwich first?'

'I'm told it's urgent.'

She sighed. 'Okay. On my way.'

The corridor, narrow at the best of times, was jammed with officers, and she had to push her way through. When she got into the interview room, she saw that Clarke was slumped forward in his seat. Feeney was kneeling in front of him, an expression Tessa couldn't read on his face.

'What's going on?' she asked.

'Take a look,' the guard said.

Tessa came over beside him, noting that Clarke was utterly motionless.

As soon as she squatted down beside Feeney, she could see why: someone had jammed a cheap plastic biro into the gangster's eye. Only the pen's blue lid was still visible. The man was dead.

'Fuck,' Tessa said.

'My thoughts exactly,' Feeney replied.

47

John Bolger arrived at Wexford General Hospital in a long black BMW at three minutes to eight that evening. Tessa was climbing out of her skin at that stage – all she wanted was to be out looking for Maggie, but with her friend and colleague missing, someone had to meet the children's father, and the reality was he had a number of questions to answer that were pertinent to the case.

When he emerged from the elevator, he had three men in dark suits with him, who hung back but glowered at Tessa, attired as she was in her parka, Led Zeppelin T-shirt and blue jeans.

John was smaller than she'd expected, probably five foot seven in shoes, which, she noted, had stacked soles. He was wearing a camel-hair coat over a black polo-neck jumper and designer black jeans. His hair was as blonde as Noa's, but his face was soft, and a roll of flesh spilled out over the neck of his jumper. When he shook Tessa's hand, she noted that his eyes had bags under them, and he needed a shave.

'Thank you for caring for my children,' he said, a very slight Wexford accent evident in his voice. 'Except for the one that's missing of course. You'll be hearing from my lawyers about that. I would appreciate it if I could take the surviving two right away.'

'You can see them in a moment,' Tessa said. 'But I'd like to ask you a few questions first. I'd hoped – expected really – that your wife would be accompanying you, taking into consideration the trauma the children have experienced.'

'My wife is... unavailable. Not that it's any business of yours.'

'Well I'll be wanting to talk to her too.'

'I don't understand. Noa, Sofie and Isaac were kidnapped from their school – I was in Amsterdam that night, which approximately twenty witnesses can verify. Neither I nor my wife knew anything about their disappearance until the police contacted me about it.'

'That's where I'm puzzled,' Tessa said. 'Your children have been missing for days. Why wasn't the school in touch?'

'Apparently they did try to contact me, but one of my employees failed to pass on the message. Most likely that was deliberate. When I find out who and why, there will be consequences.'

'Mr Bolger, why would someone kidnap your children?'

'I'm very successful. I presume the intention was to pressure me into altering my business practices or to sell one of my companies at a low price or something of that nature.'

'Did you receive any demands?'

'No, I did not.'

'Doesn't that seem odd?'

'Yes, I suppose it does. Perhaps they intended to do so when the children arrived at their destination.'

'They did, from what we can tell – or very close to it,' Tessa said. 'But something happened on that ship, which we still don't fully understand.'

'I was informed of that, yes.'

'Any thoughts?'

'Why would I have any opinion on that other than relief that my children survived the journey?'

'I don't know. This whole case makes less and less sense every time I look at it. I'm just short of asking the woman who makes the scones in the hospital café if she has any suggestions.'

'That's not very edifying to hear.'

'It absolutely isn't. Does the name Damien Forde mean anything to you?'

'No. Should it?'

'Andrew O'Dowd?'

'No.'

'Derek Sherlock?'

She thought she saw a flicker there, but it was gone in an instant.

'Okay, Mr Bolger. I'll take you to your kids.'

'Thank you.'

He said something rapidly to the three suits that Tessa didn't quite hear (she thought it sounded like *remember what we talked about* but couldn't be sure) and followed her to the children's room.

When they got there, the children were sitting on Noa's bed, Pavlov lying across them.

'Why is there a dog in a hospital?' Bolger asked sharply.

'He's a service animal,' Tessa said through gritted teeth. 'He's been a great help in comforting three very distressed and frightened kids.'

'Two now, since you seem to have misplaced one.'

'A matter that's being rectified as we speak. I'd be grateful to Pavlov there, if I were you.'

Bolger didn't respond. He made a clicking noise with his tongue to the children, who got up without comment. Noa picked up the suitcase Maggie had given them, but Bolger shot him a hard look, and he dropped it.

'Jacob will come to get that and bring it to the car,' he said to Tessa, still not looking at her.

'I can take it,' she said. 'It's not a big deal.'

'As you wish.'

Tessa took the suitcase and pulled out the extendable handle, so she could pull it behind her.

'Your dad is taking you home this evening,' she said to the children, 'so I don't know if I'll see you again. I just want to say it's been nice getting to know you.'

'Is Maggie going to be alright?' Sofie asked as they walked towards the reception area.

'Maggie is one of the toughest people I know,' Tessa assured her. 'Don't you worry. As soon as we've got her back, I'll have her call you.'

They heard raised voices ahead of them, and when they got to the waiting area, they found Bolger's three assistants squaring off against a thin blonde woman and two similarly suited men.

'I'm Detective Inspector Tessa Burns,' Tessa said, holding out her ID. 'Can I ask you to lower your voices and please tell me what in the hell is going on?'

'I'm Ella Carling, of the Child and Family Agency,' the blonde woman said. 'I have papers here, signed by the Minister for Children, placing the children in my care.'

'What does she mean?' Noa asked, looking at Tessa with an expression of terror.

'Show me the papers,' Tessa said.

The woman handed them over.

Tessa made it her business to keep herself informed regarding the various orders and writs that were part and parcel of Irish child-protection law and expected to see some variation of an emergency care order, signed by a member of the Irish judiciary, placing the children in the care of the child-protection authorities. She would have also expected this document to be accompanied by a letter from the Minister for Children, explaining why such an action had been sought.

Instead, she found herself looking at a letter printed on the headed paper of the Department of Children and Youth Affairs.

To whichever member of the Garda commissioner's task force this letter finds itself with,

It has been brought to my attention that the three Bolger children have been in your care for the past three days, and that representation has been made to you by our colleagues in Tusla, the Child and Family Agency, to deliver said children into their custody.

Earlier today, I was contacted by Ella Carling of Tusla, asking me to intervene in this matter. She explained the case to me, and I have no hesitation in granting her request.

There is every reason to believe the Bolger children have been living in an emotionally and perhaps physically abusive situation in their home, and their abduction by person or persons unknown can only have aggravated any trauma they have previously experienced. Added to this, it appears you and your team have been using them as a source of information in your own investigation, and I have heard unpleasant rumours to the effect that play and art therapy have both been utilised as a method of manipulating disclosures from them. I have also discovered that one of the children has been abducted while in your care, which surely indicates you are not suitable guardians. It seems, therefore, appropriate to place these children in Ms Carling's capable hands while more permanent arrangements can be made.

This is a complex case, and the contribution of you and your colleagues is much appreciated within the remit you have

been given. You may now stand down and allow social services
and the Wexford Gardaí to continue the investigation.

Yours sincerely,

Gillian Shaughnessy TD

Minister for Children and Youth Affairs

Beneath her printed name, Shaughnessy had signed in pen.

Tessa skimmed the letter again, just to confirm it made no reference to a custody order, was not co-signed by a judge and had, by her reckoning, no legal authority whatsoever. It seemed to her that, if they felt so strongly about the plight of the Bolger children, surely they would have pursued custody through the courts, which would have been the simplest course of action?

Tessa had to believe the lack of any such supporting paperwork meant it was impossible to procure. Which meant the contents of the letter were, more than likely, spurious.

'I don't like the look of this,' she said, handing it back to the woman.

'It's from a government minister,' Carling said.

'Yeah, but you see, I don't answer to the Minister for Children.' Tessa shrugged. 'So... sorry.'

'May I take my children now?' Bolger asked.

The man was trembling, and Tessa could see he was barely holding himself in check.

He's got a temper, does this one, she thought. *And I'm now going to test it even further.*

'Do you know what?' she said. 'No. I don't think either of you should take them anywhere tonight. I'm going to suggest you all book yourselves into one of Wexford's wonderful local hotels, and we'll revisit this in the morning.'

'You are overstepping, Ms Burns,' Carling said. 'I will speak to your superiors.'

'Go right ahead.'

'I've had enough of this,' Bolger said and motioned to his men, who took a step towards the kids. 'I'm taking my children.'

This was a mistake. As if propelled by rocket fuel, Pavlov launched himself at the closest suit, clamping his teeth on the man's genitals and hanging on for dear life. The target of the dog's annoyance wailed and lamely tried to prise Pavlov off but found this hurt even more and stopped.

'Good dog,' Tessa said.

The eyes of the group, which had all been drawn to Bolger's employee's discomfort, snapped back to Tessa, only to discover she had her gun out, holding it loosely by her side.

'Pav, let him go,' she commanded.

The terrier mix complied, dropping his front paws onto the ground – he'd been balancing on his hind legs – and trotted back over to the children, where he remained protectively in front of them.

'Now let me be clear,' Tessa said. 'I'm tired and I'm pissed off. I'm extremely worried about Isaac, who's been missing now for thirty hours. On top of that, one of my team was kidnapped this afternoon by a very dangerous man who's mixed up in all of this somewhere, and I'm worried sick about her too. If I'm honest, I strongly suspect both of you deserve some level of blame for all the crap that's gone down, and if so much as a hair on either Isaac's or my friend's head is harmed, I'm going to make it my business to see you pay for it. Am I clear?'

Neither Bolger nor Carling answered, but Tessa was certain they'd both heard and understood every word.

'The only parties in this entire mess who are completely innocent, from what I can see, are the children,' she continued. 'And I'm *fucked* if I'm going to stand back and allow them to become some kind of bargaining chip in a game I don't fully comprehend yet.'

'You're making a mistake,' Bolger said.

'Maybe I am,' Tessa said, 'but I do know this – you're not telling me the truth. I want you to think very carefully about that, and my advice is that when I see you tomorrow, you come clean. As for you' – she looked at Carling – 'I don't know what political favours have been called in, or who's in whose pocket, but my job is to make sure these kids are kept safe. And I very much doubt that even features on your agenda. So you can do your level best to take them, but just remember this: you're going to have to get through me to do it.'

Pavlov barked.

'And through Pav.'

She looked down at the two remaining children in her care. 'How about we go back to the room, order pizza and watch a movie?'

'Yes please,' Noa whispered without looking at his father.

And that's what they did.

48

As Tessa was dealing with the Bolgers and the Child and Family Agency, Danny, dressed in a black leather jacket, black jeans and boots, with a black woollen cap pulled over his hair and ears, was walking briskly up the winding lane that led to the area known as The Rocks.

A wall made of stones harvested from the wild place towered on Danny's right, the branches of high trees – oak, hawthorn, ash and larch – hanging over it and, autumn as it was, littering the path with leaves. Night had fallen by then, and the canopy the trees created made the walkway even darker. The wall had once protected a military barracks, and the housing estate that existed beyond it was called Cromwell's Fort in tribute.

To Danny's left was a metal fence, beyond which was the large campus of Wexford Garda station.

The detective had looked at maps of the area and knew that a path cut through the two walking loops that would take him to a low fence, and from there he'd have to bushwhack his way through gorse and bramble to reach Trespan Rock.

A rope was coiled about his left shoulder, and he figured he was going to need it. The cave where he suspected the Merrow was hiding out was about halfway down the face of Trespan, and the rope would be essential if he was going to get down to it.

A man walking a pit bull terrier passed him, nodding politely. Danny returned the gesture, then rounded a curve in the path, and the expanse of The Rocks opened up to him. The area in front looked to be a wide pasture, the grass well mowed and maintained. To his right, the landscape rose in a gentle hill, which he could see grew quite steep at the top and was covered in woodland. To his left, some of the rocks that gave the place its name sat, stolid and uncaring; a pond of rust-coloured water at their base had been fenced off by someone. A group of teenagers were sitting on the grass near the water, vaping.

It took him a second to find the path he was looking for, but once he did, he saw it had been covered with light gravel, making for easy footing, and he struck out at a good pace. The path wound between more rocky outcrops, Irish gorse bushes erupting from their sides in splashes of yellow.

The moon was low in the sky over Wexford town, which sprawled out below him as the path climbed higher. It wasn't quite full but gave a good light, which he was thankful for. He'd brought a torch with him but was loath to use it once he was past the fence and in the scrub: he didn't want to warn any watchful eyes of his approach. The Merrow may well be sleeping in that cave, but there was no guarantee she remained there constantly.

The path plateaued, and he hadn't gone far when he found that progress was likely to be easier than he'd expected: a way was already cut through the wild vegetation, and he moved forward without difficulty. Once or twice, a curling vine of thorns attached itself to his jeans or jacket, but he unsnagged himself easily enough.

At one point, he reached a stream and startled a big dog fox that had come to drink. He stood for a moment in the moon-light, watching its bushy tail disappear into the scrub, before continuing and felt the path begin to incline upwards. Before long, he was negotiating steps that seemed to have been worn into the rock.

In his mind's eye, Danny could see Cromwellian soldiers making this very trek, with the added burden of a huge canon that had to be hauled behind them. The thought made him aware of the weight of his own gun, nestled under his left arm.

The path wound around to the right, and then he was there, just below the highest peak of Trespan Rock. Wexford Harbour was spread out before him – he could make out its entirety from Raven Point to the north to Rosslare in the south. Behind him was more scrub and a network of fields. A pipistrelle bat flapped lazily past, hunting moths and other airborne morsels.

He climbed to the top of the rock, walked gingerly to the edge and peered over. Somewhere below was the cave he'd come to find. He sniffed the air for a second, thinking he'd caught something unusual.

At first, there was nothing, but then he sniffed again, and there it was, barely there, perhaps just a memory, but he could definitely smell woodsmoke. And was that bacon?

You're smart, Ms Merrow, Danny thought. *But you're not that clever. Dumb mistake to light a fire when you're being hunted.*

Taking the rope from his shoulder, he found a sharp outcrop and tied one end firmly to it. Then he fed its length through his hands, dropping it slowly over the edge and watching it snake downwards. Danny hadn't been able to find an exact height of Trespan Rock, but he reckoned the drop to the upper part of the hill below was about 150 feet. The rope he had was 300 feet, so he thought he was safe enough.

If he didn't let go of course.

Taking a deep breath, he arranged the rope about himself

and stepped over the edge, using whatever outcrops he could find as footholds.

The going was easy at first, but within about a minute, the face became almost sheer, and he had to force down a rising panic. He had the rope looped over one shoulder and again around his waist, and tried to execute a kind of abseiling motion, but he found the rope didn't slide through his hands as easily as he'd like, and now and then, he had to pause to loosen it, which made him feel very unsafe.

He was also worried he'd miss the cave opening.

According to the photographs he'd seen, it was supposed to be more or less in the middle of the rock, but because of where he'd tied the rope, he was very much off to one side.

Looking down, to his great relief, he spotted the cave, about five yards to his right. In two downwards jumps, he was on a level with it and executed a kind of skittering run across the rock face until he was able to reach out with his hand and grab the edge of the opening.

One lunge and he was in.

He lay for a moment on his back, staring at the low cave ceiling and breathing heavily.

I can't believe I just did that, he thought. *Tessa was right. But then, she usually is. The climbing wall in the gym doesn't prepare you at all.* Followed rapidly by: *I am not going to tell her that though!*

Having got his breath back, he sank into a low crouch and drew his gun. The cave opened onto a tunnel in the rock, which he slowly crept along. The scent of woodsmoke was stronger now, as was the smell of bacon. He came to a hard right turn and stopped. He could see light flickering against the wall ahead and knew he'd found them.

Danny counted to three in his head then stepped around the corner, his gun extended before him.

The passage ended in a wide, smoothly walled cave. In its

centre, the Merrow was sitting in front of a fire that was little more than smouldering coals. A flat piece of slate, which Danny could see from the grease stains it bore had been used as a cooking utensil, sat to one side of the fire. The woman was sitting on her black parka, which she'd folded to keep the cold from the cave floor from seeping into her thin body, and there was what looked to be a dark sweatshirt in a bundle beside it. She was wearing a grey T-shirt, one arm of which she'd torn off and turned into a pressure bandage, which she'd bound to her shoulder with more strips from the garment – her midriff was bare, and Danny could see frayed edges where she'd removed the lengths of cloth.

A collection of foraged ropes and cable lay in one corner, some tins of beans, soup and meat and what looked to be a bag of apples in another corner, as well as a children's storybook.

Isaac was asleep, wrapped in a grubby blanket against the far wall.

'I've come to take you in,' he said, and the woman, whom he realised had actually been asleep (or maybe passed out from shock and loss of blood) raised her head to look at him.

She was perhaps forty and rail thin, with dark shadows under her eyes. She had a strong, finely boned face, her hair was black and long, and her skin very pale and smooth.

'I think we've done this dance before,' she said.

'I'm the only one with a gun this time.'

'If you fire that thing in here, it'll do one of two things,' the Merrow said.

'Do tell.'

'It'll ricochet off every rock it encounters and kill us all.'

'Or?'

'Or it'll bring the whole cave down on top of us. Either way, it's not a good idea.'

Neither of these possibilities had occurred to Danny, but that didn't make them seem any less plausible.

'Is the boy alright?'

'He's fine. I've taken good care of him.'

'Living in a cave? He's used to mansions and private schools.'

'Better a cave and someone who cares about you than a mansion and a man who would sell you off.'

Danny wanted to drill down into that statement, but now wasn't the time. 'I'm taking him. If you want to try and stop me, go right ahead. You're a third my size and you've been shot. I don't fancy your chances.'

'Are you going to give the children back to their father?'

'He's their father. Why wouldn't we?'

'He's a bad man.'

'Bad how?'

'You and I and Isaac are all in this cave because of decisions he made.'

'Tell it to me at the station. I'm taking the boy now.'

The Merrow nodded in resignation. 'My Julian had red hair.'

Danny shook his head. 'Who?'

The woman laughed a tired, pained laugh. 'It doesn't matter. Take him. I can't stop you. Just promise me you'll make sure he's alright. That all of them are.'

Danny thought he heard tears in her voice just then, and he paused, looking at her. 'I will. It's what me and my team do.'

She cleared her throat and nodded. 'Alright then.'

Danny scuttled past her and shook the sleeping child. 'Isaac, it's me, Danny.'

The boy looked up at him sleepily. 'Have you come to camp with us too?'

'I've come to take you back to Noa and Sofie.'

He yawned and allowed Danny to lift him onto his shoulder.

When the detective turned, the Merrow was gone.

Cursing under his breath, he grabbed a length of rope from the bundle the woman had collected and used it to lash the boy to him. Then he climbed back to the top of Trespan hand over hand, sweat making his hands slippery and unreliable, but sheer anxiety getting him through.

'Tessa,' he said into his handset as he strode back along the path to his car, Isaac – who seemed utterly unaffected by his time in the cave – dozing on his shoulder, 'I've got him.'

'I knew you would. And the Merrow?'

'She gave me the slip again.'

He heard Tessa sigh. 'You have Isaac – that's the most important thing.'

'It is, isn't it?' Danny said.

And feeling somewhat positive for the first time in days, he jogged on through the night towards his car.

49

Tessa and Danny sat in the hospital administrator's office nursing glasses of Scotch. It was 10.30 p.m. and the sounds of the hospital going about its business reached them through the door. They were both exhausted, but neither was under any illusions the night was over.

This was a temporary respite.

The reunion between Isaac and his siblings had been an emotional one, and after he'd been given a clean bill of health by the doctor, he'd happily snuggled down in his old bed and gone to sleep.

Garda Blake, who'd been on duty when Maggie was taken, had refused to leave at the end of his shift and was guarding their door again.

'So our dark woman is in the wind again,' Tessa said. 'I bet Maggie would laugh at the fact the both of you let her slip past you.'

Danny laughed sadly.

'She would, at that.' He looked at Tessa. 'We'll get her back. O'Dowd will call soon.'

'I know. I'm going crazy with the waiting, is all, which is probably what he wants. Tell me how you lost the Merrow. It'll keep my mind busy.'

'She disappeared virtually under my nose. I could have gone after her, but...'

'Your priority was the young lad. You did the right thing,' Tessa reassured him. 'Did she say anything before she ran?'

'Just that Mr Bolger isn't a suitable parent. And something about someone called Julian.'

'Julian?'

'I don't know what she was going on about.'

Tessa sipped her drink. 'This case is a tangle of loose strands,' she said. 'So far they all seem to be crossing over, but none are directly linking. The only way to join them is to get each one and lay them out individually until we can see where they connect.'

'How do we do that?'

'By taking hold of whichever piece is visible and yanking the damn thing out. For example, the Minister for Children signed this letter that was given to me this evening. When I'm finished my drink, we're going to go and find out who asked her to corrupt the course of justice.'

'I can hazard a guess,' Danny said.

'Me too. So we'll start by calling on him.'

'Damien Forde?'

'Who else? I'll finally have something concrete I can confront him with. And he'd better have a good fucking answer, because if I'm left with even a sliver of doubt, I'm going to bring him in for questioning. And then we'll see how tight-lipped he'll be.'

'In custody might not be the safest place to be,' Danny said. 'Do we know what happened to the guy who died in the station yet?'

'They've ruled it as a suicide, but I'm not sure. I think someone killed him.'

'And by someone you mean one of our guys?'

'It has to be. Which means whoever's behind all of this has someone on the inside. Among our ranks. The cameras were shut off, Danny. That didn't just conveniently happen. He was stabbed in the eye with a pen. Who uses that as a way of committing suicide?'

Danny swallowed what was in his glass and held it out for a refill. 'So a guard murdered a suspect, someone who almost certainly had information that would have helped us?'

'In a nutshell, yes.'

'I have to ask if that puts my parents in danger.'

'No. No one knows where they are except you, me, Dawn and the two guys guarding them. And that's the way it'll be until this is over.'

'It's hard to know who to trust,' Danny said ruefully.

'Do you trust me?'

'Completely.'

'And you trust Dawn and Maggie and Pavlov. I trust the two men who are watching over your folks. Right now, that's all we need. It's enough to get the job done.'

'Okay. I can live with that.'

'Speaking of Dawn, she called me about an hour ago. We know who the Merrow is. The blood she left behind allowed us to put her DNA through the system. And we got a match.'

'Okay.'

'By which I mean we have a name – Tara Wall. The reason she hasn't popped up before, when organised crime was looking for her some years back, is that it's such an old case.'

'How old?'

'The 1980s. She was reported missing in 1988.'

'She must have been a tot,' Danny said.

'Four years old. It looks like the story Del Finnegan told me might be true. The Merrow is, herself, an abducted child.'

'Makes you feel kind of sorry for her.'

'It does, but she still needs to be brought in.'

'How do we do that?'

'She failed in her attempt to kill Forde,' Tessa said. 'I'm sure she'll try again, but if she's intent on protecting the kids, there are others she might go for first. There are two other suspects: Andrew O'Dowd, the man who has Maggie, is the obvious choice.'

'And the other?'

'The kids' parents – well, their father at least. Their mother seems to be inexplicably missing. I mean, what kind of mother wouldn't come to pick up her kids after they'd been abducted?'

'Not a good one anyway,' Danny agreed.

'There's something not right about Mr Bolger.'

'So you're suggesting that he didn't report them missing because he'd arranged to have them abducted himself?' Danny asked. 'Do you think that's likely?'

'Stranger things have happened. We have to consider it as a possibility.'

'This case is messed up,' the big detective sighed. 'Why would he do that?'

'Any number of reasons: drum up sympathy; hiding money, if a ransom did come into play; draw police attention onto a rival... do you want me to go on?'

'No. It's all too depressing.'

'Drink up,' Tessa urged. 'We have some government ministers to roust.'

Danny downed the last of his dram.

'How are you doing, Danny?' Tessa asked. 'You look fit to drop.'

'You're not looking so hot yourself.'

'Yeah, but I'll look better tomorrow,' Tessa said with grave seriousness. 'You'll still look like crap.'

'I can't argue with you there,' Danny groaned.

Tessa flashed him a grim smile. 'I think it's time we go and annoy some politicians.'

50

They'd just got into Tessa's Ford Capri when her mobile phone rang.

It was a withheld number.

'Yeah. Tessa Burns here.'

'Good evening, DI Burns.'

Tessa immediately knew she was speaking to Andrew O'Dowd.

'What do you want?' she asked without preamble.

'To give you proof of life.'

There was a scuffling sound, and then, to Tessa's overwhelming relief, she heard: 'Hi, Tessa. It's me, Maggie. I'm okay. Tell everyone I'm okay.'

'I will, I promise. Just hang in there...'

The phone was taken back before she could say anything else.

'Detective, I'm going to work under the assumption that you want Wheels here back.'

'If you've hurt her, I'll kill you.'

'I can promise she's unharmed. But that won't be the case for long unless you follow my instructions precisely.'

'Tell me what you want me to do.'

'There's a beach on the left just as you cross Wexford Bridge called Kaats Strand. If you walk to the end of it, you'll come to a salt marsh. The footing is treacherous, but I've left markers to show you the way through it. In the middle of this marsh is a shack that's used by hunters during the duck season. Be there tomorrow at 8 a.m. Alone.'

'That's it?'

'I'll tell you my terms when I see you. Goodnight, Detective Burns. I'd get some sleep if I were you. Tomorrow will be a very busy day.'

'I'll be seeing you,' Tessa said.

'I can't wait. Bye for now.'

And then he hung up.

Tessa gazed at her phone and then at Danny in shock.

'Did you hear that?'

'I did. You know that if you do it his way, you'll be walking into a trap.'

'Of course I know that. Which is why I'm not going to do it his way.'

51

Damien Forde lived three kilometres from the village of Taghmon. The house had three storeys, a manicured and landscaped garden and an electronic gate that was locked but offered very little security: Tessa and Danny simply climbed over it. It was just after 11.10 p.m., but there was a light on in the downstairs hallway and in what they took to be either an office or living room to the left of the front door.

Tessa rang the bell but banged sharply on the door with her fist for good measure. Danny offered a quizzical eyebrow.

'Trick I learned when I was on the beat,' she explained. 'Irritates whoever is inside – they think it's an overzealous Jehovah's Witness or a food delivery person in a hurry – and when they open the door and see it's the Gardai, they get really flustered. Which never hurts, does it?'

The door was opened by Clohessy in his shirtsleeves. He did, indeed, look more than a little alarmed to see Danny, who was holding out his ID.

Tessa smiled sweetly. 'Good evening. We'd like to speak to Minister Forde.'

'I'm sorry, he's with someone at the moment.'

'This won't wait.'

'I'm sure he'll be free soon...'

Tessa continued to smile. 'Graeme, which bit of "this won't wait" did you not understand? Can we come in please?'

'Um... yes, I suppose so.'

Tessa and Danny did so.

'Now, is he in there?' Tessa motioned to the door on the left.

'Yes, but he's with...'

'Thank you, Graeme. You've been a wonderful host.'

And ignoring the protestations of the unfortunate Mr Clohessy, Tessa pushed open the door, and she and Danny stepped inside.

The room they entered was long and high ceilinged, with burnished wooden floorboards set off by a couple of patchwork deep-pile rugs. A desk littered with papers, among which nestled an old-school desktop computer, sat at the end of the room, but closer to the door were three chairs arranged around a coffee table complete with a silver coffee pot and a fine china tea set. On the chairs were seated Damien Forde, Junior Minister for Foreign Affairs; Gillian Shaughnessy, Minister for Children; and the man who'd told Tessa his name was Devlin before fleeing her office earlier that day.

'Well, this is unexpected,' Tessa said jovially. 'And it saves us an extra trip and a few more days of a manhunt.'

Shaughnessy and Forde stared at the two police officers with shocked expressions.

Devlin simply shook his head. 'I didn't expect to see you again so soon, Detective.'

'Me either,' Tessa said, closing the door behind her. 'You're in esteemed company, Mr Devlin.'

Forde began to make a spluttering noise and started to stand, but Devlin placed a hand on the minister's shoulder and pushed him back into his seat. This evening, Forde had removed his suit jacket and was clad in a waistcoat that looked fit to explode and an open-necked white shirt.

'Sit *down*, Forde, you feckin' eejit.'

'Might I inquire as to the meaning of this visit?' Shaughnessy asked, regaining some of her composure. She was a stern-looking middle-aged woman in a grey business suit.

'Well, the reason changed in the few seconds since we came in,' Tessa admitted.

'What exactly do you mean?'

'I was planning to question Forde here about his connection with a grounded ship and the three children found aboard, not to mention why the woman who was paid to care for those children during their voyage tried to shoot him earlier today. Danny and I would also like to ask you why you signed a letter asking my team to hand the Bolger children over to the authorities and then stand down from an open investigation into child trafficking and murder. But *now* I want to know why you and Minister Forde are meeting with a wanted fugitive, a man who came into my office today under false pretences, tried to steal a computer, pulled a gun on me and shot a member of the force while escaping.'

'He forced his way in!' Forde blurted out. 'He forced his way in and has been holding us hostage.'

Tessa looked at Danny, who shrugged.

'I don't see a weapon,' she said.

'Shut up, will you, Forde?' Devlin said, looking deeply exasperated and perhaps a little embarrassed.

'It's true,' Shaughnessy said, realising there might be a way out of the mess they found themselves in. 'He told us he has a gun.'

'I don't believe this,' Devlin said.

'I was going to arrest you anyway, Mr Devlin,' Tessa said, stepping forward. 'This has just sped proceedings up a bit. Get on your feet so I can frisk you.'

The man stood but, as he did so, pulled a handgun from inside his jacket. Before he even had his arm extended, Tessa punched him full in the face, lifting him off his feet and sending him crashing over the chair and onto the rug behind it. By the time Devlin had his eyes open, the detective had her own weapon out, as did Danny, and they were both standing over him.

'Now that was a dumb move,' Tessa said. 'I think I broke your nose, and that could have been avoided.'

'I want to see my lawyer,' Devlin said, blood running from each nostril and down his cheeks before it soaked into the fibres of the rug.

'That's probably an excellent idea,' Danny agreed.

52

Danny handcuffed Devlin to a radiator, then he and Tessa sat down with the two politicians.

'I have to be honest with you, Ministers,' Tessa said conversationally, 'that story you told about Mr Devlin forcing his way in and holding you hostage doesn't exactly have the ring of truth to it.'

'I assure you, it's completely true,' Shaughnessy said. 'I was afraid for my life.'

'That I can perhaps believe,' the detective said. 'Was Devlin behind the sending of the letter regarding the Bolger children and the Child and Family Agency, or was that all Mr Forde's idea?'

'I haven't got a clue what you're talking about,' Forde protested.

'Mr Forde, do you recognise my colleague, Detective Inspector Danny Murphy?'

'Of course I do.'

'I should fucking hope so. He's the person who saved your life earlier today, for which you haven't even thanked him. Don't you think you might owe him the truth about all of this?'

'I've told the truth.'

'Why do you think that woman tried to murder you today?' Danny asked.

'With respect, Detective, isn't it your job to ascertain that?'

'Minister, this is the same woman who landed here on a ship whose entire crew was missing, the ship that brought the Bolger children back to Ireland,' Tessa said, 'the same children thugs tried to warn us off helping, and when one of them was pressed to divulge who had hired them to do so, the name we were given was that of your personal assistant.'

'We're starting to think this woman might still be trying to protect the children,' Danny said. 'So the fact she wants you dead could suggest she doesn't think your intentions towards them are exactly honourable.'

'I don't have any intentions towards those kids,' Forde snapped.

'Why does your name keep popping up in this case then?' Danny asked.

Forde snorted. 'Because I'm good at my job. That makes some people nervous. My position means I have to deal with all kinds of extremists. I assume the poor woman who tried to shoot me belonged to one of those factions.'

'Minister, does the name Andrew O'Dowd mean anything to you?' Danny asked.

'No. Not at all.'

'What about the Merrow?'

'No.'

'Derek Sherlock?'

'No. I'm sorry.'

'And you, Minister Shaughnessy?'

The woman just shook her head.

'Ministers, people are dying,' Tessa said. 'I would strongly advise you to reconsider your policy of remaining silent.'

'Why did you write that letter asking for the Bolgers to be

placed with the child protection authorities?' Danny asked Shaughnessy.

'I received a call from the head of Tusla. I explained as much in the letter.'

'And you had nothing to do with this?' Tessa asked Forde.

'Why would I?' he sneered. 'It's a bit outside my remit, wouldn't you say?'

'So is gunrunning,' Tessa said wryly. 'But that didn't stop you.'

'That was a long time ago, and my name was cleared.'

'Doesn't mean you didn't do it,' Tessa said. 'I might be a simple copper, but I'm not blind to the failings of our legal system. Or how open to corruption it can be.'

'I believe we're wandering into the realm of slander,' Forde growled.

'Not at all.' Tessa grinned. 'I'm simply thinking aloud. Hypothesising.'

'The Child and Family Agency had no legal order supporting their request this evening,' Danny said to Shaughnessy. 'Don't you find that strange?'

'I was under the impression they were bringing one.'

'Wouldn't an order like that be essential for the state to take children into care?' Tessa asked.

Shaughnessy shrugged. 'I don't believe so. I mean, once the paperwork is obtained at some stage...'

'They were actually in their father's care at the time,' Tessa said incredulously. 'For that situation to change, some kind of care order would need to be produced. You're the Minister for Children. Shouldn't you know this stuff?'

'I was acting in what I believed to be the best interests of the children, I assure you,' Shaughnessy said primly.

'What about you, Mr Forde,' Tessa asked. 'Are you acting in the best interests of these children?'

'Like I've already said,' Forde replied without emotion. 'I

have no interest in these waifs at all. If you continue to bother me about them, I'll bring a case of harassment against you. And your pet gorilla.'

'Do your worst, Minister,' Tessa said. 'I have a feeling you and I aren't finished this wee dance by a long way, so let's just see where the music takes us.'

53

They had just arrived back at the hospital and Devlin was getting patched up when Danny's phone rang. It was Moran, the journalist he'd spoken to about Forde.

'Hello, Detective Murphy!'

'Hello, Mr Moran. What can I do for you?'

'Sorry for the late call, but I've been informed the children found on that ship that ran aground are the Bolger kids. Their father and his shenanigans keep my paper in stories. He's a successful man.'

'Successful and honest?'

Moran laughed. 'I don't believe such a man exists. Have you met one yet?'

'No. I'd say I probably haven't.'

'Have you encountered Mr Bolger?'

'My partner did earlier this evening.'

'Did he like him?' Moran asked.

'She. And no, I think it's fair to say she didn't.'

'And I daresay Bolger didn't seem to like her, if his usual behaviour towards women is a yardstick.'

'You're right there. I don't think he much likes his kids either.'

'I didn't like my father,' Moran said. 'And not getting on with your children isn't a crime, even if it perhaps should be.'

'Can I speak to you off the record?' Danny asked. 'I usually wouldn't share with local journos, but I could use a fresh perspective on what's going on here, and you have more local knowledge than most. But I want to stress, Mr Moran, this is completely off the record.'

'All of it?'

'I'll give you what I can. But if you want to help, there's some stuff that can't go into print. Not yet anyway.'

'Alright. My digital recorder is switched off.'

'Good. Social services arrived this evening too and tried to take the kids – they had authorisation from the Minister for Children.'

'Really? I didn't think that happened with rich families.'

'Me either. They're saying someone complained about us questioning them, but they were being well cared for. What is going on?'

'It wouldn't be the first time social services has been used as a weapon in a criminal case.'

Danny laughed grimly. 'That's true.'

'What do you think is going on, Detective?'

'I know a lot of stuff; I just don't understand any of it.'

And Danny laid out the case in as much detail as he could: Rosslare being a hub for smuggling of all kinds, Tessa's theory that the ship being grounded where it was might not have been an accident; the presence of the Merrow on the *Dolphin*, and the captain's logs and journals; the Merrow showing up at the hospital but not hurting Maggie, even though she could have done, and taking Isaac; Andrew O'Dowd and Del Finnegan, local gangsters and child abductors being used as recipients and handlers of the children before they were to be moved on;

Damien Forde, an Irish government minister and a successful businessman in his own right potentially being behind the children's abduction and movement to Ireland, and how the team were being put under pressure to step away from the case.

He told Moran about Derek Sherlock, the ship's cook, a former gang member who owed some sort of debt, being on board the *Dolphin*; Eric Stafford, Farnogue Freight's enforcer, who'd informed them his company didn't know that their ships were being used to traffic children, although he'd had his suspicions; a second government minister stepping in to support child services' claim on the children, and yet again looking for the team to walk away from the case. He finished by telling him about Maggie being taken by O'Dowd, and how Tessa was to go to a cabin in the marshes at first light to see if she could get her best friend back.

'That's a lot of information,' Moran agreed. 'I'm a bit worried my brain will melt trying to process it all.'

'I know the feeling,' Danny said.

'Will I give you my tuppence worth? The reason I was calling?'

'Please do.'

'Well after our chat, I worked out that you were most likely investigating the *Dolphin* case and thought I'd do a little digging in case I could help. I have a few useful contacts... Anyway, Farnogue Freight seems to be clean. Their accounts have been looked at by the forensic accountants in the Criminal Assets Bureau several times in the past and they've never found anything amiss. Every cent is accounted for. I don't think they knew anything criminal was happening under their nose.'

'So they're in the clear, you think?'

'The evidence suggests as much.'

'So that leaves Forde and the Bolgers,' Danny said.

'Yes. John Bolger is an interesting man. His politics are, shall we say, a little bit disturbing.'

'How so?'

'He's donated money to a number of organisations that are swimming very much in the right lane of the swimming pool. The far-right lane at that.'

'Maggie mentioned that. You think he's a fascist?'

'I don't believe that term is used much anymore. He's what the Americans would call alt-right.'

'The kids have talked a bit about their mother...' Danny said.

'She used to be a very public figure, involved in various high-profile charities, but over the past few years, she's vanished completely from the media and the press – it's as if she suddenly stopped all the charity work she'd been involved in, though I've heard that she's been seen locally, mostly being driven in and out of the Bolger homestead. Rumour is that John has recently had her committed to an institution.'

'The kids said their father blames them for their mother's illness.'

'That doesn't seem fair. Or even accurate,' Moran replied.

'Not fair at all. So Bolger was involved in politics, and we have a number of politicians and a high-ranking civil servant involved.'

'You do.'

'Do you find that interesting, Mr Moran?'

'Well it does make me think.'

'My partner refused to hand the kids over to either of them.'

'I think that was the right course of action,' Moran concurred. 'The web is very tangled, but that doesn't mean there isn't a spider at its heart.'

'Thanks for your help,' Danny said.

'Keep me posted,' Moran said. 'Only on the record next time.'

54

Devlin wasn't talking.

They'd packed his nose in A&E, and he was now in the same interview room Clarke had been in earlier that day. Which Tessa wasted no time in telling him.

'He lasted two hours in here,' she said calmly. 'I still don't know who did it. The local guys want to believe he shoved a pen in his own eye, but I'm not so sure. Cameras were switched off, you see, not just in here, but out in the hallway too. The killer didn't do a good job of it either. Poor old Clarkey probably survived a good ten minutes with his brains oozing out of his eye socket. Nasty business.'

Devlin grimaced. 'Is that supposed to scare me?'

Tessa held his gaze. 'Does it?'

'No, DI Burns, it does not.'

'Funny, because you *look* scared. What the fuck is all this about, Devlin? You strike me as a professional, as someone who isn't used to a lot of nonsense. I could see how embarrassed you were by the conduct of Forde and Shaughnessy. Whatever this job started out as, it's degenerated into a shitstorm of chaos. Do yourself a favour: tell me who you work for and what's going on, and I'll see to it that you do a little time in one of those open prisons where you might as well be in a holiday camp.'

'A tempting offer,' Devlin said. 'But alas, I'll have to decline.'

'Can you tell me anything?'

'Why should I?'

'I dunno – form recognises form maybe? Look, for me, this is all about keeping those children safe. I don't care about any of the rest of it. Honestly, I don't.'

'You don't care about the dead crew? About the dead body found in an old office building on the quay? About the fact one of your task force is currently being held hostage? I bet you care about *her* life, Detective.'

Tessa wanted to reach out and smack the man, but she kept her emotions in check. 'You're very well informed,' she said.

'I like to keep up to speed on things.'

'What are you trying to tell me?'

'If you want Maggie Doolan alive to see sunrise, let me go.'

Tessa's stomach turned over. 'You're not backwards about coming forward, are you, Devlin?'

'Coyness serves no one,' he replied.

Tessa stood.

'I trust you're going to get the paperwork necessary for my release.'

'Then you'd trust wrong,' Tessa said. 'I'm going to take a shit. Being in your company has messed up my digestion terribly.'

She left him in what she was starting to think of as 'The Interview Room of Death' and hoped Maggie was doing okay.

55

An hour later, Tessa followed Jim Sheils as he navigated a canoe along the shoreline of the beach called Kaats Strand. She'd called him primarily to ask about the landscape she'd be expected to navigate, and the pair had decided that waiting for O'Dowd's deadline was unwise.

'We might as well strike while the iron is hot,' the chief officer had said.

Danny had very much wanted to come, but someone had to remain to watch Devlin, so the big detective had begrudgingly agreed.

It was just after 2 a.m., and the moon was casting enough light for them to manoeuvre by, and luckily it was a still night, so the river, which spilled out to the sea only a quarter of a mile to their backs, was virtually still. Behind them, the lights of Wexford town twinkled, the silhouette of the steeples of the twin churches reaching towards the cloud-stained sky as if they were imploring God for help.

Tessa knew how they felt.

Ahead of them was the salt marsh.

Pavlov sat in the prow of Tessa's boat, watching the shoreline as it snaked past: a narrow strip of beach dotted with drift-wood and slimy-looking seaweed. Sheils had been dubious about taking him, but there was no way Tessa was leaving him behind.

'Maggie will want to see him anyway,' she said. 'He needs to be a part of this.'

The river curved, and they followed it. Ahead of Sheils, a heron was stock-still in the shallows. A curlew stood on one leg, its curved bill seeming almost out of proportion to its body.

As they rounded the corner, Tessa noticed the river seemed to open up ahead, the expanse of water almost doubling in width. She blinked for a second then realised what she was actually seeing was the beginning of the marsh itself.

'It's tidal this close to the ocean,' Sheils explained. 'So when we're at high tide, like we are now, a large portion of it is under-water. As the tide ebbs, more of it becomes uncovered.'

'So where the hell is this shack O'Dowd is talking about?'

'I know it,' Sheils said. 'When the water is high, it's basically on a little island in the middle of the marsh. Our mutual friend won't expect us to come when the shack is only accessible by boat. Hopefully, we'll have the drop on him.'

'That would be good,' Tessa said. 'The tactics we used during our last meeting weren't successful.'

Sheils laughed dryly and moved his canoe to the right, guiding them through a maze of reed beds and shallow sand-banks. The place smelled of damp vegetation and stagnant water. Something rustled in the beds to Tessa's left, and Pavlov whined.

'What the fuck was that?' she whispered.

'Probably a bird,' Sheils replied. 'Water rail maybe, or a redshank.'

'It sounded bigger,' Tessa said.

'Fox then. Possibly a seal.'

'You don't know, do you?'

'Nope. I'm kind of focused on getting us close to the hunter's cabin.'

'What if we get eaten by something first?'

'We won't.'

It felt like they were moving through the channels of that marsh for hours. Some of the streams they traversed seemed barely wide enough for the canoes to pass through, and Tessa worried they'd become stuck. But Sheils moved with confidence, and they made their way without incident.

Finally, the reed beds began to grow thinner and less dense, and there, in front of them, was what looked like a raised patch of white sand, and in the middle of that a rickety-looking shed. Some disused lobster pots and fish crates were scattered around it.

Light spilled from the windows, and smoke curled from a chimney that sat off-kilter on the roof.

'There she blows,' Sheils murmured.

'Brilliant,' Tessa breathed.

'So what's the plan this time?'

'One's just forming in my head as we speak,' Tessa replied.

'Why does that not fill me with comforting thoughts?' Sheils said ruefully.

56

Tessa pulled herself across the cold, damp sand on her belly. When she reached the wall of the cabin, she skirted around so she was on one of the sides without a window. The walls were made of rough boards – some plywood, some better quality – all loosely hammered together in slats. She could just about get the toe of her boot into the cracks between them and, with a little effort, pulled herself up onto the roof of the shack.

She could hear the structure creak as she did so, and she froze, hoping those inside would believe it was just the little building moving in the wind. She remained stationary for three long minutes, then slowly – oh so slowly – she edged forward until she could reach the chimney. Up close, she could see its base was half corroded – it was little more than a metal pipe, and smoke came out the hole at the top but also out a rusty tear at the base.

If her plan was to have maximum effect, both holes would need to be plugged.

She took a piece of tarpaulin Sheils had given her from her pocket and, using her penknife, cut it in two down the middle. She then stuffed one part into the hole the chimney was supposed to have and the other into the tear, making sure both were airtight.

Then she drew her gun and waited.

Within thirty seconds, she could hear someone swearing inside. A minute passed, and she could hear coughing. Another minute and there was a shouted conversation, after which the door of the cabin was flung open and the tall figure of Andrew O'Dowd burst out, coughing and choking. Another man followed, and to Tessa's joy, she saw he was carrying Maggie.

She waited to make sure there was no one else inside, then delayed things no more.

'O'Dowd, this is Tessa Burns. I have a gun aimed at your head. An associate of mine is close by and has a weapon trained on your friend. Place Maggie on the sand *gently*, then put your hands on your head and step away from her.'

O'Dowd didn't move. 'You're a fool, Burns. This was a simple thing. You didn't have to go and make it so complicated.'

'There's no complication,' Tessa said. 'Tell your man to put Maggie down, then step back from her towards the reeds.'

'Just remember I tried to do this in a civilised way,' O'Dowd said and raised his hands over his head.

And a shot rang out from somewhere in the depths of the salt marsh and took a chunk out of the roof right beside Tessa's ears.

'Sniper!' she yelled at the top of her voice and rolled hard, coming off the roof and landing hard on her side. She felt a crunch and knew she'd dislocated her shoulder, but she didn't have time to think about it, because O'Dowd was on her in a second, grabbing her by the scruff of the neck and lifting her into the air. She was aware of her gun dropping from her useless hand, then she was being shaken like a dog shakes a rabbit.

'You brought this on yourself, you stupid fucking copper!' he seethed.

Tessa kicked as hard as she could, trying to get him in the

ribs, but her blows seemed to have no effect on the man. It was as if he was made of stone.

Somewhere behind, she could hear Pavlov barking and the sounds of shooting – she was sure Sheils was returning fire.

'You disrespect me in my own home,' O'Dowd growled and struck Tessa a backhanded blow that caused her to see stars. 'You renege on an arrangement that would have seen an end to all this stupidity, so we could all get back on with our lives!'

He struck her again. For a moment, things went totally black, but only for a moment.

'You have no idea what you're meddling in, and you've become a thorn in my side to such an extent, I can't concentrate on sorting it all out.'

He hit her a third time – something gave in her jaw – and then threw her against the wall of the shack with such force, she felt the boards breaking behind her.

'Well enough is enough,' O'Dowd said, picking her gun up off the sand and pointing it at her. 'I won't pretend I never thought about killing you, but I had decided to opt for another way. You, however, are leaving me no choice.'

Tessa prepared herself for the shot, but then a hole appeared in the middle of Andrew O'Dowd's forehead, and he made an odd sound, as if he was trying to speak but couldn't find the word, then he tipped over face forward onto the sand.

Standing behind him, dressed in black and holding a Glock handgun, was the Merrow. She stood there for a second, her dark hair blowing in the light breeze, and then she was gone.

57

Devlin's lawyer had arrived shortly after 1.30 a.m.

This wasn't usual, but then, there was nothing usual about the case, so Danny shrugged it off and drank coffee and waited to hear from Tessa that Maggie was safe.

It was 2.15 a.m. when there was a knock on the door of the office Danny had borrowed for the night.

'He wants to talk to you,' the detective in charge of the interview rooms said. 'Claims it's urgent.'

Danny hauled himself out of his seat and went down to see what the fuss was.

Devlin was sweating when they got there, although the room wasn't warm.

'Good meeting with your legal eagle?' Danny inquired.

'Very enlightening,' Devlin said. 'Reading between the lines of what I've just been told, I'm not going to live to see morning. So I've decided that I want to deal.'

'Okay,' Danny said. 'What have you got for me?'

'Nah,' Devlin said. 'I want on the earliest plane out of Ireland. Somewhere far away from here, and I want *you* to book it yourself and your word no one will know about it. This place has more holes than a golf course.'

'I can do that,' Danny said. 'But I need to know what I'm buying.'

'I'll tell you who's behind the whole thing, and how all the players link up,' Devlin said. 'And why. But not until I'm in Departures and ready to go.'

'You know it's not as simple as that.'

'So make it simple,' Devlin said, and the big detective could see he was scared out of his wits.

'I'll see what I can do,' Danny said and got up to go.

'No, don't leave me alone!' Devlin hissed.

Danny paused. 'I can use my phone to make the call to the commissioner and to look at tickets,' he said. 'So yeah, I can stay.'

'Thank you,' Devlin said. 'You don't know what you're mixed up in. You have no idea.'

'I don't think it much matters,' Danny said. 'It's all about the kids. None of the rest of it means an awful lot.'

'That's where you're wrong,' Devlin said. 'The kids are only window dressing. It's everything else that's important. Those children are just a distraction.'

At that moment, Danny's phone rang. It was an unknown number.

'Excuse me,' he said and put the handset to his ear.

'Danny Murphy?' a voice he didn't know asked.

'Yes, this is he.'

'I need to talk to you about cover for the safe house your parents are staying in.'

'Who is this?'

'I'm DI Bruce Davison.'

'Okay, hang on one moment.'

He stood up and said to Devlin, 'I'll just be outside, okay? I need to deal with this.'

Devlin's face took on a look of panic. 'Don't leave me! It's a trap. They want me on my own.'

'I'll literally be outside the door – and it has a window. I'll see everyone coming and going.'

He went out and closed the door behind him. The interview rooms were on a basement level of Wexford Garda station, and late at night the corridor was illuminated by bare electric bulbs hanging from the ceiling. It gave the space a cold, eerie feel.

'Yeah, I'm back. I'm not sure what I can do to help with that issue,' he said. 'It's not really in my pay grade. You should talk to the commish.'

'She's not that easy to get though,' Davison said. 'I mean, you could be ringing for hours and not get a response.'

That had never been Danny's experience, but he figured that maybe he and his team had special dispensation.

'Well I can ask her to call you. What's your number there? You're coming up as withheld.'

Just then, Feeney, who'd volunteered to stay on to help Tessa and Danny, arrived, carrying a pot of tea and biscuits on a tray.

'I'll just leave these in, Danny,' he said.

Danny nodded and held open the door for him.

'Yeah, I'll text that to you,' Davison said. 'I'd appreciate it if you'd get the commissioner to call. We're stretched a little thin here.'

'I will of course,' Danny said. 'Is there anything else I can do for you?'

'No, no. That's all for now.'

'Okay, take it easy.'

He hung up and turned back to the interview room in time to see Feeney throw himself at Devlin, a knife in his hand, which the prisoner was desperately trying to wrestle from his grip. Danny swore and went to open the door, only to find it locked from the inside.

Standing back as far as the hallway would allow, he delivered a powerful kick to it, just where the handle was, but it had almost no effect.

He tried once more then abandoned it as a waste of time and energy, drew his gun and fired three shots into the locking mechanism. It came asunder, and he kicked the door again, relief spreading through him as it swung open.

Devlin was in the corner, using the tea tray as a shield, holding his abdomen with his left hand to staunch the flow of blood from a wound. Feeney had a bruise coming up on the left side of his face.

'Feeney, drop the knife *now!*'

'We both know that's not on the cards.'

'Whatever this is, we can work it out.'

'No we can't. I've been on the payroll of some very bad men for a long while. Even if you hadn't been here, it's just a matter of time before they worked out it was me that did Clarke.'

'Shoot him!' Devlin wheezed, swaying even crouched as he was, blood pooling on the floor.

'Let us help you, Feeney,' Danny said. 'Tell us who you're in hock to and we can fix it!'

Feeney turned to look at Danny for a moment, and the big detective saw tears in the other man's eyes.

'I was a good cop once,' he said.

'I don't doubt it,' Danny said. 'And it's not too late to make this right.'

'I can't tell you who they are,' Feeney said. 'They'd kill my family. My kids.'

'We'd protect you,' Danny said. 'I'll protect you.'

'Like you protected him?' Feeney asked, raising the knife and rushing at Devlin.

Danny shot him in the head before he'd taken two steps.

58

Tessa dragged herself up and ran towards the spot where the Merrow had stood.

There was a trail of small footprints heading into the reeds, but as soon as Tessa stepped onto the silt, her foot sank up to her ankle, with no sense of reaching the bottom any time soon, and she pulled it out – fast. If they were going to pursue the woman, it would have to wait until daylight.

Another shot rang out, whizzing past her cheek and hitting the wood of the shack. Turning, she saw Maggie trying to get to her feet, the man who'd been carrying her lying on the ground, seemingly unconscious.

A bullet kicked up sand right next to Maggie's leg, and Tessa threw herself forward, grabbing her friend and pulling her upright.

'What kept you?' Maggie asked. 'I was beginning to think I was going to have to swim out of here on my own.'

'You can't swim,' Tessa retorted.

'I never said it was a good plan.'

As they moved towards the reed bed where the canoes were tethered, Sheils came out of the undergrowth, a rifle at his shoulder, firing in the direction of the shots. Pavlov was at his heels, and the little dog launched himself at Maggie, who caught him in one arm and kissed him on the top of his head.

'It's good to see you boy,' she said. 'It is *so* good to see you.'

Sheils paused, scanning the dark horizon. 'I think we've scared them off.'

'Let's hope so,' Tessa agreed.

But she spoke too soon.

A barrage of automatic weapons fire sprayed the tidal island, and the three of them dove for cover. Tessa and Maggie landed half-in and half-out of one of the canoes, and Sheils was fully in the mud, one arm wrapped around the other boat to prevent himself from sinking.

'We have to get out of here,' he shouted over the noise of gunfire. 'We don't know how many of them there are, and we don't have the firepower to deal with machine guns.'

As he said these words, the reeds above them were shredded by more fire.

'They're closer,' Maggie said.

'Let's go,' Tessa agreed. 'Stay low.'

Sheils hauled himself into his canoe, and they began to move back down the tributaries towards the river, using the oars more as barge poles than for their intended purpose, trying to build up as much speed as they could. They hadn't got far when the sound of an engine starting shattered the silence, and they heard what sounded like a boat with an outboard motor moving through the water parallel to them.

'That's not good,' Tessa said.

'Keep moving,' Sheils hissed. 'Our best bet is to get out of the marsh then make a run for it into the farmland behind the beach. I know the land. There are places we can hide. We're sitting ducks if we stay on the water.'

They continued to propel themselves feverishly through the foul-smelling waterways. Every now and then, the boatman would fire, chopping the vegetation to pieces, usually far enough away not to be a danger, but once or twice coming uncomfortably close.

As they drew nearer the open river, they could see a light shining through the reeds.

'He's got a floodlight,' Sheils said.

'We can't hide from that,' Tessa observed.

They came to a dead stop, knowing they were beaten. Tessa wanted to scream in fury. She'd known this was potentially a suicide mission, and she'd gone in half-cocked and dragged Jim into it too. Now they were all in deadly peril.

'Jim, switch canoes,' she said.

'What the hell for?'

'I'm going to go out and see if I can't reason with him.'

'How the hell are you going to do that?' Maggie asked.

'I don't know yet,' Tessa admitted. 'But the least I can do is buy you some time. Jim, is there somewhere in the marsh you can hole up and wait out the night if you have to?'

'One or two spots yeah.'

'If this goes wrong, go to one of them.'

'Tessa, this is mental. Let's all go.'

'We don't know how many men there are, or what weapons they have, or even what kind of boats,' Tessa said. 'Also, they don't know how many of us there are alive. You two might have been hit. If I go out there, it gives you a chance. You know it makes sense! Now go!'

Sheils, swearing colourfully, scrambled into the canoe Tessa had been sharing with Maggie and Pav, and she climbed into his.

'You've got your phone,' she said to the coastguard. 'If I can, I'll call you.'

'Tessa,' he said. 'I... I just want to say...'

She grinned at him. 'I know,' she said. 'Me too. Now go on. I have to go and see a man.'

59

'You're building up your frequent flier miles in the hospital today, aren't you?' Danny said to Devlin – it was a little after 3 a.m. and they were in a private examination room in A&E. He was frighteningly pale from loss of blood, but the blade hadn't pierced any major organs, and the doctors had decreed he'd live to fight another day.

'What can I say?' He laughed then stopped, wincing. 'I'm a terrible hypochondriac.'

'What am I dealing with here, Devlin?' the big detective asked. 'I've faced down a lot in my time, but this one scares me. Now I think you're as good a candidate as anyone for witness protection – I see no reason why the powers that be won't see the sense in hiding you in some village in the back end of South America or wherever you want to go. I can put in the application tonight. But I need to know what my people and I are up against.'

'John Bolger,' Devlin said, 'is attempting to get a far-right party into the Dáil in Ireland. He's been funding them for a long time, and they're linked to quite a number of similar parties right across Europe. They're getting a very small portion of the vote at the moment, but their election organisers believe that, if some members of the opposition parties were discredited, not to mention some members of the European Parliament who've spoken out against them, their chances in the next general elections would be greatly improved.'

'How in the hell does this involve you?'

'I work for Andrew O'Dowd. Mr O'Dowd does business with certain big business interests, and certain individuals within the Irish government, which have cosy agreements with people who have an interest in causing political unrest in Europe. So when Bolger formulated his plan, my employer was contacted to help set it in action.'

'And how are the kids involved in all of this?' Danny asked.

'Ah,' Devlin said. 'The children. Bolger hit on the idea that these days, one of the most sure-fire ways to smear a politician or a businessman is to involve them in even the rumour of child abduction. The church has been linked to illegal foreign adoptions, and this has caused a furore in the Irish press. Two of the politicians he sees as the greatest opponents of his fascist party are major shareholders in Farnogue Freight. And as luck would have it, his criminal friends had someone on the inside, a crewmember on a ship coming to Ireland, who had experience of trafficking.'

'Derek Sherlock?' Danny asked.

'Exactly. He didn't want to be involved, but he owed O'Dowd a debt.'

'You're really good guys, aren't you?' Danny said, shaking his head in disgust.

'This was a way to kill a number of birds with one stone,' Devlin continued, ignoring the detective. 'Damien Forde has spoken out against Bolger in the house, and Bolger hates him for it. Wanted to have his name destroyed completely. So the whole deal was set up to make it look like he, Forde, had ordered it.'

'And I thought he was just a scumbag,' Danny said.

'He is,' Devlin said. 'But his politics maybe aren't as bad as they could be. His assistant, Clohessy, was on our payroll for quite some time. He helped us make the whole thing look convincing.'

'He seemed like an innocent gobshite,' Danny said. 'He's a better actor than I gave him credit for. It looked for all the world as if you gangsters were trying to protect Forde!'

'We wanted it to look that way,' Devlin said. 'Really paint him as a criminal. We figured it would make you dig even deeper, and then you'd find the trail of clues we'd left.'

'So you're telling me that Bolger was prepared to have his own kids trafficked to achieve his political ends?' Danny asked, genuinely horrified.

'He wanted to be able to paint himself as the victim. To show that the people standing in opposition were far worse than he was.'

'And how do social services fit into it all?'

'That, I'm afraid, I don't know,' Devlin said. 'You'll have to ask them.'

'What about Del Finnegan?' Danny asked. 'Tessa said he was advising you on how to deal with the kids from the start.'

'Yes, and he was going to deal with the handover, I believe,' Devlin said. 'Look, I want to say here and now that I don't approve of any of it. But we were being paid a lot of money, and there were talks of large-scale international deals opening up off the back of the whole thing. So we put up and shut up. O'Dowd always insists the adoptions are genuine, to rich families who really want kids, so they'd have been going to a good home. Most probably a far better one.'

'Yeah, but you're saying the kids were really going to be sold?' Danny asked. 'Bolger wasn't going to secretly pick them up at this end?'

'No. The children were going to disappear. That image of

the grieving parent was one he was looking forward to playing, I believe.'

'My God,' Danny breathed, disgusted.

'And it all would have gone off without a hitch if it weren't for that woman,' Devlin said.

'Tara Wall. The Merrow.'

'Whatever happened on that ship, it caused everything to go to hell,' Devlin said. 'We've been playing catch-up ever since.'

'I'm going to need you to testify to all of this.'

Devlin sighed a deep sigh. 'I don't see as I have much choice, do I?'

'Not really, no.'

'Okay then. So what's left to do?'

'I believe I'm going to go and arrest Mr Bolger.'

60

Tessa pulled the canoe up onto the sand as she reached the beach and came out of the reeds with her hands aloft. 'I come in peace!' she called.

The floodlight was blazing, and she couldn't see a thing.

'Drop the gun!' a voice called out. 'Take it out – slowly!'

'My shoulder is dislocated,' she said. 'I can only use my left hand. Just so you know.'

She reached into the back of her belt and took out her weapon, then tossed it onto the sand in front of her.

'Where are the others?' the voice called.

'Dead,' Tessa said. 'It's just me.'

'Get on your knees.'

'Why?'

'Do it!'

Tessa did as she was asked.

She heard engines rev and a crunching sound, and then a figure emerged out of the light, carrying an M15. She recognised him as one of the men she'd seen in O'Dowd's house the evening she and Sheils had visited. It felt like a lifetime ago, even though she realised it had only been the previous night.

'You are one troublesome bitch,' the man said, raising the machine gun.

'That is no way to talk to a lady,' a voice said from the darkness behind Tessa, and a shot rang out, hitting the man on the bridge of the nose and spinning him. A sputter of bullets came from the gun as his finger convulsed on the weapon, and Tessa threw herself to the side to avoid it.

When she raised her head again, Eric Stafford was standing above her, dressed in what looked for all the world like a black safari suit, offering his hand.

'We meet again, and once more in the nick of time,' he said. 'Would you like me to pop that shoulder back in for you?'

61

Stafford had parked his Volvo at the edge of the strand. Once Sheils and Maggie had joined them, they all gathered around it while he offered coffee from a flask.

As they sipped, Tessa called Danny. She listened gravely to the information her partner had to convey.

'The Merrow is here,' she said in response. 'She killed O'Dowd. I'm guessing Bolger will be next.'

'You'd best get over there then,' Danny said. 'I was just away to go and stick the cuffs on the fucker myself, but it's probably better that it's you.'

'Why?' Tessa asked. It wasn't like Danny to swear.

'Because I'd probably kill him.'

'We're on our way,' Tessa said and hung up.

'You have news?' Stafford asked.

'I do. We'll all fit in this boat of a car of yours, so why don't you drive, and I'll tell you all about it. Looks like you're going to be with us at the end after all.'

. . .

John Bolger and his entourage were staying in the Clayton Whites Hotel in Wexford town's Cornmarket. The Clayton was a large, glass-fronted hotel with a large and welcoming foyer that, during the day, offered punters a bustling coffee house and meeting place. The night manager, a tall, impeccably groomed man with a thick head of white hair and a well-groomed moustache listened to Tessa quietly and calmly and said he would show them to Bolger's suite. Without missing a beat, he cast a glance at Stafford, who was carrying Maggie in his arms.

'Might I be so bold as to offer the lady a wheelchair? I have one in the storage room which would probably suffice.'

Maggie grinned. 'That would be most welcome, thank you.'

'My pleasure.'

The elevator took them to the top floor and a short corridor to a door labelled 'Presidential Suite'.

'I'll unlock the room then withdraw and allow you to do what you must,' the night manager said.

'Thank you,' Tessa said. 'We'll try not to make too much of a mess.'

The tall man slid a key card into a slot, a light on the door flashed green and Tessa turned the handle.

Inside it was dark, but a large window overlooked Wexford's quay, and the street lamps offered plenty of illumination. They were standing in what looked to be a lounge area, with a large-screen television, a suite of plush furniture and a coffee table upon which a near-empty bottle of wine sat, along with a plate of cheese and grapes. Two glasses rested at opposite ends of the table

Sitting on the couch was John Bolger, wearing a black silk robe over black pyjamas.

Sitting on the coffee table, a gun trained steadily on the businessman, was Tara Wall. The Merrow.

'Take one more step and I'll shoot him,' she said.

'Detective, help me!' Bolger shouted, and the Merrow

clubbed him across the forehead with the barrel of her gun, knocking him unconscious.

'Shoot him and we'll shoot you,' Tessa said. 'Is that the end you were hoping for?'

'It's the end I expected,' the Merrow said.

'It doesn't have to be that way.'

'Yes it does.'

Tessa looked at her companions and saw Stafford slide a small handgun – she assumed it was a .22, from the pocket of his trousers.

'So where does this leave us then?' she asked.

'You all back out,' the Merrow said. 'Leave me to do what I have to do, then I'll give myself up.'

'You know I can't do that,' Tessa replied.

'If you don't, I'll kill him and yes, I know you'll shoot me, but I guarantee I'll take at least two of you with me before I die.'

Tessa had no doubt the woman was telling the truth. 'What if the others step out, but I stay and we talk some more?'

The Merrow gave Tessa a hard look. 'I need to see you hand your gun over to Maggie.'

Tessa did.

'Okay. You can stay and Bolger's going nowhere. Everyone else goes.'

They began to file out. Maggie was last, and before she left, the Merrow called out to her, 'Maggie, thank you for everything you did for the children.'

The family liaison officer paused. 'It was my privilege. They're great kids.'

And then she trundled out.

'Can I sit?' Tessa asked. 'It's been a long few days.'

The Merrow nodded, and Tessa pulled up one of the armchairs.

'I feel like we know each other,' she said. 'You've been occupying a lot of my time.'

The woman gazed at Tessa. The detective gazed back.

She'd thought of the Merrow as something superhuman, something *other*, but now, sitting in front of her, saw that she was just a woman. And an exhausted and pained one to boot. Tessa took in the fine, striking features and thin mouth, the dark rings under the clear, intelligent eyes. Red patches stood out on her cheeks, garish on her pale face, and Tessa suspected a fever – the result of an infection from the gunshot wound Danny had delivered.

She was clearly nearing the end of her endurance.

'You were a soldier,' the Merrow said to her.

'Yes. Irish army. Served for nine years.'

'You liked it?'

'Very much.'

'I was a soldier too. Though not for the military. The gang raised me to be loyal to them. It's all I've ever known.'

'Yeah. I've heard some stories about you. Why do you call yourself the Merrow, if you don't mind my asking?'

'The job I'm most known for is escorting children by boat from one port to another. A ship's captain once told me I was O'Dowd's very own merrow – his mermaid. It stuck.'

'You clearly don't mind.'

'I was flattered,' the woman said. 'It gave me an identity.' She smiled sadly. 'Do you know I had a child once?'

'I didn't know that.'

'It's true.'

'Once?' Tessa asked.

'He was taken from me when he was six months old.'

'They sold him.'

'Yes. He had red hair. I called him Julian.'

'I can help you find him, if you want.'

The woman shook her head sadly. 'What could I offer him? This life I lead? The things I've done? He's better off believing whichever family has him is his own.'

'I take it you took Isaac because he reminded you of him.'

'I did. I wanted him to know love, at least once in his life. His father isn't a man who even knows what that is. I thought I would wait until people weren't looking for me anymore then take him somewhere and make a life.'

'You could still have one,' Tessa said. 'Yes, you're going to prison, but we could make a case you were trying to protect the children. You might get a very light sentence.'

'I don't deserve a light sentence. I took countless children away from their families and handed them over to be sold like swine. I have a debt to pay, and I intend to pay it.'

Tessa cast about desperately for something to entice the woman. 'We might find your parents.'

The Merrow laughed. 'I found them ten years ago. They were already dead.'

'I'm so sorry,' Tessa said.

'It seems I was considered a valuable resource by my employers. My parents were murdered by professionals. A neighbour told the police he saw someone going into their house, but he didn't get a good look. He said the light was poor, and that it looked like the man had no face.'

Tessa froze then swallowed softly. 'I've had some dealings with the men with no faces myself. In fact, I wondered if you might be one of them.'

The Merrow smiled sadly. 'No. I'm just small, and I know how to wear a hood and cut my hair to good effect.'

'Did you go looking for the person who killed your family?'

'I did... It's a pity we didn't meet under other circumstances,' the woman said. 'We might have had much to share. But perhaps we should deal with the elephant in the room before we talk about our personal commonalities.'

Tessa nodded. 'We'll continue that conversation later,' she said.

'If there is a later,' the Merrow countered.

'Here's what I know,' Tessa said. 'You were employed to take the children from school, get them to the ship and then escort them to Ireland,' she said. 'What I don't know is what happened on the ship to cause you to... well, to do what you did.'

'I was employed to make sure those kids were brought here, where I was led to believe they were being placed with an adoptive family,' the Merrow said, and Tessa could hear an edge of real anger in her voice. 'We were only a few hours at sea when a crewmember discovered the kids. I'd gone to get water, and Sofie went wandering. A crewman found her and brought her to the captain. A debate followed amongst the crew, which I overheard. They wanted to sell the children to the highest bidder themselves and divide the spoils.'

'Wow,' Tessa said. 'I have to admit, I didn't see that coming.'

'An agreement was struck between them. I questioned the cook, Derek Sherlock, who was my contact on the ship – he'd been in O'Dowd's gang when he was younger and owed them a debt – about all of this, and he told me it was true – and that he'd told the captain everything, I suppose to get back at O'Dowd. I planned to killed him, but the captain beat me to it. O'Dowd insists the children he traffics go to decent families. The crew, however, didn't care where they went.'

'O'Dowd cares where these kids go? That doesn't seem like the man I met at all.'

'Andrew O'Dowd is a survivor of abuse. He didn't care for children, but he wasn't going to send a child somewhere it might be harmed. He put a lot of resources into that.'

'But the crew had less scruples?'

'None at all, from what I could tell.'

'Did you kill the rest of the crew?'

'No. The captain was responsible for most of the deaths. It seems he didn't want to share the money, and one by one, he murdered his crewmen and threw them overboard. I'd hidden myself by then. But by a stroke of bad luck, I was spotted by the pilot and was forced to deal with him. By the time we were halfway to Ireland, there was only the captain left.'

'He wrote a journal blaming you for everything,' Tessa said.

'I know. I didn't much care, to be honest. He sabotaged the navigation systems, and I knew his plan was to steer us away from Rosslare, where the pre-arranged pickup was to take place, land us somewhere else and take the children into his own custody. I was... I was afraid of what he might trade them into. He was going to sell them to the highest bidder, and that could mean... bad things. Very bad things.'

'So you killed him.'

'Yes. I took a kitchen knife and cut his throat.'

'You were going to facilitate the sale of the children yourself. Why were you so appalled at what the captain was planning?'

'I know what I've done for most of my life is awful, in that many children were taken from families who cared for them and raised not knowing who they really are. But I can say no child I escorted was sent into abuse.'

'If Bolger was planning on a clean, safe adoption, why are you here now?'

'Before he sabotaged the ship's communication systems, the captain emailed Murray – Derek had told him he was the contact person for O'Dowd. He left the screen open when he went to throw the bodies overboard, and I was able to read the message. Oliver informed Murray he had the children and was going to make his own sale, but that he was going to give the children's family a chance to make an offer on them before he did.'

Tessa knew what was coming but was still appalled when she heard the words.

'Murray emailed back ten minutes later,' the Merrow said.

'He informed him that the children's father hoped Oliver made a decent profit.'

'He washed his hands of the whole thing,' Tessa said. 'Even though his children might have been sold to bad people.'

'Yes.'

'So you planned to kill him for it.'

'Yes, and I feel no guilt on that front.'

'Without navigation systems, how did you manage to ground the ship in Ballymoney?'

'It was the nearest landfall. I know the tides and the currents and knew that, even with no navigation systems, we would probably wash up somewhere on the Wexford coast. Even without all the tech, I could still steer the boat – I didn't want to risk the children being washed out to sea, which could happen if a riptide hit them. So I waited until I could see houses on the shore, so I knew people would come quickly and the children would be in the care of the emergency services before too long. Once the ship was in the grip of the tides, I jumped overboard.'

'Why didn't you take them with you?'

'The little ones – I was afraid they might drown.'

'You hung around to make sure they were safe though?' Tessa asked.

'Yes. Once I was certain you were all good people, I set about righting what had been done. But... I had to return for Isaac.'

'It took us a while to untangle it all,' Tessa said. 'You know Damien Forde is innocent – of this at least? Mr Bolger was trying to frame him.'

'I know,' the Merrow said. 'I had a gentle conversation with his assistant before coming here. He told me everything – eventually.'

'Where will we find his body?'

'In his apartment.'

'Why'd you kill Murray?'

'He was the access point for people who wanted to buy children. He did all the vetting. I wanted to know who'd arranged the sale of the Bolger kids and where they were supposed to be going. He wouldn't tell me. I gave him a choice. He made the wrong one.'

'You left Isaac outside on the landing while you... questioned him.'

'I didn't want the child seeing what was likely to happen. He'd had enough trauma as it was.'

'So what are your plans now?'

'I'm going to kill this man, who would, for his personal gain, have sold his children.'

'The kids are safe,' Tessa said, sitting forward. 'They're never going back to their father. I'll see to it that he spends the rest of his life in prison.'

'You can't promise that,' the Merrow said. 'Rich people don't go to jail.'

'I'm not so sure,' Tessa said. 'But he won't be in there for long anyway. The people he's in bed with financially will probably make sure he doesn't last more than a month.'

'That's true...' the Merrow said.

'It is. He'll be far more frightened this way too. People like Bolger find jail really hard. And the ones who come for him, they won't put one shot in him. He'll go hard. I'm not saying that with any pleasure. It's just a fact.'

She watched the Merrow considering this new information.

'You make a good argument,' she said eventually.

'I'm glad we agree. So where does that leave us?'

'At an impasse, I'm afraid. You're not taking me in; I won't go to prison.'

'I can't just let you go.'

'I know.'

'My friends are outside. The first sound of a struggle and they'll be in here.'

'Tessa, I'm tired,' the Merrow said, a tear slipping down her face. 'I've done my best, but I'm all used up. I want to be with my parents.'

In a rapid movement, she stood, raising the gun so it was pointed at Tessa, and just as quickly, Stafford, who it seemed had not exited the room at all, stepped out of the hallway and put a bullet between her eyes.

62

One of Bolger's entourage was a private medic, and he treated his employer's injuries, after which the businessman was taken to Wexford Garda station.

The Merrow was taken to Wexford General, where a post-mortem would follow.

'Well this has been a tough one,' Danny said as they watched the patrol car pulling away, Bolger handcuffed within.

'We're not done yet,' Tessa said. 'This man still owes us some answers.'

'Let's go and get them then,' Maggie agreed.

Maggie, Sheils and Stafford sat in the observation room while Tessa and Danny settled down opposite Noa, Sofie and Isaac's father.

'We know all of it,' Tessa said. 'And we have one of Andrew O'Dowd's crew ready to testify. I'm going to have our money guys in the Criminal Assets Bureau sit down with their opposites in Interpol and have a long hard look at the money trail you've laid during this sordid little affair. I have no doubt it'll be a difficult mess to unravel, but these guys live for the chase.'

'I wish to speak to my lawyer,' Bolger said.

'I've only got one question,' Tessa said.

'I will answer nothing without my lawyer.'

'He's coming. But here's the thing: I can understand your desire to change the political landscape – I might not agree with your politics, but I get that you'd want to. I can understand your wanting to stage an abduction, if your plan was to have the kids picked up at the other end and taken to safety. I don't agree with the methods, but I can see how playing the sympathy card might work, particularly if you'd framed your opponents to look like they were people-trafficking scumbags. I don't like it, I think it's dishonest and conniving, but I understand it. What I *don't* understand is that your plan was to *actually* sell your three children. That I cannot get my head around. What would possess you to do that?'

'The bitter irony,' Danny said, 'is that it's that very thing that brought your plan crashing down. The Merrow cared more for your kids than you did.'

Bolger sneered at the detective's declaration. 'Those children – I had to rid myself of them. They carry a sickness in their blood.'

'Seriously?' Tessa asked incredulously. 'What sickness are you referring to?'

'The same sickness that took my wife. Schizophrenia. It's hereditary, a taint in their DNA that I won't tolerate in my progeny. I thought my wife was the perfect choice. I was wrong. So I've removed her, and the children needed to be gone as well.'

'You removed her?' Tessa said warily.

'She's gone, yes.'

'What did you do to your wife, Mr Bolger?' Danny asked.

'I put her out of her misery,' he said. 'Had her euthanised in Sweden. It was perfectly legal, I assure you.'

'I'll have Interpol look into that,' Tessa said, disgust clear in her voice. 'So you're telling me you were prepared to sell your children because they might carry hereditary traits for mental illness?'

'She was weak, and her children are too. Such individuals need to be eradicated. It's as simple as that.'

'I think we've heard all we need to,' Danny said.

'I know I have,' Tessa agreed.

63

They sat around a desk in the squad room, passing a bottle of Jameson the desk sergeant had procured for them between themselves. Sheils took a slug and handed it to Stafford.

'We said we'd have a drink when this was over,' the coast-guard said. 'I'm glad we were able to, in the end.'

'As am I,' Stafford agreed.

'The Merrow pretty much died by suicide,' Tessa said. 'I know you're not a guard, Eric, but it was more or less suicide by cop.'

'She'd done what she set out to do, I suppose,' Danny said. 'She got those children to the right people and made sure the ones responsible for the plan to sell them paid for it.'

'What happens to the children now?' Tessa asked.

'We still need to have a chat with our friends from social services,' Maggie said. 'Has it occurred to any of you that they may have actually been trying to do the right thing by those kiddies?'

'Not until recently,' Tessa said. 'Let's just say I'm beginning to wonder if I might have been wrong about them.'

Danny put his hand on Maggie's shoulder. The family

liaison officer was cuddling Pav, who'd fallen asleep in her lap. She looked over at the big detective and gave him a tired smile.

'How are you, Maggie? Were you very badly treated when O'Dowd took you?'

'Not really. They seemed to believe that, once I didn't have a wheelchair, I wasn't really a flight risk. Him and one of his crew took me out to that hunter's shack by boat, and I was thrown in the corner and left there. The other one left, and O'Dowd sat in a chair by the door with a James Patterson novel for a bit, but he fell asleep after an hour or two, and when he did, I started to work on the boards behind me. I figured if I could get out, I might drag myself into the reeds and get far enough away to hide. Of course, then another one of his cronies arrived, and he kept a closer watch on me. So that was my plan scuppered, but then Tessa, Pavlov and Jim arrived, and you know the rest.'

'What do you think he wanted?' Tessa asked. 'Why did he take you?'

'Oh, he told me,' Maggie said. 'It was another attempt to get us to walk away. It looks like this deal was huge for him. He saw it as his legacy. The pinnacle of his life's work.'

'Well that didn't go too well for him,' Danny said.

'He was paranoid,' Maggie said. 'Convinced he was being watched – not just by us but by others as well. He sat by that window, muttering to himself, half reading his book but mostly watching the water and scanning the reeds and brush, looking for the people he was convinced were coming to get him.'

'Well he was right, wasn't he?' Tessa said.

'I might have allowed him to see me just for a moment,' Stafford said. 'I've found that keeping targets like Mr O'Dowd jumpy is desirable.'

'You had him jumping at shadows,' Maggie said.

They paused for a moment and passed the bottle around one more time.

'What's next for you then, Mr Stafford?' Danny wanted to know.

'I'll oversee the return of the *Dolphin* to our dry dock in Dublin,' the enforcer said. 'A crew shouldn't be too difficult to find. Once that task is complete and the ship is deemed ocean worthy, I'll go wherever the company sends me next.'

'There's some paperwork I'm going to need you to fill out,' Tessa said. 'We've got two corpses to account for due to your handiwork.'

'And you, Tessa, are alive,' he said. 'Both killings were justified.'

'If I have any further questions, I'll know where to find you,' Tessa said, winking at him and taking the bottle as he passed it to her.

'I shall look forward to future conversations with you,' Stafford said. 'For now, though, I hear my bed calling.'

'I think we all do,' Tessa said.

They said their goodbyes to the desk sergeant and made their way out to the car park.

The sergeant had organised for their vehicles to be brought in, and Tessa and Sheils stopped beside her Capri.

'Well, you really know how to show a guy an exciting time,' he said with a laugh.

'You can't say I'm boring company,' Tessa agreed.

'I know you must be exhausted, but would you like to come back to my place?' he asked.

Tessa grinned. 'Funny, suddenly I don't feel all that tired.'

64

Maggie, Tessa and Danny sat with Ella Carling in the conference room of Wexford General the following morning.

'I think I may owe you an apology, Ms Carling,' Tessa said. 'You'll have to understand, I had a lot of conflicting information coming at me, and I simply didn't know who I could trust. In a situation like that, I usually opt for trusting no one.'

'Of course. You were placing the children's welfare first, and I commend you for that.'

'Why didn't you have any legal paperwork with you?' Maggie asked.

'Much like yourself, I didn't know who *I* could trust. As soon as I learned that three children had been found, I suspected they were the Bolgers. When it was discovered they'd been taken from their schools, Europol's child protection branch was contacted – they attempted to contact John Bolger but kept being passed from one employee of his to the next. In desperation, a Europol operative called my department. The children being who they are, the file was passed up the line to me. I immediately went to my superiors, but to my horror, they refused to take the situation seriously.'

'Someone in a position of power was already involved in Bolger's plan,' Danny said.

'I believe so, yes. He's a powerful man, and his pockets are deep. People everywhere were on his payroll.'

'So we've learned,' Tessa said.

'When it was confirmed that your three castaways were definitely the Bolgers, I tried to get a care order, but no judge I approached would hear the case. So I called my friend, Gillian Shaughnessy, and asked her if she might intervene for me.'

'You might have more luck getting that care order now,' Tessa suggested.

'One of my colleagues is working on it at the moment.'

'What are your plans for the children?' Maggie wanted to know.

'There's a wonderful foster family waiting to take them,' Carling said. 'They're not averse to the idea of adopting them, if the placement goes well.'

'They don't know their mother is dead yet,' Tessa said. 'Maggie's going to tell them later today.'

'They have a long road ahead of them,' Carling said. 'But they'll have all the love and support they need.'

'They're going to need a lot,' Maggie said.

65

John Bolger was held awaiting trial for a litany of crimes, including conspiracy to commit multiple homicide, people trafficking, involvement in illegal adoptions, bribing of numerous public officials, links to organised crime and quite a few more.

Even before his case was on the books of the Central Criminal Court, an army of lawyers were lining up to represent him. Tessa wondered if the Merrow hadn't been right, and that the deranged man might not serve any prison time at all.

Del Finnegan went back to Wheatfield Prison, an extra ten years added to his previous sentence.

Two days after the shootout in the salt marsh and their confrontation with the Merrow in the Presidential Suite of Whites Hotel, Tessa received a text message from an unknown number:

I have formed my crew and set sail at midday. It has been a pleasure working with you, and I wish you and your friends very good luck. I also hope your relationship with the coastguard proves to be a beneficial one for you. He seems a good and honourable man. By sending this, I'm giving you my number. If you should need a man of my talents in the future, please feel free to call me. I will answer. All my good wishes, Eric Stafford.

66

Three days after everything had come to a head, Tessa, Maggie and Pavlov sat in the children's room in Wexford General. Danny had excused himself, as he hadn't had the opportunity to get to know the children particularly well.

'Have you met the family we're going to live with?' Noa asked.

'I've had a Zoom call with them,' Maggie said. 'They seem really nice, and they're excited to meet you. The dad is an architect, and the mam is a teacher, but when you go to live with them, she's going to take some time out of work so she can be there for you. Which I think is a really good idea. It'll give you a chance to get to know one another.'

'What if she doesn't like us?' Sofie wanted to know.

'She will,' Tessa said. 'You're impossible not to like.'

'Daddy didn't like us,' Isaac said.

'Your dad did some mean things,' Tessa said. 'But I don't think that was because he didn't like you. Your father had got himself mixed up with some bad people who had really messed up ideas, and he'd let those get all muddled up in his head. That made him act in ways that weren't kind. I'm hoping he's going to have some time to think about all of that, these next few years.'

'Will he go to prison?' Noa asked.

'We don't know for sure, but some of the things he's done could land him in jail, yes.'

'Will he be scared?' Sofie asked.

'Were you scared on the boat, sweetie?' Maggie asked.

'Sometimes, yes.'

'And were you scared when you were brought here with lots of people you didn't know?'

'Yes. I was.'

'And were you scared when Isaac was taken?'

The little girl nodded.

'Well then, maybe it would be good for your dad to know what that feels like. So he'll understand he shouldn't do those things again.'

That seemed to satisfy her, and while Noa remained quiet and contemplative, it seemed they were ready for what came next.

Ella Carling arrived just after lunch, and Tessa, Maggie and Pav walked with them down to the car that was to take them to their new home.

The two younger kids gave hugs and cried over leaving Pavlov, but Noa remained aloof, standing a little to the side. When his two siblings were in the car, he approached Tessa and shook her hand.

'Thank you, Detective, for everything you've done for us.'

He suddenly seemed so much older than his ten years and it made Maggie's heart ache.

'You're welcome, Noa,' Tessa said. 'You take care.'

She ruffled his hair, nodded at Maggie and walked back towards the hospital.

'Maggie,' the youngster said, offering his hand again.

'You know, you don't need to try to be so tough,' Maggie said.

'I'm not trying to be tough.'

'Yeah, you are. You think now your dad's been busted and your mam's gone that you need to be a man. You don't. There's a lovely family waiting to meet you, and they want you to be able to be a kid for once, and to not have to worry. You can let your guard down, Noa.'

'I'm fine, really.'

'I don't believe you. You've had an awful time, and you've just learned you've lost your mam and that your dad tried to do... well, something no parent should do. You've looked after those two little ones and been the best big brother they could possibly ask for, and you've barely shed a tear through any of it. Now you're going to a new family and a new life, and that's terrifying. I know it is. And it's okay to admit that.'

Noa cleared his throat and looked at his shoes for a moment, and when he looked at Maggie next, she saw that tears were running down his cheeks.

'What if it doesn't work out?' he asked her, panic in his voice. 'We've got nowhere to go, and no one to turn to. What if these new parents try to hurt us or they decide we're bad kids and throw us out? What do I do then, Maggie? What should I do?'

And then he was crying hard, loud, gasping sobs coming from deep inside.

Maggie held him, and Pavlov licked his tears away.

'Noa, I'm not going to lie to you,' Maggie said, 'I can't promise that bad things won't happen in your life again, but I do think things are about to take a very positive turn. I will say this to you though. Are you listening?'

The little boy's head was buried in her shoulder, but she felt him nod.

'Good. Now here's what I'm going to say. If at any stage in

your life you feel scared, or worried, or something happens to you or your brother or your sister and you can't think what to do, you can call me. Or Tessa. Or my friend Danny – I know you don't know him as well as Tessa or me, but he'll be there to help if you need him. Ella will give you all our numbers, and we'll take a call any time.'

'But you might be anywhere in Ireland helping other kids.'

'Yes, but we can be there in half a day if you need us. So you see? Things aren't so bad.'

Noa lifted his head, and for the first time since Maggie had known him, his face lit up with the beginnings of a smile.

'That's better,' she said, and Pavlov gave a happy bark. 'Noa, you and your brother and sister have a lot of people who care about you. And you have foster parents waiting in Tipperary who can't wait to meet you. Yes, you've had a dark time, which I suspect has been going on for a while. But you're in the sunshine now. Let yourself enjoy it.'

And they hugged hard.

EPILOGUE

'When you fish for love, bait with your heart, not with your brain.'

— MARK TWAIN

67

After the Bolger children left for pastures new with Carling, Dawn told the team to take the rest of the day off.

Tessa called Sheils. 'I'm at a loose end for the rest of the day. You got any plans?'

'You might be amazed to learn that, as a chief officer in the Irish coastguard, I'm normally quite busy with my own cases.'

'Ha ha. Point heard and understood. I'll entertain myself, so.'

'Hold on, DI Burns. As it so happens, I am due some time off. I can take a day if you'd like me to show you some of Wexford's beauty spots.'

'How about taking me for breakfast and then to bed?'

'That works too.'

Later that day, they lay entwined with one another. The Gloaming were playing gently through a speaker Sheils had attached to his phone, and the light played across their naked bodies from the half-open blinds.

'I'm leaving Wexford tomorrow,' Tessa said.

'I figured you would.'

'Want to talk about what that means?'

'Okay.'

Neither of them spoke for a while.

'You first,' Tessa said.

'Oh, right. Well... I'd like to see you again.'

'I'd like to see you again too. But I have no idea where I'm going to be sent next. Me and Danny and Maggie and Pav, we go where the cases are.'

'I know.'

'How do you feel about a long-distance relationship?'

'I'd prefer it if you were living closer and I could see you every day, but I'm open to giving it a go.'

'I don't want to stop you from meeting someone who could give you a more... well, a more normal life.'

'Tessa, we're both in law enforcement. We don't lead normal lives.'

'You know what I mean though. You might meet someone who could offer you far more than I can.'

'I've been divorced for eight years. I've had partners in that time; I'm not a monk. But there's been nothing even close to long-term. And I never felt about any of them the way I feel about you, even though we've not known each other long.'

She lifted her head so she was looking into his eyes. 'Honestly?'

'Truly. I... I really like you, Tessa.'

'I'm pretty fond of you too.'

They kissed, and the kissing turned into caresses, and then they were making love again, and this time it was frantic and hungry, and each felt the need for the other, a need they'd had before they'd even met but which they now recognised as fulfilled.

Somehow, they'd been waiting for something, and it was only now they knew they'd found it.

When it was over, they slept for a time, then Sheils made them some pasta with peppers, mushrooms and chorizo, which they ate with crusty bread and ice-cold white wine.

'So we're a thing,' Tessa said.

'Looks like we are.'

They toasted their new reality, and as they did, Tessa's phone buzzed.

She picked it up. 'Hey, Danny.'

'Tessa, I'm... well I'm parked outside.'

'Outside where?'

'Jim Sheils' house.'

'Danny, I'm not going to pretend this isn't just a little bit weird.'

'No! The commissioner asked me to come and get you. We've been called to a case, and we need to leave right away.'

'So much for a day off,' Tessa sighed.

'I know. Some kid is in a cell in the Anglesea Street station in Cork in connection with two murders.'

'A kid?'

'Yes. Twelve years old.'

'And they think he killed these people?'

'It's a girl and they know she didn't. But she told the guards the murders were going to happen. Got her parents to bring her into the station so she could give them the information.'

'Which of course they dismissed.'

'Oh yeah,' Danny replied. 'Told her folks to get her some therapy. But then the murders happened. Exactly as she said they would.'

'And now they've got no choice but to take her seriously.'

'That's it. The boss wants us down there post haste.'

'Can I finish my dinner?'

'What are ye eating?'

Sheils, who was watching Tessa with a raised eyebrow, cut

in. 'I'm not eavesdropping, but I heard that. Danny, would you like to come in and have a bite before you go?'

'Did you hear that, Daniel?'

'I'm on my way in!'

Tessa looked at Sheils with a soft expression. 'You're a good man, Jim Sheils. And a patient one.'

'You open the door. I'll get an extra plate.'

A LETTER FROM S.A. DUNPHY

Dear reader,

I want to say a huge thank you for choosing to read *Only the Children*. If you did enjoy it and want to keep up to date with all my latest releases and other news, just sign up at the following link. Your email address will never be shared, and you can unsubscribe at any time.

www.bookouture.com/s.a.dunphy

I hope you loved *Only the Children*, and if you did, I'd be extremely grateful if you could write a review. I'd love to hear what you think, and it makes such a difference helping new readers to discover one of my books for the first time.

I love hearing from my readers. I wouldn't be able to do what I do without you. If you'd like to, you can get in touch through social media or my website. I'm pretty active on social media, and value each and every interaction with my readers.

So thanks again, and I look forward to sharing more stories with you very soon.

Very best,

Shane (S. A. Dunphy)

KEEP IN TOUCH WITH S.A. DUNPHY

https://shanedunphyauthor.org

 facebook.com/shanewritesbooks

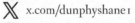 x.com/dunphyshane1

instagram.com/shanewritesbooks

AUTHOR'S NOTE AND ACKNOWLEDGEMENTS

I wrote *Only the Children* during one of the toughest periods I've experienced in quite some time.

The story probably reflects that – the team are dispersed, exhausted, fighting for the survival of the Bolger children but also for their own skins, against odds they can only barely comprehend. They don't know who to trust, and all they have to go on is a desire to live and come out the other end of it all.

Just like all my novels for Bookouture, and indeed the Dunnigan books that went before them and inhabit the same world, the locations described in this book are all completely real (I grew up in Wexford), and you can visit them with ease. Ballymoney Beach, where the *Dolphin* runs aground, is exactly as I've described and is a very pleasant spot to spend an afternoon swimming or birdwatching.

Kaats Strand is a place I dearly love and have spent many happy hours. The salt marsh at the end of the strand is really there, and a treacherous spot for sure. I've been told about a duck-hunters shack existing in the heart of the place, accessible only by boat, but I've never been there. I thought it might be an interesting location for a stand-off between Tessa and O'Dowd though.

I've been fortunate to have experience of large ships, particularly during the making of my radio documentary, *The Sinking of the* St Patrick, and the details of how the *Dolphin* was piloted, how it functioned in high water and how the bridge was laid out came from sailing on various vessels. If you want to know more, I'd highly recommend www.marinein-sight.com.

The details of the people-trafficking business, which effectively amounts to the modern slave industry, are known to me from my history in child protection and from much of the work I did as a journalist. If you want to know more, my audio-original true-crime book *The Bad Place* has a lot of information and statistics, as well as accounts from survivors. I can also recommend the harrowing novel *Harvesting* by Lisa Harding, which deals with the subject in unflinching detail.

The research Maggie did on the mythology behind the Merrow mirrors an evening I spent in my rented office space in Waterford just before Christmas of 2022, during which – alone in the building long after everyone else had gone home – I successfully managed to scare myself. All the texts I reference are available online, and I recommend *The Dindsenchas,* which is probably the richest source of their lore, but Joe Kerrigan's *Old Ways, Old Secrets: Pagan Ireland* is also well worth a look.

There are many resources that examine the culture of Irish gangs, the history of their evolution and their evolution in post-recession Ireland. Might I direct those interested to any of my good friend Paul Williams' books. They're all full of remarkable detail and nuance.

Darkness was a feature of the writing of this book for me too.

As I wrote the first title in the Tessa Burns series, my marriage of thirty years had come to an end, and as I began this one, my family were trying to adjust to that. It was far from easy, and took a lot of patience and no few tears from everyone involved, and while I tried to use my writing as a way of escaping the pain of it all, the honest truth is I found I couldn't write. My brain wouldn't tune into the frequency needed to access Tessa's and Danny's and Maggie's world, and I felt bereft and stupid.

And that was only half of it.

I had successfully dodged Covid-19 during the height of the pandemic and had – in that arrogant way men tend to rationalise things – come to believe I was immune. Don't get me wrong, I was still careful and didn't do anything stupid, but when one of my college classes asked about extra medical leave in case they contracted the virus, I laughed and told them Covid was over, and not to worry.

Famous last words. That weekend I got what I thought was a flu, but when I took a Covid test, those two lines popped up almost immediately, and to my horror, I was informed by my doctor that I had a 'heavy viral load' in my blood. And, as if the universe was laughing at me, it went on and on, morphing into long Covid, which threw every symptom possible at me. At one stage, I genuinely began to think my heart was under pressure, only to be told that this was another symptom of the dreaded illness (I'd climbed the stairs in my house and was so out of breath by the time I reached the top, I thought I would surely pass out). I broke out in a rash. I had weird, fever-like dreams. I had to take three months away from my college, and my writing schedule was put on hold, all deadlines removed.

I began writing *Only the Children* in October of 2022, and I'd taken the story as far as the arrival on Ballymoney Strand of the remarkable Eric Stafford. I had a nice rhythm going, my characters felt familiar and the dialogue was singing.

Then everything went to hell.

I'm blessed to have an editor like Susannah Hamilton, who, after my having to break several promises to her that I would have the completed manuscript in her inbox 'within the next week or so', simply told me to take a break and get it to her when I could.

'Your physical and mental health are more important,' she told me. 'We can move things around. Just get your life in order and send me the first draft when you feel able to.'

I'm on record as saying that Bookouture are a publishing house who put the needs and welfare of their writers first, and here is yet another example of that. Susannah behaved not as an editor but as a friend. I will always be grateful for that.

I'm also lucky to have the best literary agent out there, Ivan Mulcahy. Ivan was with me every step of the way, as a listening ear and a confidant as much as an agent. Knowing he's always at the end of the phone with a reassuring word or the suggestion that I cop myself on and get on with what needs doing is always a comfort.

I should stress that Ivan is also a gifted editor in his own right, has a love of books and a delightfully eclectic taste, and is a great writer too. (You should check out his blog at @myagentsecret – it's really wonderful.)

I want to thank my children, Richard and Marnie, for putting up with me and for loving me enough to stick with me, even during the hard times. And of course my grandson, Rhys, who is one of the bright spots in my world.

Particular thanks and love to Kristina and Jess, who had to put up with me during the writing of this.

And finally, thanks to you, my dear reader. I feel a huge well of gratitude when I realise I have such a number of supporters who come back again and again to share these stories. The world of Tessa and Danny, Maggie and Pavlov, Jessie and Seamus, Dawn and Terri, Dunnigan and Miley has come alive because you've engaged with it and given it a heartbeat. Nothing I do would have any purpose if it wasn't for you.

As I write this I'm preparing book three – the team are on their way to Cork and there is a very dangerous adventure waiting for them there. I know you'll be there to support them.

Wexford
Waterford
Tramore
October 2022–April 2023

PUBLISHING TEAM

Turning a manuscript into a book requires the efforts of many people. The publishing team at Bookouture would like to acknowledge everyone who contributed to this publication.

Audio
Alba Proko
Sinead O'Connor
Melissa Tran

Commercial
Lauren Morrissette
Jil Thielen
Imogen Allport

Contracts
Peta Nightingale

Cover design
Blacksheep

Data and analysis
Mark Alder
Mohamed Bussuri

Made in United States
Orlando, FL
29 April 2024

46327792R00203